THE UNBREAKABLE CODE

A Gift For: *Miss Pasket*

From: *Ryan J. Lee*

THE UNBREAKABLE CODE

Jennifer Chambliss Bertman

WITH ILLUSTRATIONS BY Sarah Watts

SQUARE
FISH

Christy Ottaviano Books

HENRY HOLT AND COMPANY • NEW YORK

SQUARE
FISH

An imprint of Macmillan Publishing Group, LLC
175 Fifth Avenue, New York, NY 10010
mackids.com

THE UNBREAKABLE CODE. Text copyright © 2017 by
Jennifer Chambliss Bertman
Illustrations copyright © 2017 by Sarah Watts
All rights reserved. Printed in the United States of America by
LSC Communications, Harrisonburg, Virginia

Square Fish and the Square Fish logo are trademarks of Macmillan and
are used by Henry Holt and Company under license from Macmillan.

Our books may be purchased in bulk for promotional, educational, or
business use. Please contact your local bookseller or the Macmillan
Corporate and Premium Sales Department at (800) 221-7945 ext. 5442
or by e-mail at MacmillanSpecialMarkets@macmillan.com.

Library of Congress Cataloging-in-Publication Data is available.
ISBN 978-1-250-15839-0 (paperback)   ISBN 978-1-62779-661-3 (ebook)

Originally published in the United States by Henry Holt and Company
First Square Fish edition, 2018
Book designed by April Ward
Square Fish logo designed by Filomena Tuosto

3   5   7   9   10   8   6   4   2

AR: 5.8 / LEXILE: 840L

Dedicated in memory of Michelle Begley,
to her daughter Ellen,
and to Kate DiCamillo,
because Michelle would have liked that.

"Gold represented the possibility of starting anew, of being a new person, inventing a new self. It's a metaphor for hope."

—Isabel Allende, *American Experience: The Gold Rush* documentary

THE
UNBREAKABLE
CODE

Angel Island

Alcatraz

Treasure Island

San Francisco

SAN FRANCISCO
BAY

N
W   E
S

CHAPTER 1

THE PHOENIX blended in with the staggered group of people waiting for the bus. He held a paper cup in a gloved hand and checked his watch. Any eyes skimming past would judge him as average, unexceptional. That's how it was and how it had always been. People underestimated him.

That was a mistake.

The 41 rounded the corner and eased to a stop in front of Washington Square. Before joining the line that assembled to board, the Phoenix raised his cup to his lips and took his last pretend sip. Then he removed a gum wrapper from his pocket, dropped it inside the cup, and left them behind on the park bench next to a green zippered pouch.

He was the last person to board the bus. With two leaping steps up the stairs and a flash of his card to the driver, who barely looked his way, he headed down the aisle past people too absorbed in their cell phones, their paperbacks, their newspapers, their tablets, the static beats that pulsed in their ears, to pay him any attention. People were so willing to not pay attention.

He sat in the back by a window so he could glimpse the distant bay as they slugged up the hill. A deep smoky blue had taken over the sky and pushed the dying embers of sunset below the horizon. Alcatraz was a black lump on the shimmering water.

As he took in the view, he thought about the litter he'd left behind. His paper cup that had held water, not the dregs of coffee. The gum wrapper that hadn't been crushed flat but held a small silvery-white cube. He thought about the water soaking the piece of paper, working its way through the waxy coating until it reached the cube.

And then it would explode.

It wouldn't be sensational like in the movies. It shouldn't be, at least. He couldn't be responsible for what somebody else left behind. The explosion would make a noise—a pop loud enough to startle nearby people, dogs. The fire would start small. Flames would eat away at the cup, then spread quickly, crawling across the zippered pouch beside it.

Someday he might stop and watch. He'd never done that before. But not tonight. Tonight he was running late for a book party.

CHAPTER 2

"THE CLOCK'S TICKING!" Emily called down the empty hallway. She drummed the heels of her boots and adjusted the Book Scavenger pin on her dress. She wasn't really a dress person, but tonight was a special occasion. Her mom had found her a knit one with a hood, so it didn't feel too far off from her typical hoodie and jeans, and the boots were flat. Good for walking the hills of San Francisco.

"C'mon!" she urged her absent family.

Matthew's door opened. It was a long, narrow apartment so he only had to take two steps across the hallway before he joined her at the top of their interior entry stairs. Her older brother wore jeans and a T-shirt designed to look like the front of a tux. His hair had been dyed jet-black and was styled straight up. Emily pointed to his head with a questioning look, and he replied, "Modern-day top hat."

At the opposite end of the hallway, their dad hopped out of their parents' bedroom and into the kitchen, all while pulling on a sock.

"Do I need a tie?" His voice came around the corner and down the hall.

"Dad has ties?" Matthew asked.

"He keeps them in the kitchen?" Emily replied. She stepped backward down a stair, inching herself closer to their front door, as if that would hurry her parents along. Her best friend, James, who lived upstairs, would be there any minute with his family to walk with them to Hollister's bookstore.

Emily's dad carried out a cardboard box that still hadn't been unpacked, even though the Cranes had lived in San Francisco for three months. He set it in the hall and pulled out a colander, an art book about Diego Rivera, and a wad of fabric that unrolled itself to reveal two ties. He stood in the hallway outside the tiny bathroom and looked at his reflection in the mirror, holding up first the blue tie and then the red one. "These are kind of wrinkly."

Emily's mom strode out of her bedroom, a long skirt swishing around her ankles and her camera draped over her sweater like a necklace. "You'll want a jacket, Matthew," she said. "It'll be chilly on our way back."

Matthew returned to his room, and the doorbell rang. Emily flexed her hands in exasperation.

"The Lees are here," she said, taking another step

down the stairs and toward the door. "Forget the tie, Dad. You look great."

His concerned expression melted into a smile. "Thanks, sweetheart." He tossed the ties back in the direction of the cardboard box. "I'm ready, then."

Matthew rejoined the family just as the bell rang a second time.

"Finally," Emily said.

Her mom snapped her fingers. "The camera battery. I left it in the charger." She hurried down the hall.

Emily sighed.

The Cranes and the Lees made quite a procession as they tromped down the hill. James's grandmother led the way, a petite force marching with swinging arms, sidestepping brown-needled Christmas trees left out for curbside pickup. Emily, James, and Matthew followed behind. When they walked under a street lamp, Matthew's "top hat" cast a shadow that made him look like Frankenstein. The mothers were next, deep in discussion about photographing food. James's mother ran a Chinese cuisine catering business with his grandmother, and Emily's mom was a graphic designer and photographer on the side. James's father, whom Emily had only ever met one time before, and her dad brought up the rear.

Night settled onto the city as they walked, but it

never seemed to truly get dark in their neighborhood. When Emily lived in New Mexico, the night sky was inky black, and more and more stars appeared the longer you stared, like an invisible hand pricking new holes to let light shine through. In San Francisco, windows glowed warm amber in the three- and four-story residences that huddled along the street, lighting their way, along with street lamps and headlights. Stars, when you could spot them, were an afterthought.

The families turned onto Polk Street, and the jitters in Emily's stomach amped up. She couldn't tell if they were from nerves or excitement. They were headed to a book party thrown by Bayside Press in celebration of a previously unknown Edgar Allan Poe manuscript that Emily, James, and Matthew had found—rescued, really—a couple of months earlier. The three of them were going to be honored.

In the brightness of restaurant and shop windows, Emily noticed sparkles in James's hair.

"Is Steve wearing glitter?" Emily asked. *Steve* was what James called his cowlick, a piece of his hair with a mind of its own. Steve was most often found in a "ta-da!" stance on top of James's head, and the sparkles suited him well.

"He wanted to look dressy, too," James replied. Matthew nodded with understanding.

The group reached Hollister's. The view through the large picture window was normally that of a cozy, tranquil bookstore, but for this event the bookcases had been moved aside and the open space was filled with people. As Emily imagined each of those heads swiveling to stare when she walked through the door, her dress shrank seven sizes. Was she going to be expected to say something in front of all those people?

James's grandmother pushed open the door. The buzzing conversations drowned out the bells that normally jingled. Most of the people in the bookstore were grown-ups, the bland everyday sort, which made the ones dressed up as Edgar Allan Poe stand out all the more in their old-fashioned suits, scarves knotted at the neck, and tiny mustaches. One man had a fake raven on his shoulder, and another—with blood-spotted, bandaged fingers—carried a birdcage with a real raven inside, in honor of one of Poe's most famous poems.

There were kids, too, some very little, in their parents' arms or holding on to a hand. Older ones bent over a table to solve puzzle challenges or rubbed temporary tattoos of gold-bugs on each other. Matthew nodded to a group of teenagers lingering near the food and drinks and crossed the room to greet his friends.

As Emily scanned the crowd, she noticed one thing that united nearly everyone: the small gold Book Scavenger pin. The same pin Emily herself wore every day. Book Scavenger was a book-hunting game that she had played for the past few years. People hid used books in public places and posted clues about how to find the books on the website. The pin wasn't really a part of the game; it was just a trinket people sometimes wore, like a

secret symbol so you could recognize fellow players without having to ask. Emily had never seen so many pins displayed prominently at one time. The glints of gold should have relaxed her, knowing she was surrounded by Book Scavenger fans like herself, but it wasn't as if she recognized anyone. If people could wear their Book Scavenger avatars, that might be a different story.

Emily craned her neck, trying to spot Mr. Griswold, the creator of Book Scavenger and the publisher of the new Poe book. With his great height and habit of dressing in the Bayside Press colors of wine and silver blue, he had a way of being noticeable. She saw a flash of those colors and thought she'd spotted him, but it was only Jack, Mr. Griswold's assistant, talking with someone across the room.

On the edge of the party, a man fiddled with a large video camera and a woman in a dress suit did neck rolls and what Emily could only describe as kissy-face gymnastics. This woman held a microphone loosely at her side. Emily's stomach flip-flopped as she realized the pair must be from one of the news outlets Hollister had said would be at the party.

Where *was* Hollister? Emily finally spotted his back across the crowded room. He was speaking to someone in an animated way that made his gathered ponytail of dreadlocks hop across his sports coat. Someone tapped him on the shoulder and pointed in Emily and James's direction. Hollister turned, and a smile split his face. He threw his arms wide like he was sending them a hug and crowed, "The kids of the hour!"

The voices in the room dulled. Just as she'd imagined, every face turned and stared. Her cheeks warmed at the collective cooing. She fiddled with her Book Scavenger pin. James held up his hand in a hesitant wave. Matthew came back to join them, raising a power fist to the crowd. When Hollister reached them, he pulled Emily, James, and Matthew into a group bear hug.

"You excited?" he asked.

Terrified, she thought to herself, but for Hollister she nodded. "Is Mr. Griswold here yet?"

Something washed over Hollister's face—concern or guilt?—and he shook his head. "Couldn't make it. I'm sure he wanted to be here, though. Jack is stepping in to be master of ceremonies."

Hollister turned to greet their parents, and James raised an eyebrow at Emily. Hollister and Mr. Griswold had been the best of friends a long time ago, but then they'd had a falling out. When they had learned Mr. Griswold was throwing a party for the new Poe book at Hollister's store, Emily and James had hoped that meant the two old friends had made up. But if Mr. Griswold wasn't here, maybe that hadn't been the case after all.

"Point us to the books, Hollister," Emily's dad said. "The proud parents want some extra copies."

"You do?" Emily asked.

Because of her family's frequent moving in the past, her parents weren't big on material possessions, books included, even though they loved to read. "That's what the library is for!" her dad always said. For most of her lifetime, her parents had been consumed with their quest to live once in each state. It was only recently that Emily had persuaded them to call San Francisco their home indefinitely, instead of looking ahead to where they would move next. So it was a small but significant gesture that her dad wanted to buy a second copy of the new Poe book.

"I'll have Charlie bring you some," Hollister said.

"Who's Charlie?" James asked.

"You haven't met him yet?" Hollister looked around the room, trying to spot this person. "He's been here a few weeks. New employee. I saw him come in not long ago, so I know he's here. . . ." Hollister shook his head. "Ah, well. I'll grab extra copies."

As Hollister stepped away, Jack stepped through a trio of Edgar Allan Poes. His burgundy and silver-blue sweater vest and the backdrop of Poes made him look like the lead singer of a very bizarre band. He gestured to the blown-up cover of *The Cathedral Murders* that hung above the front counter.

"This book wouldn't exist without these kids—I hope you know that," Jack said to Emily's and James's families.

Mr. Lee pressed his hands onto James's shoulders. "I wish I'd been so lucky when I was young. But I wouldn't have had time to hunt for something like that anyway— my mother kept me too busy doing serious things."

Emily looked curiously at Mr. Lee. His face emanated pride, but his words sounded mocking. It wasn't luck at all that had led her and James to the undiscovered Poe manuscript.

James noticed Emily's expression and tossed his shoulders in a *Grown-ups—what can you do?* kind of shrug.

"Well, we should get started." Jack rubbed his palms together. "All these people are eager to hear more about your adventures and meet you."

Emily and James took a step closer to each other, but her brother straightened his posture, ready for duty. Matthew was always up for the task of entertaining potential fans.

Jack leaped onto a platform at the front of the store that normally served as the base for window displays but tonight was a small stage. A white screen on an easel stood next to him. He tapped the microphone, which squealed, and spoke into it. "Hello, everybody!" Jack's enthusiasm, and his tall, slender build reminded Emily of a younger Mr. Griswold. She felt a pang of disappointment that made her forget her nerves for a second. She'd been looking forward to seeing him tonight—she'd met her idol only once before.

"Welcome to Hollister's magnificent bookstore!" Jack said. "Thank you for hosting us, Hollister!"

The crowd erupted in cheers, and Hollister waved them away good-naturedly.

"While Mr. Griswold couldn't be here in person, he

did want to make an appearance. So without further ado . . ." Jack gestured to the screen next to him, and Hollister flipped off the bookstore lights. The screen lit up, and there was Griswold's face. He leaned closer, closer to the camera filming him until his frameless glasses, bulbous nose, and bushy mustache were all that filled the screen. Then he sat back and smiled.

"Greetings, scavengers!" Mr. Griswold said, and the room filled with cheers.

CHAPTER 3

EMILY LOOKED AROUND, not sure if she was more surprised by the roaring enthusiasm or by the prickles of jealousy she felt about sharing Mr. Griswold with so many other people.

"I'm recovering nicely, I'm happy to report," Mr. Griswold said. On the day Emily and her family had moved to San Francisco last October, Mr. Griswold had been attacked in a BART station and was hospitalized for some time. "However, I'm not yet up for a party, so please forgive me for staying home.

"It gives me great pleasure to introduce you to this new work by Edgar Allan Poe, a work that you quite possibly wouldn't have had the opportunity to read without the smarts and perseverance of three kids." Those prickles of jealousy softened into pride, and Emily got lost in Mr. Griswold's words. People in the audience would glance at Emily, James, and her brother as Mr.

Griswold recounted the story behind the Poe novel, but they weren't asked to give a speech or anything, and for that, Emily was grateful.

Mr. Griswold held up a glass of water in a toasting motion and said, "Enjoy the festivities!" The video clicked off, and the bookstore filled with hoots and applause. As the lights went on, so did the conversations.

"Let's check out the puzzle table," James said.

The thought of focusing on puzzles instead of the strangers who continued to stare at them was a huge relief to Emily. They had started to move when one of the Edgar Allan Poes stopped them.

"Would you sign my book?"

Emily and James looked at each other. "Us?" Emily asked.

"Of course!" he said. "You're Book Scavenger celebrities."

Emily accepted the book and his pen, and suddenly felt like she'd forgotten how to write her name. The arches in her *m* smooshed together, and then she felt self-conscious as she tried to use her best cursive to finish her signature. She handed the book to James, and he took equal care writing out his name.

James had only just handed the book back when a girl with orange-framed glasses and a Book Scavenger pin stepped in front of them. "I go to Booker Middle, too," she said softly.

James studied her. "Aren't you in my science class? Your name is Misha, right?"

"Nisha," she said.

"Right. Nisha. Sorry about that."

Nisha offered them her book and a pen, but just as Emily was about to press the pen to the page, Nisha blurted out, "Could you sign it in code?"

"Code?" Emily said.

Nisha nodded, and Emily thought for a second before she wrote *UNBWD*. James wrote *RTNUS*. They were using the cipher they'd made up together and memorized until it became their own secret language. Nisha took the book back with a wispy "thanks." Emily watched her disappear into the crowd and wondered how many more Book Scavenger players were at their school that she didn't know about.

The words *Emily* and *James* were repeated over and over above the hum, making it apparent they were still very much the center of attention. Voices swirled and heads turned their way. Emily felt dizzy.

"I need to go the bathroom," Emily said. "Be right back."

She left the crowded front of the store and immediately felt comforted by the walls of books that lined her pathway to the back of the shop. She stopped to check on Herb, a bookmark in the shape of a famous San Francisco writer named Herb Caen. Emily and James liked to hide Herb around the store so customers would randomly come across his eyes peeking out from behind a row of books. Herb was where they'd left him, nose and eyes rising above a set of old Nancy Drew hardbacks. He had kind, moon-shaped eyes. She imagined him saying, *It's okay, kid. Crowds make me anxious, too.*

It was tempting to pull one of the Nancy Drew mysteries off the shelf, go around the corner to where her favorite overstuffed purple chair was tucked in a nook, and forget the party and read. But she couldn't abandon James. She continued with her mission to the bathroom, even though she didn't really have to go, but when she stepped into the intersecting aisle, she was surprised to see her favorite chair was occupied.

Occupied by a giant floral-print purse, but still, occupied.

A man stood nearby with his back to her. Emily instinctively retreated behind the bookcase, and then felt silly for being so jumpy. She peeked around the corner and realized there was something familiar about this guy.

"Oh" escaped from her mouth.

It was her social studies teacher, Mr. Quisling. Emily knew Mr. Quisling played Book Scavenger, so it shouldn't have been a surprise for him to be here at the book party, but it was weird to see a teacher outside of his natural habitat. And back where nobody else was hanging out. Maybe her teacher didn't like crowds, either?

She realized that if Mr. Quisling noticed her now, hiding behind a bookcase, he would assume she was spying on him when she hadn't been. She needed to move. She stepped forward with purpose, planning to act surprised if Mr. Quisling noticed her, but when she glanced his way, she saw him look to his right, his left, then plunge a hand inside the purse.

Now she really was spying on her teacher, because she couldn't tear her eyes away. Why in the world was he fishing around inside a bag that obviously did not belong to him?

Mr. Quisling pulled out something thin and small— was it money? She couldn't tell. He looked at whatever it was briefly, and then disappeared into a parallel aisle, presumably heading back to the book party.

Did she just see her teacher *steal*?

Emily forgot her nerves completely, as well as her mission to the bathroom, and hightailed it back to the party to find James. He was bent over the puzzle table, and she grabbed his arm.

"James," she said.

"Hold on, I've almost got this sudoku solved," he said.

"It's Mr. Quisling."

"He's here?"

"There," Emily said, spotting their social studies teacher standing at the fringe of the crowd. His arms were crossed over his chest, and he surveyed the bookstore with a stoic expression, just as he did when students filed into his classroom.

"I guess we should go say hi," James said.

"Wait." Emily gripped his arm once again, holding him back. "I saw him stealing from someone."

James wrinkled his nose. "You saw him what?"

Emily looked to either side to make sure nobody was eavesdropping and whispered, "Stealing."

"Mr. Quisling?" He shook his head. "That can't be right. He's the most rule-abiding guy in the history of the universe."

That was true. Their teacher was pretty strict and black-and-white on his dos and don'ts. If she hadn't just seen what she did, there was no way she would have believed herself, either.

"I'm telling you, there's a purse back there. Someone left it on a chair. And Mr. Quisling took something from it."

James frowned. She could tell he still didn't quite believe her. "Well, let's go say hi."

They sidestepped a man in a turtleneck and a woman with a gray ponytail that reached her waist, who were arguing about how Poe died, and then another group trading stories about puzzle quests they had completed through Book Scavenger. When they reached the spot where their teacher had been standing, he was gone.

"Where did he go?" Emily asked.

They spent a moment eyeing the people in the room. Finally, James said, "There he is."

A hand rested on Emily's shoulder, and she jumped. It belonged to the reporter she'd spotted when they first entered the store. The woman leaned in like a gossiping friend, but her grip felt possessive. "I've been chatting with your brother. What a hoot!" The man with the video camera stood behind her, looking bored.

Matthew was across the room tossing grapes in the air and catching them in his mouth to the applause of his friends. What could her brother have said? On the opposite side of the room, their teacher was making his way through the crowd, heading toward the door. Emily strained to see what he held in his hand.

"He must keep you endlessly entertained," the reporter said. Emily wasn't sure if she meant Mr. Quisling or Matthew.

"My brother?" Emily finally said.

"Yes! He—"

Her words were drowned out by the screeching wail of a siren. For a second, Emily wondered if the police had been called about Mr. Quisling stealing from a purse, but then the interior of Hollister's bookstore flashed red as a fire engine passed by. The movement and voices in the store froze. Once the sirens softened, conversations flared up even louder than before.

The reporter studied a message on her phone. "Looks like a fire in Washington Square," she said to her cameraman.

"A fire?" James repeated.

Typing madly with both thumbs on her phone screen, she muttered, "Nothing to get worked up over. Probably something small, but you never know when something small might turn into something huge." To the cameraman she said, "We have enough material to work with here. Let's go."

The woman charged toward the door, the cameraman trailing behind. They crossed in front of the shop window under the white twinkle of lights strung in the trees outside Hollister's store. The corners of the glass were fogged up, giving the illusion of frost even though the late December weather was hardly frosty that evening.

Emily and James again followed the path of their teacher. It seemed hopeless that they would head him off before he reached the front door. But then a man intercepted Mr. Quisling. They were a couple of feet away now and could hear the man say, "Brian Quisling?"

Mr. Quisling wasn't facing them, so she couldn't see his expression, but Emily heard him say, "Yes?" in a calm and curious voice. His arm swiftly folded behind his back, and Emily saw a flash of white in his hand. Was this what he'd taken from the purse? She assumed her teacher meant to tuck the card into his pocket, but unbeknownst to him, it missed and fluttered to the ground, where it sat among the shuffling feet of people milling about the bookstore.

"Brian," the man said to their teacher, "it's me—Harry Sloan? We reconnected at the Book Scavenger literary labyrinth last September? We used to teach together many years ago."

Emily tap-tapped James's arm and pointed to the white card on the floor.

Mr. Quisling said, "Harry Sloan? The literary labyrinth?"

James extended his foot, toe pointed, and tapped the tip of his shoe to the paper, drawing it toward them and away from Mr. Quisling. James had started to bend over to pick it up when the man Mr. Quisling was talking to—Mr. Sloan—leaned to the side and looked Emily directly in the eye.

Oh no, were they about to get caught for stealing a card from their teacher, who had stolen the card from a purse? This time her dress shrank about twenty sizes. She could hardly breathe until Mr. Sloan said, "Don't tell me you're the lucky guy who teaches these kids."

James hastily grabbed the card and shoved it in his pocket before Mr. Quisling fully turned.

"It's good to see you, Mr. Quisling!" Emily nearly shouted, in a voice that was way louder and way more enthusiastic than she ever talked. A little snort of laughter burst from James.

"Did you know this man was a celebrity last fall?" Mr. Sloan said. "Just like you two today."

"A celebrity?" Emily asked. She felt grateful for this stranger who was keeping what could have been a very bizarre or awkward exchange with their teacher headed down a normal track.

Mr. Quisling sighed. "*Celebrity* seems a bit much."

"Always humble, always humble," Mr. Sloan said, clapping him on the arm.

Mr. Quisling grimaced and looked toward the door.

"Are you two familiar with the literary labyrinth event?" Mr. Sloan said. "Garrison Griswold built a maze with walls entirely constructed of books. You had to enter, find and solve three puzzle stations hidden inside the maze, and leave within a certain amount of time." The man gave Mr. Quisling's arm a little shake. "Your teacher here left everyone in the dust in the adult round. How quickly did you get through it? Fourteen minutes and thirty-six seconds?"

"Something like that," Mr. Quisling said.

"The next-fastest time was around twenty-five minutes. I didn't even come close to that." Mr. Sloan dug in his pocket and removed a wallet. "I mentioned this when I saw you last September, Brian, but I'm getting back into teaching. Subbing for now." He extended a plain business card. "I probably gave you one of these, but I know how easy it is to misplace them."

When Mr. Quisling didn't reach for the card, Mr. Sloan pressed it into his hand. "In case you need a sub. You can call me."

"I don't get sick," Mr. Quisling replied.

Mr. Sloan whistled low. "You've done it now. You've jinxed yourself!" He tapped the card resting on Mr. Quisling's open palm. "Hold on to that, my friend. I can cover any subject. Math, history, English . . . Took the GRE recently and got a perfect score, can you believe that?"

"I'm sorry, but I should get going," Mr. Quisling said, accepting the business card. To Emily and James he nodded and said, "Congratulations, you two. See you in the New Year."

As their teacher made his way to the exit, Mr. Sloan bent toward Emily and James. "Is it just me, or is he not much of a party person?"

Emily and James grinned. "It's not just you," they answered.

Mr. Sloan winked and slipped into the crowd.

"So?" Emily asked, once they were alone again in the sea of people. "What was the paper?"

James held it forward, and they examined it: a note-card with a bird on the front, wings spread, and a long tail of feathers. Inside was a handwritten note that read

Remember the Niantic? I sure do. To figure out my message, that is your clue.

GTTSAJN AJ LTPQKJ WAFF ET
QWTTSTP KJMT WT'VT QKFVTB SIT
UJEPTRDREFT MKBT

Solve the puzzle and leave the solution with the next book, and maybe you will change my mind.

"'The Niantic'? What's that mean?" James asked.

"I'm more curious about the cipher," Emily said. "And why our teacher stole this out of a purse."

"And what does 'leave the solution with the next book' mean?" James added.

"Pardon me."

They looked up to see an Edgar Allan Poe standing before them. He bowed his head, and his caterpillar-like mustache sprang from his lip to the floor. The Poe swore, picked up the mustache, and turned his back to them. When he faced them again, the mustache had been reapplied, but crookedly. "Apologies, my fair children." Poe held his book out for them and smiled, his mustache dropping from the top lip to his chin.

They signed the Poe's book and watched him slink over to the snack table.

"What a weird night," James said.

"You can say that again," Emily replied.

CHAPTER 4

EMILY HAD RETURNED home from the book party hours ago and was supposed to be getting ready for bed, but she was still buzzing. Fortunately, James was up, too.

Thud. Thud-thud-thud. Thud.

Prompted by James's knocking on the floor above, Emily went to her open bedroom window. James's room directly over hers cast a narrow rectangle of light on the wall of the neighboring building only a few feet away. For a moment, Emily could see the shadow of the tin pail being lowered down by the pulley system that ran between their windows.

Once the bucket reached her, Emily removed the notebook paper they'd been passing back and forth. She skimmed the chain of messages written in their made-up secret code. She had the key written in her notebook, but she rarely had to refer to it anymore:

A	B	C	D	E	F	G	H	I	J	K	L	M
T	H	E	Q	U	I	C	K	B	R	O	W	N

N	O	P	Q	R	S	T	U	V	W	X	Y	Z
F	X	J	M	P	S	V	L	A	Z	Y	D	G

It didn't take Emily long to understand what James had written:

EPTEOUQ BV! "PUNUNHUP VKU
FBTFVBE" BS VKU OUDZXPQ
*(Cracked it! "Remember the Niantic"
is the keyword.)*

A keyword cipher! Emily groaned. Why hadn't she guessed that? James hadn't written out the solution, so she flipped to a new page in her notebook and tugged free the pencil she kept tucked in her ponytail.

A keyword cipher was a type of substitution cipher, similar to their secret code. Emily wrote out the regular alphabet, and then underneath she wrote *Remember the Niantic*, leaving out any repeated letters. After that, she filled in the rest of the alphabet to come up with the key:

A	B	C	D	E	F	G	H	I	J	K	L	M
R	E	M	B	T	H	N	I	A	C	D	F	G

27

N	O	P	Q	R	S	T	U	V	W	X	Y	Z
J	K	L	O	P	Q	S	U	V	W	X	Y	Z

Now all she had to do was look up each letter from the coded message to see what it translated to in the key. She looked again at the puzzle in Mr. Quisling's note:

Remember the Niantic? I sure do. To figure out my message, that is your clue.

GTTSAJN AJ LTPQKJ WAFF ET
QWTTSTP KJMT WT'VT QKFVTB SIT
UJEPTRDREFT MKBT

She slowly read each word out loud as she deciphered the message: "Meeting . . . in . . . person . . . will . . . be . . . sweeter . . . once . . . we've . . . solved . . . the . . . un . . . breakable . . . code.

"The unbreakable code?" Emily said again.

There was no better way to hook Emily's interest in a cipher than to say it couldn't be broken. Her skin prickled, electrified. This was the feeling she got when a book sucked her into the zone of no return. Like the time she was reading *When You Reach Me* and her parents gave up trying to get her attention to come to dinner and she ended up eating cold spaghetti after she finally finished the book.

Only this wasn't a book. There were no pages to turn to find out what the mysterious message meant by the unbreakable code.

James's voice carried down the narrow gap from his window above. "You'll never guess what the *Niantic* is! I looked it up online."

Emily leaned her head out the window and said to the dark, "What happened to our 'no talking when we're using the bucket' rule?"

"This is too cool to wait," James called back. "Guess what the *Niantic* is."

Emily tried to think about what might get James so excited. "A supercomputer? A code left by aliens?"

A distant foghorn rose above the white noise of the city at night. Emily waited for James to reply. Finally, he said, a bit wistfully, "Well, a code left by aliens would be much cooler."

Emily snorted. "Tell me already."

"The *Niantic* is an old ship that's buried under the city."

"There's a ship buried under San Francisco?"

"According to Wiki, there are about fifty ships buried under the city. They're from the Gold Rush."

"Seriously?" She imagined an enormous cave underneath San Francisco with stalactites hanging down and pirate ships parked in every nook and cranny. But James had said "buried" not abandoned in a cave, so maybe it was more like a ship graveyard.

"Why would they bury ships?" Emily asked.

"I'm not sure. Wiki says there's a chunk of the *Niantic* on display at a museum down by Fort Mason."

"Do you think we could find out more about this unbreakable code there?" Emily asked.

A window slid open in the building next door, slicing the night with its screech. Emily froze. A man bellowed, "Do you know what time it is?"

"Sorry," Emily and James said in unison.

The window groaned shut, and the lingering silence was heavy with the embarrassment of being caught.

Emily scribbled a message to James:

ZTFV VX EKUEO XLV VKU
FBTFVBE VXNXPPXZ?
(Want to check out the Niantic *tomorrow?)*

She placed the paper in the bucket and raised it up, cringing with every *squeak, squeak* of the pulleys. She knew James's reply would come quickly, so she waited by the window, and sure enough, the paper was returned within minutes.

DXL OFXZ BV!
(You know it!)

CHAPTER 5

THE PHOENIX sat in a restaurant whipping an empty sugar packet through the candle flame on his table. Back, forth, back, forth. He meditated on the flame, watching it grasp for the packet with every pass and miss.

"Not now," he scolded. "*I* control when you'll be fed."

Smirking at this little joke of fire as his pet, he returned his gaze to the television screen behind the bar and mindlessly continued to swing the sugar packet through the flame. Back. Forth. Back. Forth.

On the TV, a reporter stood at Washington Square. He couldn't hear her words, but it was obvious she was discussing his fire. An uncomfortable feeling brewed in his stomach, and he didn't like it. *If you think you're so smart*, an imaginary voice chirped, *then why are you working so hard to prove it to others?*

No connection appeared to have been made between

this fire and his last. That was good. Wasn't it? The doubt flashed across his mind before he could stop it, and he snapped his hand into a fist, balling up the sugar packet. Questioning yourself was for the weak. He had made a plan, and he was sticking to it.

"I control you," he whispered to the flame. He extended the packet and could almost hear the fire hiss with relief as it ate the paper. The edges curled in on themselves, brown, then black. He dropped the flaming piece into the candle cup, where it would wither and die.

His waitress returned with his bill and gave the blackened lump of char resting in the votive holder a double take.

"Nervous habit," the Phoenix explained.

The waitress cleared his plate and glass from the table. "I bite my nails. We've all got our quirks."

CHAPTER 6

THE NEXT MORNING, Emily and James headed out to the Maritime Museum. Emily had searched the Internet for information on the unbreakable code while she ate her cereal, but there was no way of telling if Mr. Quisling's note referred to the McCormick cipher or the *Kryptos* sculpture at CIA headquarters or any of the dozens more unsolved codes that had turned up in her online search. She'd had no idea there were so many unsolved puzzles out there in the world.

They walked from their building down the sloping streets until they reached Fisherman's Wharf. The final hill was so steep, their steps turned into a scuttling run until they reached the bottom. In the distance, a massive ship that could've been straight out of a pirate movie was anchored at the end of the Hyde Street Pier. The ship had been there the entire time Emily had lived in San Francisco, but today she saw it with new eyes.

"Do you think the *Niantic* was as big as that ship?" she asked James.

"Probably," he said.

It was hard to imagine a ship that big buried under the city, let alone fifty of them.

The Maritime Museum was a white stucco building with curved ends and porthole-shaped windows, making it look like a cruise ship. Inside, a large, open room was filled with display cases and a small sailboat. Floor-to-ceiling windows looked out to a slender beach. In the bay she could see Alcatraz and a larger island behind it.

The *Niantic* remnant was a jagged chunk of green-tinged copper wrapped around wood beams. It was as long as both Emily and James put together if they stood side by side with their arms outstretched, and very narrow. It was barely as wide as Emily's shoulders. She had a hard time imagining how it had been part of a large ship.

Reading from the museum displays, Emily was surprised to learn that many Americans on the East Coast had sailed all the way around South America in order to get to the West Coast during the Gold Rush. For some reason, she had imagined people traveling only by covered wagon in the olden days. When she was seven and her family moved from New York to South Dakota, they listened to *Little House on the Prairie* in the car, and Emily had imagined that was what they were doing—heading west huddled together in a covered wagon. It had seemed a fitting fantasy for how long and tedious that road trip had been.

Emily also learned that the ships that came to San Francisco not only brought gold seekers from the East Coast, they also brought people from other countries, too, like Mexico, Peru, Chile, and China.

"How did the ships get buried?" Emily wondered aloud.

"Landfill," said a woman's voice from across the room. They turned to see a docent not much taller than they were, with gray hair styled like James's minus a

Steve. The woman crossed over to them, but her right foot was in a walking cast. It took great effort for her to move it forward with every step.

"All that used to be water," the woman said as she approached, wagging a finger at a map hung behind them. It showed the shoreline of San Francisco Bay today overlapped with the shoreline during the Gold Rush. The docent reached the map and used her index finger to trace an oval around several miles of the outer perimeter of San Francisco.

She tapped the map. "This area was called Yerba Buena Cove," she said.

"Isn't that where downtown San Francisco is?" Emily asked.

"Yep," said the docent.

Downtown San Francisco was where the skyscrapers and biggest buildings were. The idea that those buildings now stood where it had once been only water seemed so weird. Unstable somehow. Like the water might find a way to creep back where it belonged and uproot everything.

James pointed to another area of the map. "And there's North Beach."

"No wonder!" Emily said. "I couldn't figure out why they named it a beach when there isn't any water there. But there used to be, a hundred and fifty years ago."

James studied the map a minute longer. "I didn't know this was possible," he said. "To just fill in part of a bay like it's a swimming pool or something. I wonder what else got buried under the city besides a bunch of whaling ships."

The word *buried* made Emily think of dead people. "What if there are bodies down there?"

James considered this. "It's been well over a hundred years, so they'd be long gone if there were. No threat of a zombie apocalypse. Decomposed bodies are hard to bring back from the dead."

The docent barked a laugh. "Zombie apocalypse. That's good. I'm using that on my next tour."

"But why did the ships get buried?" Emily asked.

"Well." The docent clasped her hands in front of her stomach. "The first thing you have to understand is the population explosion that happened here when word got out about gold being discovered. Prior to that, this area was a small settlement, not a city. There was no infra-structure here—no homes for people to move to, no paved roads, no railroad to transport people or supplies. Most everything—people and goods—arrived via ship, and the San Francisco Bay was the main port of entry for those ships coming and going. See how crazy it got?" The woman tapped a black-and-white image of the bay jammed full of ship masts. "That was Yerba Buena Cove. It's been said a person could have crossed the water by stepping from ship to ship, that's how crowded it was.

"Those ships were often left abandoned. The crews were so eager to get to the gold, they hightailed it out of there and headed up to the mining country. The abandoned ships were sometimes broken down for their materials. Other times they were brought aground and converted into stores and hotels. That's what happened to the *Niantic*.

"Wharves were built for better access to these ships. The shallow water between the wharves was gradually filled in. It was the most desirable land for development because of the convenience to ships bringing in goods. The waterfront was the commercial heart of the city."

"Does any of this have to do with something called the unbreakable code?" James asked.

If the docent's eyes could have popped out of her head, they would have. She took a step back, her injured foot dragging to catch up with the other.

"Oh, no—I'm not talking about that. Nope. Nope. Nope. Not to you kids."

Emily looked to James. Had they done something wrong? The woman had been so eager to tell them everything else.

"You two don't need to get mixed up with that old code," the docent said.

"Why?" Emily asked.

"Because it's cursed."

CHAPTER 7

"CURSED?" Emily and James repeated.

"It causes fires. That's what people say. It survived one that destroyed the *Niantic*, as a matter of fact, back in 1851. And then . . ." The docent waved her hand. "I've said too much already. It's not even worth discussing. What you should be interested in are these *Niantic* artifacts."

She pointed to a plate of glass on the floor that covered a gaping hole filled with dirt, blackened bottles, and pickax-looking tools. "This is a simulation of the dig that happened in 1978. Those are actual items found in the buried hull. . . ."

Her voice became a background hum as Emily's mind ran away with thoughts about the unbreakable code. Being told it was cursed only made her want to know more, but she could tell the woman was done talking about it. Emily was ready to leave, but then a photo caught her eye. It was part of a series that showed the 1978 excavation: a large dirt plot surrounded by office buildings, a dozen or so people in '70s flared pants, digging with shovels or standing in small groups talking and watching the work being done.

It was the close-up of one person in particular that had stood out: a man—a teenager, really—with his arm thrown around a teenage girl's shoulders. The girl was laughing, and the man had his head angled down, smiling at her. Another man in the background squinted at the camera like he wasn't sure if he was in the shot or not.

"James, look."

"Those are volunteers who came to help the Maritime Museum with the excavation," the docent said.

"That's also our social studies teacher," Emily said.

"It is?" James leaned close. "Mr. Quisling?"

"Read the caption."

The caption said *Volunteers Brian Quisling and Miranda Oleanda help the Maritime Museum with their excavation project.*

"Miranda *Oleanda*? That is seriously someone's name?" James said.

"Our teacher was randomly at this historic dig, but what you're focusing on is his old girlfriend's name? Really?"

"How do you know she was a girlfriend?" James asked, studying the photo.

"They just seem . . . boyfriend-girlfriendish. I mean, the way he's looking at her. Have you ever seen Mr. Quisling look at something that way, ever?"

"Maybe a . . . sandwich? A really good one?"

The docent shook her head and smiled. "You kids today."

After their visit to the Maritime Museum, Emily felt stuffed up with new information, but none of it explained the unbreakable code. She added *fire curse* to her online search, but it still didn't draw up anything useful. For the next two days, Emily and James continued to deliberate what the code could be.

"At least we know it actually exists. That's something," Emily said. They were sitting on their front stoop, waiting for her brother to finish getting ready so they could go downtown for their first Book Scavenger advisory meeting. "Do you think Mr. Quisling has known about the unbreakable code since that *Niantic* dig in 1978?"

"Maybe," James said. "But the docent said it survived a fire on that ship in 1851, not that it was discovered during the excavation."

That was slightly reassuring. Even though they still didn't know what the unbreakable code *was*, Emily had grown attached to her fantasy of being the one to break it. It was harder to believe that might happen if their puzzle-expert teacher had been spending the last thirty-odd years trying to crack the code with no luck.

"We could always ask Mr. Quisling about it when we're back in school," James said.

Emily snorted. "I'm sure that would go over well." Mimicking herself in a high-pitched and hyper voice, she said, *"Um, Mr. Quisling? We saw you steal something at the book party, and then you dropped it, and so we picked it up and deciphered your secret message, and now we know about something called the unbreakable code. Do you know anything about this, and if so could you please tell us?"*

James laughed. "Hey, there are no dumb questions—doesn't he say that all the time in class?"

"I think what he says is 'There are no dumb questions, only poorly thought-out questions.' This would probably fall in the poorly thought-out category."

The front door opened, and Matthew joined them on the stoop. "Ready to get my book nerding on," he announced.

Emily stood up and took in her brother's appearance. His hair was still dyed jet-black from the book party, but instead of sticking straight up, it was slicked back in an über-preppy style. He wore thick-rimmed black glasses and a T-shirt that said I LIKE BIG BOOKS AND I CANNOT LIE.

"Oh, brother," Emily said.

"You called?"

Emily slugged Matthew's arm in response.

The three walked down the hill to where they would catch a bus downtown. Church bells rang as they crossed a busy street toward the large green expanse of Washington Square.

"What happened there?" Emily asked.

A red rope cordoned off an area under a large tree. What appeared to be shade from a distance was actually a blackened swath of grass. A bench charred at one end sat among the gaping remains of burnt shrubs. The tree overhead rustled ever so slightly, and a tiny leaf came free, fluttering down to the ground, its green neon against the black.

"It looks like there was a fire," James said.

They crossed the street to their bus stop, but Emily couldn't help looking back over her shoulder. She passed this park all the time. Sometimes it was lively and filled with crowds or an art festival. Sometimes it was tranquil, with people sitting on benches or practicing tai chi or other exercises. And now there was this scar, reminding her that anything you took for granted could change at any time.

CHAPTER 8

AT BAYSIDE PRESS, the three signed in with the security guard and pushed the elevator button for the sixth floor. As they rode in silence, Emily daydreamed about what sorts of things the Book Scavenger teen advisory might do. Since Mr. Griswold had invited them a month ago to launch a teen advisory committee for Book Scavenger, she and James had been brainstorming ideas for cool Griswold-esque events they could help plan. She hoped that would be their first task.

The elevator doors opened, and they were blasted with burgundy and silver blue. The walls and carpet of the lobby were boldly adorned in Bayside Press colors. The receptionist paged Jack, and he soon appeared wearing a wine-colored sweater with a teal collar popped out.

"Does Mr. Griswold make you wear those colors?" Matthew asked.

Jack laughed. "Just a fashion trend I thought I'd follow. Promotes a team spirit, don't you think? And the colors suit my complexion." Jack made a fishy face and struck a model pose before leading them down the hallway.

While this was Emily's third visit to Mr. Griswold's office, it was only the second time she would be seeing the man himself. She'd watched him in plenty of Book Scavenger videos and had read various articles about him and posts from Book Scavenger users who'd met Mr. Griswold at events. When she'd met Mr. Griswold for the first time, he'd been as warm and colorful as she'd imagined he would be, even though he'd just been released from the hospital.

Jack held up a hand for them to stop just before the hallway opened into the large cubicle-filled space.

"I should probably tell you guys . . ." Jack slid his fingers into his hair and squeezed, pulling the hair up so he had a momentary faux-hawk. "Mr. Griswold is doing much better than before, but there's . . . a lot of recovery still ahead. His physical recovery is on track, but the incident last fall . . . well, it rattled him. As would be expected, of course." Jack's chuckle seemed forced, and he swallowed it uncomfortably. "I just don't want you guys to be disappointed if he seems a little off today. It's not you kids. He's happy you're here, trust me, and I think seeing you will be good for him. He just needs some time to get back to his old self."

Back to his old self? Emily wiped her hands on her

sides and shoved them in her hoodie pockets, suddenly uncertain about who they would find when Jack opened Mr. Griswold's office door. When Jack's hand rested on the doorknob, three deep barks erupted on the other side, followed by a sharp, high-pitched one. Emily jumped.

"Dogs?" She and James looked at each other, wide-eyed. That was about the last thing she'd expected.

"Technically they're service dogs." Jack bent his fingers into air quotes when he said *service*. "They're harmless."

He swung the door open, and two dogs came racing out: one sleek and brown, who nearly came up to Emily's chest, and the other small, scruffy, and white.

"Aww!" Emily and James cooed over the dogs. Matthew dropped to one knee, held out a hand, and clicked his tongue, but both dogs ignored him. The large one ran in a figure eight around them while the small dog came to a halt just outside the office, gave one perfunctory yip, then raced back inside. Jack shooed the big dog to return to the office, but that seemed to only encourage his trotting figure eights.

"Claus," Mr. Griswold's voice called from inside. The dog's ears perked at the crumple and rattle of treats, and he abruptly turned and went back into the room.

Mr. Griswold's office was big and sunny with a view of downtown skyscrapers framing the Ferry Building clock tower and the bay beyond. A bust of Edgar Allan Poe posed in front of the window wearing a golden

46

rabbit medallion. The bookshelves were overstuffed with toys and puzzles as well as books. Marbles *click-clack*ed through a glass-encased contraption that consisted of ramps and rotating buckets and other obstacles designed to keep them moving.

The office was just as Emily remembered, but Mr. Griswold was not. The man she'd met in November had seemed much more like the Mr. Griswold she knew from the videos on the Book Scavenger website. Today, the publisher appeared frail and washed out in his oversize gray sweater and slacks. Even though Jack had warned them, seeing this diluted, *normal* version of her idol was like pulling back the curtain on the Wizard of Oz.

Their surprised reactions must have showed, because Mr. Griswold brushed his clothes and said, almost apologetically, "My usual suits aren't so comfortable right now." To Jack he said, "I suppose my casual wear could use some brightening, couldn't it?"

"You look great, Old Book Dude," Matthew said. Ordinarily this was the sort of comment that would make Emily thwap her brother, but Mr. Griswold chuckled at the nickname Matthew had coined a couple of months ago.

"You met my new pups?" The big dog continued to lick Mr. Griswold's palm after gobbling up his treat. "This one is Claus, and the little one is Angel."

Angel curled up in a basket in a corner with one furry eyebrow raised, watching the room skeptically. Having finished his treat, Claus pranced to the couch, gingerly nipped the corner of a throw pillow so it dangled from his mouth, then trotted away with his head held high like he was showing off a newly won trophy.

"Claus likes to imagine himself in a parade, I think," Mr. Griswold said, his mustache lifting with his smile.

They all laughed, and it felt good, like a breeze of fresh air sweeping through the room.

"Are those cameras?" James pointed to the ceiling where plastic bubbles encased shiny black equipment.

Mr. Griswold nodded. "A new addition since . . ." He gestured to himself with a flourish. "You can never be too cautious these days. This might interest you three. I know you like electronics, James." With the help of a cane, Mr. Griswold crossed the room to open a panel of bookcases that revealed a secret room they had seen once before. The small room was filled with computer equipment. Emily stepped inside. Mechanical whirring surrounded her like a swarm of invisible robotic bees. Four new monitors showed black-and-white footage of Mr. Griswold's office, the Bayside Press reception area, what looked like the front entry of an apartment building, and a rooftop patio. "To help me keep an eye on things here and at home," Mr. Griswold explained.

"Wow . . ." Emily said, her voice hushed.

"I suppose it is impressive, isn't it?"

But Emily wasn't in awe. The guard dogs and the surveillance cameras . . . It bothered Emily that a pendulum could swing into Mr. Griswold's life and leave his personality and spirit dented.

They exited the room, and Mr. Griswold swung the bookcase closed. He limped back to the couch. Claus climbed up next to him, dragging his pillow, and plopped both pillow and head onto Mr. Griswold's lap. The dog whimpered and nibbled at the corner of the pillow.

"He looks like he'd be ferocious, but he's the biggest baby you'll ever meet," Mr. Griswold said, stroking Claus's head.

From his basket, Angel snorted, as if in agreement, and dropped her head onto her paws.

"Now, the teen advisory committee!" Mr. Griswold smiled. "I've been wanting to organize this for a while. Your young perspectives will be invaluable for Book Scavenger."

Emily couldn't help but think that hearing their ideas might be exactly what Mr. Griswold needed to get back to his old flamboyant, game-scheming ways. She jumped right in. "We're really excited. James and I already have a plan. We thought there could be an obstacle course around Golden Gate Park—"

"With puzzle stations," James added. "The competitors would complete a puzzle station, then go down the cement slide, then run to the next puzzle station—"

"And then paddleboat across Stow Lake to the next puzzle station."

Matthew hadn't been part of their brainstorming, but he was nodding along with everything they said. "We should end the whole thing at a live concert! I wonder how much it would cost to have Flush play."

Mr. Griswold's eyebrows rose up and up and up. "Oh, dear," he finally said. "Well. That certainly sounds ambitious. And it's something I might have done . . . before." Mr. Griswold sighed. "Those days are behind me now. The elaborate games and events were fun while they lasted, but—" Mr. Griswold shook his head and wrinkled his nose, his mustache scrunching up like he'd tasted something sour.

"Oh." It was all Emily could muster to say. Of course Mr. Griswold would be reluctant to do a big event again. But how could he give them up altogether? She remembered the video he'd posted to the Book Scavenger website recounting the reverse egg hunt he'd hosted. Contestants wore large, inflatable egg-shaped suits and ran around a park bumping into each other as they found hidden paperback books to fill their baskets. In the video, Mr. Griswold started laughing so hard he couldn't talk. Clearly, planning those events had made him happy. Emily could understand why he might be scared now, but how could you give up something that had been such a big part of who you were?

Jack chimed in. "Our idea for the advisory had been for you to start off generating content for the website, maybe feature book recommendations or tips for book hunting. We'd also like to set you up as website admins to help model and maintain an encouraging and collaborative atmosphere. And you could help with forum housekeeping—deleting inactive threads, booting trolls off the site, that sort of thing."

Mr. Griswold rhythmically stroked Claus's head as Jack spoke. The dog had fallen asleep.

"Oh. Sure!" Emily said, maybe a bit too brightly. The obstacle course she and James had envisioned seemed like it could be so much fun. Maybe in time Mr. Griswold would come around to doing it.

After a little more discussion about their teen advisory responsibilities, James said, "Hey, Mr. Griswold, did you know there might be an old ship buried under your office building?"

Mr. Griswold smiled. "I did know about that, as a matter of fact. I take it you've learned part of the city was built on landfill?"

"On landfill? Like on trash?" Matthew said. He walked to the window as if he'd be able to see evidence of this outside.

"Have you heard about something called the unbreakable code?" Emily asked. She leaned forward in her seat, eager to hear his answer. If Mr. Griswold knew about the buried ships, maybe he'd know about this, too.

"The unbreakable code?" Mr. Griswold studied his hand resting on Claus's neck.

"Isn't that the Mark Twain cipher?" Jack said.

Emily and James looked to Jack in surprise, then each other.

"The writer?" Emily asked. The Maritime Museum docent hadn't said anything about Mark Twain. Of course she hadn't wanted them to know about the unbreakable code in the first place.

Mr. Griswold continued to study sleeping Claus, but Jack nodded enthusiastically. "Yeah, yeah—I'm fuzzy on the details, but I remember hearing about this a while back. You can view the code at the main library. They have the original document there."

"It's at the library?!" Emily and James looked sheepishly at each other. They'd spent the last two days debating what the code could be and doing random searches on the Internet. Why hadn't it occurred to them to ask at a library?

"You have to request to see it at the History Center," Jack replied. "But yeah, I'm pretty sure it's there."

"We are so totally checking this out," Emily said.

CHAPTER 9

A SHORT WHILE LATER, Emily, James, and Matthew were riding a streetcar down Market Street on their way to the main library.

"Jack didn't say anything about a fire curse," Emily noted.

"Maybe that docent was pulling our leg," James said.

"What's the fire curse?" Matthew asked.

They filled her brother in on the odd way the woman at the Maritime Museum had acted when they asked about the unbreakable code, and how she'd said it was cursed.

"She said the code survived a fire in 1851. That means it's over a hundred and sixty years old. How cool would it be to crack a cipher that couldn't be solved for that long?" James asked.

Matthew placed an earbud in one ear. "You two get excited about the weirdest things."

The main library was a silver-and-gray grid of concrete and windows—about as exciting as graph paper—so it surprised Emily to walk into a vast, sun-filled lobby crowned with a round sunroof high overhead. Emily's head spun looking up and around at the balconied hallways that ringed every level. All those hallways and doors led to different sections of the library. If they weren't on a mission to see the unbreakable code, Emily would have wanted to randomly pick a floor and wander.

Once they found their way to the History Center, Emily had imagined they would browse shelves like she normally did in a library, but they were stopped at the front desk by a librarian.

"What can I help you find?" The woman's name tag read REGINA LINDEN, and she looked nothing like what Emily imagined when she thought of the word *librarian*. She had green-streaked hair threading through an otherwise black ponytail. The color surprised Emily most of all because the librarian was old. Not old-old, like little-old-lady old, but colorful hair was something Emily thought of teenagers and college kids having, and Ms. Linden was older than that. Maybe even older than her parents. And then there were the tattoos wrapping around her forearm that peeked out from the cuff of her blouse.

"Cool sleeve," Matthew said, noting the tattoos.

"Thanks." Ms. Linden smiled, and pushed up the fabric so they could have a better look at the collage of images. It was like an I-Spy game with flowers, a feather, a lightning bolt, a cat—Emily thought it would take her an hour to make out all the pictures. An airplane carried a banner that read *Tell me, what is it you plan to do with your one wild and precious life?*

"Great quote, don't you think?" Ms. Linden asked. "It's from the poet Mary Oliver. So you tell me"—she pressed her hands together like she was praying, pointed her fingers toward them, and said—"what do *you* plan to do with your one wild and precious . . . visit to the History Center?"

Emily laughed nervously. James shifted his feet, and they looked at each other, daring the other to speak up first. There was something about how vibrant and bold Ms. Linden seemed that intimidated Emily.

"They want to see the unbreakable code," Matthew said. "I'm just along for the ride."

Ms. Linden's eyes lit up. "Treasure hunters, are you? You'll appreciate this, then." The librarian lifted her necklace to show them an odd-looking coin strung on the chain. "This is from a dive through an old shipwreck off the coast of Florida."

Emily and James collectively breathed out the word *wow*. Matthew leaned an elbow on the counter. "You dive?" he said. "I've been wanting to try that."

Emily snorted. Matthew freaked out in aquariums, so she was pretty sure he hadn't considered scuba diving until that very second.

"You'll love it," Ms. Linden said. "I've got a J-Boat I

take down to Monterey every so often when I'm itching for a local dive." She typed into her computer. "Okay, I'll bring the code to you, but you all need to sign this first." Ms. Linden slid over a sheet of paper stating they wouldn't destroy or steal any of the materials. "And I'll keep your bags up here with me."

"Can I bring my notebook?" Emily asked.

"Sure. Notebooks are fine. Pens, pencils, even cameras—but no flash on historical documents. No photocopying, of course."

Ms. Linden led them to a long empty table in the middle of an intimidatingly quiet room lined with sleek, glass-fronted bookshelves. There were three other people in the room reading.

"So, I'm curious," Ms. Linden said. "What exactly do you know about the unbreakable code?"

"Not very much."

Emily hesitated to say any more, but her brother blurted out, "We know it's cursed, but that sort of thing doesn't scare us." He shrugged nonchalantly.

Who *was* this guy showing off for the librarian? Emily hadn't even been sure Matthew had been listening when they'd told him about their conversation with the Maritime Museum docent, but obviously he had. She hadn't been sure if they should mention the curse. The museum docent had refused to talk about it for that reason—what if Ms. Linden changed her mind about letting them look at it?

"We also know it's called the Mark Twain cipher," James added. That made Ms. Linden's eyes light up.

"So then you know about Tom Sawyer?" she asked.

"The book?" Emily knew the title because she'd hunted it before through Book Scavenger. It was the first hunt she went on in San Francisco, actually, only another player had found the book before her.

"Not the book." Ms. Linden smiled. "Ah, this will be fun. You'll love this story. I'll be right back."

Ms. Linden left them for a moment and returned with two folders in hand. "Before we get to the code, I want you to meet someone." She flipped open one folder to reveal a black-and-white portrait of a man with a mustache, goatee, and sideburns. A tall firefighter hat topped his head. "This is Tom Sawyer. He lived here in San Francisco in the late eighteen hundreds."

"That guy? He lived here *that* long ago?" Matthew scoffed. "He looks like a hipster. With a big hat."

Ms. Linden gave the photo a second look. "I guess some trends come back around. In any case, this guy was a hero of early San Francisco. He helped organize one of the first fire companies for the city."

"If his name is Tom Sawyer, then does he have anything to do with the book?" Emily asked.

Ms. Linden nodded. "That's where the story gets interesting. Our Tom Sawyer claimed Mark Twain— that's the author of the book—named the character after him, although Twain never said one way or another if that was true. They did know each other, though, when Twain worked as a reporter here in San Francisco. He was Samuel Clemens then, of course." Ms. Linden paused, studying their wrinkled foreheads, then explained, "Mark Twain was a pen name.

"Tom Sawyer and Twain were good enough friends that Sawyer visited him when he lived in Virginia City, one of the mining towns up north in Nevada. It was when the two were together up there that Mark Twain supposedly won the unbreakable code while gambling. The man who lost didn't have money to settle his bet and offered the code instead. He claimed that, once broken, it would lead to a stash of gold buried near San Francisco."

"Really?" Emily caught James's eye. Could that be what Mr. Quisling was after? Buried gold? If they broke the unbreakable code, would they beat their teacher to the treasure?

"Really," Ms. Linden replied. "Twain was a sucker for a good story, so he accepted the code as payment. He was cautioned by someone that the code was cursed—allegedly it had survived a major fire—"

"The one that burned down the *Niantic*," Emily said, remembering what the docent at the Maritime Museum had told them.

Ms. Linden raised her eyebrows, impressed. "So you do know some of the history." She nodded. "That's where the idea of a curse began. The legend is that if anyone but the original owner tries to crack the cipher and find the rumored treasure, they will suffer a fire. But Mark Twain wasn't concerned—some historians speculate that he accepted the code as payment specifically *because* he appreciated the story behind it. But then Mark Twain had a change of heart when a fire started in his hotel room."

"Seriously?" Matthew asked.

Ms. Linden nodded solemnly. "Seriously. And it spooked Twain away from the code. Tom Sawyer offered to take it off his hands. He'd been a firefighter—he wasn't afraid of a silly fire curse. Sawyer owned a saloon in San Francisco, and he saw the potential for drawing customers to his business if the code was on display. He framed it and hung it among the firefighting memorabilia that decorated the walls. He told patrons it was a gift from Mark Twain and challenged them to solve it, promising free drinks for life to anyone who could. Nobody ever did.

"But here's the kicker," Ms. Linden said. "Tom Sawyer's bar *burned down* while the code was hung on its walls. Imagine that! But guess what survived?"

Ms. Linden flipped open the second folder, revealing an aged paper sandwiched between pieces of vellum. The bottom half of the paper was filled with letters written in an old-fashioned scroll. "The unbreakable code."

CHAPTER 10

I 'LL LEAVE YOU to it," Ms. Linden said, and sashayed away.

The paper was darker around the edges, as if it had been toasted. It smelled like an attic in an old house. The only thing on the top half of the page was the faintest moon-shaped mark, like a ring left from a coffee mug. Shadows of markings on the flip side showed through. Emily slid her fingers underneath the vellum and turned the page over. There was a simple sketch—four lopsided circles and a few wormy dashes—as if someone had started a drawing and then stopped. The sort of doodle she might do in class.

"The person writes like a kid," Matthew said. "My English teacher would give that a big fat C for penmanship."

Emily sighed, exasperated with her brother. "It's *old*, Matthew," she said. "They wrote differently back then."

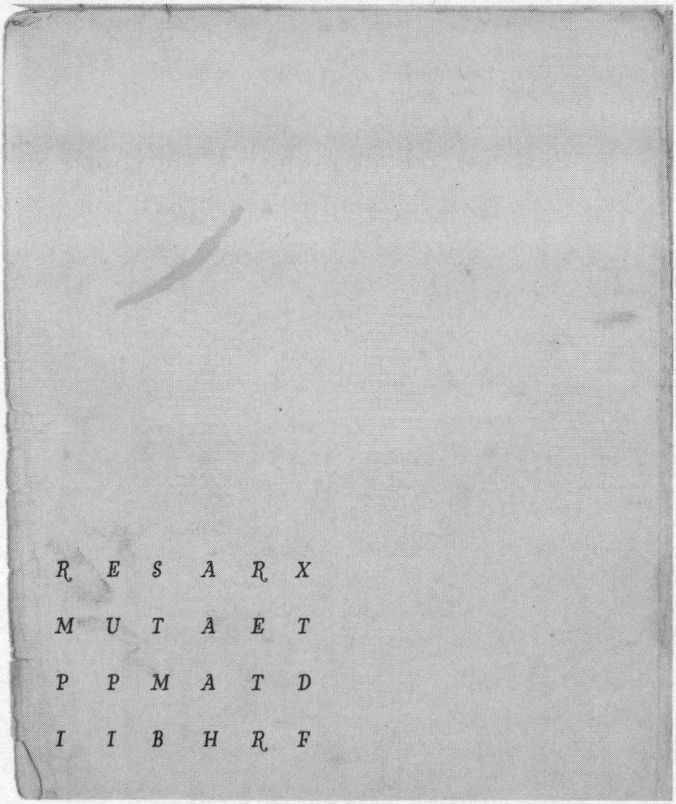

```
R   E   S   A   R   X

M   U   T   A   E   T

P   P   M   A   T   D

I   I   B   H   R   F
```

But what Matthew had observed was true. The printing was a little . . . juvenile? It looked as if someone had taken painstaking care to write each letter as neatly as they could, but just didn't have the best handwriting.

Emily twisted the pencil tucked in her ponytail, scrutinizing the grid. This felt a lot more serious than the puzzles she downloaded on Book Scavenger. "I don't even know where to start with this. Do you?"

"It *is* called the unbreakable code," James reasoned.

"It's going to take us at least a day. Why don't we copy it down so we can work on it at home?"

Emily flipped the parchment over to look at the drawing, then flipped back to the side with the letters.

"You could trace it," Matthew suggested. He pointed to the windows across the room. "We could use one of those like a light box."

Emily tore a blank piece of paper out of her notebook. She pulled the pencil from her ponytail, and the

three crossed to the window most concealed by book-cases. Not that they were doing anything criminal, but Emily didn't want to draw attention to their actions.

"I'll hold the papers," Matthew said, pressing the unbreakable code with the notebook paper on top of it against the glass. The letters were faint, but visible enough for Emily to start tracing them. When she finished, Matthew said, "You should do the back, too. You never know." He flipped both pages so the notebook paper would be oriented the same way as the unbreakable code. Emily gently sketched the outline of the drawing.

When they returned the file to Ms. Linden, Emily asked, "Does the unbreakable code get looked at a lot?" She wondered how many people besides Mr. Quisling might be trying to solve it right now.

"It hasn't been recently, I can tell you that," Ms. Linden said. "But maybe I'll start working on it, too." She winked.

The next day was New Year's Eve, and after frustrating themselves with trying to solve the unbreakable code ever since they'd found it in the library, Emily and James were happy to have a distraction from thinking about it.

The Lees cooked dinner for Emily's family, a meal James's mom had called a hot pot, which was, not surprisingly, a literal hot pot full of ginger broth that sat in the middle of the table. The Lees were patient and laughed with Emily's family as they used chopsticks to pick up an assortment of raw foods to drop into the boiling broth. When Emily's dad scooted a slippery shrimp around the serving platter instead of being able to pick it up, James said, "We have forks, too. You can use one instead."

"No, no," Mr. Crane insisted. "I'm usually pretty good with chopsticks. At least with sushi."

For a brief victorious second, he balanced the shrimp between his chopsticks, and then it shot away, landing neatly with a *plink* in the broth.

"Ayyyy!" The two families erupted in cheers, and Emily's dad grinned sheepishly, using a small ladle-shaped strainer to fish out his now-cooked shrimp.

After dinner, Emily's parents stayed upstairs to learn how to play mah-jongg, while Emily, her brother, and James played board games under a tent they'd made from a sheet in the Cranes' family room. Emily couldn't remember the last time she'd built a fort, and maybe they were too old for it now, but none of them mentioned that. It was like the three had a wordless pact not to question whether they were being immature and just enjoy the moment. It was fun to not act your age sometimes.

"Mr. Green, in the lobby, with the candlestick." Matthew held a tan envelope to his forehead, eyes closed, as he guessed his final answer to their third round of Clue.

The clatter of tiles being dumped on a table overhead and a round of laughter filtered through the ceiling.

Matthew pulled out the cards and flopped them on the board. "Yes!" He punched fists in the air and tilted back, then lost his balance, toppling into one of the chairs that supported the tent. The chair tipped over, pulling the sheet off the opposing chair so it draped onto their heads.

"Matthew!" The sheet muffled Emily's cry.

"Sorry!" Matthew jumped up, tangling himself. "Sorry." He set about reassembling the tent with James's help.

"Time for a new game." Emily extricated herself from the sheet and ran to her room to sift through the pile James had brought down with him. "Yahtzee or Taboo?" she called down the hallway. Her brother and James each yelled different games in response, so she grabbed both, hesitating before she left her room to study the blobs of foggy blue, teal, and jungle green that she'd recently painted on her walls. James's grandmother—their landlord—had given Emily permission to paint her room as long as the Cranes painted it back to white when they eventually moved out. Now that she had the freedom to have a room in any color, she didn't know which to choose.

Emily carried the two board games back into the family room. "You know how they say the way you spend the first day of a new year sets the tone for how your whole year goes?"

"Who says that?" Matthew squinted skeptically.

"Like when Mom and Dad say 'new state, clean

slate' whenever we move? It's the same idea," Emily said. "What would you want your next year to be filled with?"

"Music," said Matthew, predictably.

"It's-Its," said James.

"It's-Its?" Emily and Matthew replied in unison.

"You've lived here for three months, and you've never had an It's-It? They're . . . they're . . ." James sighed and stared dreamily at the corner of the room. "Imagine if a chewy oatmeal cookie and a chocolate-dipped ice cream cone had a baby."

"Thinking about foods mating is not very appetizing," Matthew said.

James shrugged. "They're delicious. That's what I'm saying."

"I want my year to be filled with . . ." Emily began.

"Reading," her brother interjected.

"Book Scavenger," James added.

Emily frowned. Those answers were obvious and true, but still unsatisfying. She thought about Ms. Linden with her boat, scuba diving through shipwrecks, and knowledgeable about all the unbreakable code history. Becoming a bona fide treasure hunter sounded awesome, but saying she wanted her year to be filled with treasure would be about as ridiculous as saying she wanted it to be filled with unicorns.

"I have an idea." James grabbed his laptop.

"An idea for what?" Emily saw the Book Scavenger website on his screen before James angled it away.

"I'm looking to see if there's a book already hidden in one of my favorite places to go in the city, but it's better as a surprise." He typed a few more things, then said, "Yes! Someone hid a book there. Let's go find it tomorrow. It involves music, Matthew, so you'll like it. And if the stars align, there will be It's-Its, too."

Emily hadn't been the one to offer Book Scavenger as her pick, but she had to agree it sounded like a great way to spend the day.

The next morning, Emily, James, and Matthew left for the book-hunting adventure James had planned, but they had barely walked a few feet away from their building when Emily realized she'd forgotten her bus pass.

"I'll be right back," she said, and ran up their front steps. She left the front door ajar, and her sneakers were soft on the stairs as she jogged up.

Her mother's raised voice carried out from the kitchen. "They filed for bankruptcy?"

"I know," her dad replied. "I'm as shocked as you are."

"That's one of your regular clients. This is huge, David. Why aren't you more worried about this? We've been counting on those editing projects coming in."

Her parents' voices were like a fishing line cast down the hallway, hooking Emily. They tugged at her as she crossed the hallway to her room, tugged as she found her bus pass marking her place inside *The Egypt Game*.

"I know, I know. Trust me, I'm as worried as you are. Probably more," her dad said. "But we'll figure this out. Money has been tight before and we survived. I'll reach out to my contacts, let them know I'm in need of more work."

"Money has been tight before, but we weren't living in San Francisco. Just breathing here is expensive," Emily's mom said.

There was a heavy pause. Emily knew she should untangle herself from their sharp-toned words that weren't meant for her ears and scoot back down the stairs and out the door. She knew she should do that, but she stood on the landing and listened.

"We have the advance for the *50 States* book coming," her dad said.

Emily's mom scoffed. "That will cover two months, at most, and who knows when it will arrive."

"I know this, Elizabeth." Her dad's voice was brittle.

Her mother softened. "I know you do. I'll reach out to my design clients, too. Maybe I can rustle up more work. And we can dip into our savings while we figure this out, but that will only last us so long. We didn't initially plan on being here more than a year."

Emily breathed in sharply, and the fishing line of words was cut free. She retreated down the stairs as quietly as she'd entered. Her parents were always a team, a united front. She'd heard them get in heated debates over things like whether *frenemy* was a valid Scrabble word, but up to now there had always been an undercurrent of playfulness. Worse than their tone was the reason for their argument. Her parents wouldn't be fighting right now if Emily hadn't made them promise to stay in San Francisco.

Emily closed their front door with a soft click and joined James and her brother on the sidewalk.

"You wanted a perfect first day of the New Year," Matthew said, gesturing to the crisp blue sky and the distant bay water that twinkled in the gaps between buildings as they walked up the hill. "You can't get much better than this."

They rode the bus in the general direction of the Marina. Emily gnawed on her lip and stared out the window. A loop of her mother saying *just breathing here is expensive* played over and over in her head. Beside her, Matthew peppered James with questions about how this mystery spot related to music.

"Is it a place that has shows or concerts?"

James handed over a printout from the Book Scavenger website. "This is the clue for the hidden book. That's the only hint I'll give you."

$$23 \ 8 \ 5 \ 18 \ 5 \quad 19 \ 20 \ 15 \ 14 \ 5 \ 19$$
$$13 \ 1 \ 11 \ 5 \quad 13 \ 21 \ 19 \ 9 \ 3$$

"It's Nancy Drew level," James added.

Matthew nudged Emily. "I need your help,

Sherlylocks," he said, borrowing the nickname their dad had coined because she was a puzzle lover. Emily dragged her gaze from the window and stared at the numbers. She was tempted to say *what's the point*, but then she looked at Matthew—normally too cool to hang out with her these days—scrutinizing the clue like he'd be graded on it. James fidgeted in his seat like a little kid struggling to keep a secret. Her big plan had been for their first day of the New Year to represent what they hoped the future would hold. Did she want a year of sulking? No, she did not. Emily put on her game face.

Nancy Drew was one of the easier puzzle levels for Book Scavenger, so with that as a hint, Emily guessed this would be a straightforward number substitution cipher. She pulled the pencil from her ponytail and scratched out an alphabet in her notebook, then wrote the numbers *1* through *26* underneath each letter. She quickly deciphered the clue to read:

Where stones make music.

Matthew repeated the clue out loud. "Is it someplace where the Rolling Stones had a concert?" he asked James.

"Nope," James replied.

Matthew rested one arm on the top of the seat in front of him and drummed his fingers. "The Stone Temple Pilots?"

"It doesn't have to do with a band," James said.

Emily let them go back and forth in their guessing game, her thoughts returning to her parents' argument. What could she do to make a difference? If she could find a way to help her parents, then she wouldn't feel so responsible for asking them not to move, and maybe they would see how serious she was about wanting to stay in San Francisco.

What did other nearly-thirteen-year-olds do to make money? She could babysit. She didn't know of any families with young children, but she could find some. Her dad talked about having a paper route when he was a kid. Did those still exist? Maybe Hollister could use some extra help around his store. Yes, Hollister might be the way to go. Thinking up a plan pushed her worries to the back of her mind. This was a fixable problem. Her perfect New Year's Day could still be salvaged.

CHAPTER 11

EMILY, JAMES, and Matthew had barely walked a block from a bus stop in the Marina district when James pointed to an unremarkable corner market.

"This is our first stop," he said.

"Here? This was the spectacular location you wanted to be a surprise?" Emily asked.

"We're getting necessary supplies," James explained.

She and Matthew followed him inside. They stopped at the front counter, where an older man sat on a stool, speaking loudly into a cell phone in another language. In the glass case next to the register, there were plates of baklava, spanakopita, dolmas, and a salad dotted with feta and olives and peppers, so Emily imagined the man was speaking Greek, although she really had no idea. He gave an almost imperceptible nod of acknowledgment and continued with his conversation.

Directly in front of the cash register was a freezer chest. James slid the top open.

"Behold: It's-Its. The real San Francisco treat," he said. Individually wrapped round ice cream sandwiches were stacked in piles. James plucked one from the freezer and dropped it on the counter. "Pick your flavor. I'm a vanilla guy."

"Cappuccino," Matthew said. "Fancy."

"That's the hardest flavor to find, too," James said, which was all the encouragement Matthew needed to choose it.

Emily bit her lip, wavering.

"You really can't go wrong," James said, but it wasn't indecisiveness that had her hesitating. Minutes before, she'd been sitting on the bus vowing to find a way to help her parents make money. Should she really spend two dollars on an ice cream sandwich? Two dollars wasn't enough to pay their rent, she knew that, but she could put the money in a jar and save up.

As if he could read her mind, James added, "My treat. My mom gave me cash before we left."

Emily gnawed her lip for a few seconds more before grabbing a mint sandwich. "Thanks, James," she said as the man rang them up without missing a beat in his conversation.

They stepped back outside, and Matthew started to tear his wrapper open, but James flung out a hand. "No, no, no! Your first It's-It experience needs to be savored in a memorable setting. Let's find the book. Then we dine."

Matthew looked longingly at his ice cream sandwich. "It'll melt."

"Don't worry," James said, flicking his with a finger. "They're like hockey pucks. We've got time."

They walked until the neighborhood ended at a parking lot on the edge of San Francisco, looking out at the water. The Golden Gate Bridge cables reached down from their main posts to meet in the middle like giants holding hands across the water.

"This is where the book is hidden?" Emily asked. "A parking lot?"

"You'll like this spot, trust me," James said. He led them to a miniature peninsula jutting across the water, wide enough for only a walkway. Dozens of sailboat masts bobbed in the marina on their city side, and the open bay was on the other.

"This path doesn't look like it goes anywhere, dude," Matthew said. "Are you making us walk a plank?"

"I'll race you!" James shot forward down the empty stretch. Emily and Matthew sprinted after him, passing the moored sailboats and a lone fisherman standing on the rocky edge of the bay side. Emily soon realized the walkway didn't end but turned a corner. When they rounded it, the path sloped down and revealed a lower level that had been hidden from view before.

It was a patio on the edge of a boatless stretch of the marina. Stones and cement blocks were stacked around them in odd patterns to create curving benches and walls. Stairs led up to tiers of planter boxes, and giant concrete tubes reached out from everywhere with open ends rimmed in black. They looked like mutant worms opening their mouths for food.

"Holy weirdness," Matthew said.

"What is this place?" Emily asked.

"It's called the *Wave Organ*," James said. "Isn't it cool?"

It smelled like wet rocks, briny air, and something incongruent, like the lingering aroma of old French fries. The hard surfaces and dull grays were softened every so often by a scrub of green in a planted bed or a mound of purple flowers. Some of the stones were smooth with a sheen; others, bumpy and dull. There were speckled pieces, carved and ornate blocks, chunks of columns, and what looked like broken rubble. If it all hadn't been arranged in such an intentional-looking way, Emily might have thought she was sitting in the midst of a tiny ancient building that had collapsed in an earthquake.

"Why are some of these blocks fancy and some not?" she asked.

"I think all the stones came from a cemetery that was demolished," James said.

"Cool," Matthew said at the same time Emily said, "Eww."

"What does that mean anyway—wave organ?" Matthew asked.

"Listen," James said. He leaned an ear to one of the

wormy mouths. The opening was more than half the size of his head. Emily and Matthew picked different ones and listened as well. What Emily heard sounded like water sloshing over tin cans.

"These are the organ pipes, and when high tide comes in, the water fills them and makes sounds," James said. "Like a water version of a wind chime."

"Aqua rock!" Matthew said. After listening a minute longer, he added, "That would be a good name for a band."

Emily forgot about creepy worms and cemetery vibes as they ran around pressing their ears to various tentacles, and then she stood in the center of the patio, surveying the area for book-sized hiding spots.

There were crevices and gaps between the stones, but none looked quite big enough. She climbed up the stone stairs and trailed her hand through weedy greens sprouting from planters, but didn't find a book.

Crossing the patio, she stood at the edge, facing the building-covered mounds of San Francisco across the marina. Below her, a tumble of rocks and boulders sloped to the water. Gentle waves lapped and retreated, revealing a sliver of sandy beach.

Emily's eye was drawn to a gray brick askew on top of the rocks. It was the only rectangular shape amidst a variety of rounded ones. The angle of the brick also looked unnatural somehow. Emily crouched at the edge of the patio and reached for the block, her fingertips brushing against it. She moved one foot to a large boulder, testing it first to make sure it didn't move, and then reached again. This time she was able to lift the brick, and there underneath was a clear plastic bag with a paperback tucked safely inside.

"Ha!" Emily cried.

"You found the book?" James called. He and Matthew gathered behind Emily as she pinched the edge of the bag and pulled it free. She slid open the zippered seal and pulled out a paperback copy of *The Fourteenth Goldfish*. She would have plunked herself down on one of the slab benches and started to read, but James shook his It's-It.

"Perfect time to celebrate!" he said.

The three rounded the path to sit on the rocky crust of the jetty, looking out at the bay. Dozens of kite surfers were on the water, their colorful sails arcing in an aerial dance. Emily took a bite of her It's-It. The chocolate shell cracked to reveal chewy oatmeal cookies. Semi-melted mint ice cream oozed out. It was sweet and cold with crunchy bits, all in one bite.

"This is so good," Emily said, only her mouth was full and cold, so it sounded more like "Es esho goo!"

After a few minutes of nothing but seagull shrieks, the rhythmic swishing of water, and concentrated eating of the ice cream sandwiches, Emily swallowed a bite and pointed across the bay.

"I know that's Alcatraz," she said, indicating the crag of an island with a long white building and lighthouse perched on top. "But what island is that?" The

larger mass of land near Alcatraz was shrouded in green.

"That's Angel Island," James said. "People go there to hike or ride bikes. And immigrants used to come through there, a long time ago. We have a field trip to the immigration station coming up, actually. The seventh graders go every year." James had finished his It's-It and folded his plastic wrapper into smaller and smaller squares.

"When you look on a map of San Francisco, the bay

doesn't look large enough to have two islands," Emily said.

"There's more than two. You can kind of see another one down there. It's called Treasure Island. The Bay Bridge runs through it."

James pointed to the peak of the Bay Bridge, which looked like a miniature toy from so far away.

"*Treasure* Island?" Emily repeated.

Matthew chomped on his It's-It. "Did someone find buried gold there or something? Like that code you looked at in the library?"

James stared toward the island like he was seeing it in a new way. "I always assumed it was named after the book."

"Even if someone did find *a* treasure, that doesn't mean it was the unbreakable code treasure," Emily said firmly. She hadn't realized how hopeful she'd been about the prospect of finding long-lost treasure until she was faced with the possibility of someone having beaten her to it.

"That's true." James nodded. "The code hasn't been cracked, we know that for sure, so if the unbreakable code really does lead to gold, it must still be hidden."

"What would you buy if you found this long-lost gold?" Matthew asked. "I'd buy a Gibson Les Paul."

"A what?" Emily asked.

"A cool guitar," Matthew explained.

"I'd buy a new computer," James said.

"But you already have three!" Emily said. "Four, including your laptop."

James shrugged. "I'd replace one with a better model. But my parents would tell me to save the money for college. What would you spend it on?"

Emily was thinking about the discussion she'd overheard between her parents, but she didn't want to tell Matthew and James about that. Instead she said the next thing that popped into her head.

"Night-vision goggles, maybe?"

"Night-vision goggles?" Matthew and James said in unison.

Emily shrugged. "So I could go book hunting at night."

James laughed and shook his head.

The three stood up and walked their wrappers to a trash can encased in stone rubble from the old cemetery. Emily hadn't even noticed it when they ran past before.

"What's the verdict?" James asked as they walked away. *"Wave Organ* and It's-Its—a good start to the New Year?"

Emily hesitated for a split second, still weighed down by her parents' words. Golden light winked off the windows of distant buildings, and Emily imagined it was the spirit of lost treasure beckoning her to come find it. She straightened her posture and smiled. *Think positive, and it will be positive.* "It's a great start," she said.

CHAPTER 12

THE FIRST DAY back to school after winter break, Emily and James walked past Hollister's bookstore. A closed sign was propped in the window next to a display of *The Cathedral Murders*. It had been only a week since the book party, but somehow it felt like months. Today would be the first day back at school since the news went public about them finding the Poe book. Looking in the store window, Emily remembered the stifling attention at the party, and she wondered how kids were going to act toward her and James at school. She imagined the hallways of Booker narrowing and students staring or asking them to sign things, just like people had at the book party. She wanted to ask James how he thought kids would be, but she didn't want him to misunderstand and think she *wanted* the attention.

"Look at what my grandma found." James swung

his backpack off one arm so he could hold it in front while he dug out a column cut from a newspaper.

"A couple found a bottle stuck in the wall when they were renovating their house," he summarized.

"That made the newspaper?" Emily asked. "They must be desperate for stories." She remembered the reporter who had been at the book party and how eager she'd been to leave at the suggestion of a small fire somewhere in the city.

"It wasn't just any bottle. It was really old—from the Gold Rush. It turns out some of them are rare and collectible, and this one was worth five thousand dollars!"

"A bottle can be worth five thousand dollars?" Emily asked.

"This one had a chip in it. If it had been perfect, it would have been worth even more. Can you imagine that? It made me think of the *Niantic* and those bottles they found."

Emily took the article from James and skimmed it as they walked. The couple said finding the bottle ended up paying for their new bathroom. She wondered if there might be a Gold Rush era bottle stuck in the walls of her apartment. Of course since they were renting, any money from a found bottle would probably belong to James's grandmother and not the Cranes.

The *slap-slap* of feet on concrete rushed up behind them, and James was spun sideways as a kid raced by.

"Watch it!" James yelled.

Three more kids ran past, shouting in another language. Emily would have been worried for the first kid, except all four had been laughing together, like they were playing a game.

Up ahead loomed Booker Middle School, a massive redbrick building that looked more like a sprawling mansion where murder mysteries were solved than a school. Emily watched as the first boy hurdled a shrub and landed with a roll on the skinny rectangle of lawn in front of the building. The boy jumped to his feet and made a V with his arms.

Kids approached the school from all directions, filing off the city bus, unloading from cars, or arriving on foot like Emily and James. With all her experience being the new girl over and over again, she'd perfected the art of swiftly fading into the background. She wasn't used to being the center of attention, and all those people at Hollister's were only a tiny fraction of how many kids went to Booker. Emily dragged in a slow, deep breath and exhaled through her nose.

"You okay?" James asked.

She nodded. Better to get the students' reaction over with, whatever it may be.

By lunchtime, Emily was glad she hadn't mentioned her nerves to James and felt silly for being anxious in the first place. Nobody had said a word all morning about the Poe book. Not one student. Not even a teacher.

"Am I invisible?" she asked James when they met by the drinking fountain at lunch.

"What?" James asked, confused.

Emily hinted at a smile. "Nothing. Dumb joke."

Even Nisha, the girl who had been at the book party and asked them to sign her book in code, hadn't acknowledged Emily in the hallways. Admittedly, she may not have *seen* Emily—she'd been studying a notebook while she walked by, and Emily didn't call out to her or anything. But still.

Emily didn't understand how she could want two contradictory things at the same time. She didn't want people to pay too much attention to her, but then when literally no one paid attention to her or mentioned her role in discovering the Poe book, she was disappointed.

"Uh-oh," James said. "Vivian must be prowling for volunteers." He nodded to their class president, who zigzagged the hall, having brief conversations with individuals and groups that ended with the students shaking their heads and walking away.

"Volunteers for what?" Emily asked.

"I think we're about to find out."

Vivian strode up, a clipboard pressed to her chest. She smiled widely, showing off the rubber bands on her braces in school colors. "We need volunteers for the Presidents' Day dance committee. Can I count on you to help?"

"There's a Presidents' Day dance?" Emily asked.

"On Saturday, February fourteenth," Vivian replied.

"But that's Valentine's Day. Why not have a Valentine's Day dance?" Emily asked.

Vivian rolled her eyes. "Polled students overwhelmingly rejected the idea of promoting a blatantly commercial holiday and voted instead to celebrate something more inspirational and academic, like our presidents."

"There was a poll?" James asked. "I don't remember a poll."

Vivian became preoccupied marking notes on her clipboard.

"Are you sure you polled the *entire* student body? Not just your friends? Or yourself? Do I need to talk to Principal Montoya about this?" James teased.

Vivian's eyes widened. "You can't do that!" She pressed her clipboard so tight against her blouse, Emily wondered if a rectangular impression would be left behind.

James laughed. "Relax, Vivian. I'm kidding. I would have voted anti V-Day anyway."

Vivian's shoulders dropped, and she smiled sheepishly. "So? Can I count on your help?" she asked.

"Well . . ." Emily began.

For as long as she could remember, Emily had been defined by the same box—a moving box. The older she got, the harder it became to be the new girl again and again. She wasn't like her brother, who could make conversation with a stop sign. It had become comfortable for Emily to stay in the background and not put herself out there. There was less risk of rejection and embarrassment that way. But befriending James these last few months had opened her eyes to what she missed out on by holding herself back. Maybe it was time to step outside the moving box and get involved in her school. Was a dance committee the right choice, though? What if it wasn't her thing? She'd never even attended a school dance before. Maybe she should do that first before she helped plan one.

Vivian added, "The ticket price will be waived for committee members."

"It costs money to go to the Presidents' Day dance?" Emily asked.

"How else could we afford the decorations and music and everything?"

Money. Of course.

"So?" Vivian held her pen poised, ready for her answer.

"I'm in," Emily said quickly before she could second-guess herself any longer.

"You are?" James asked incredulously.

Vivian scribbled down Emily's name, solidifying the commitment in ink. If she wanted to see what it was like to be involved in school activities, then she'd have to jump in at some point. And this way, she'd be saving her parents money, too.

"And you, too?" Vivian was already starting to write down James's name.

"Uh, I guess. Sure," James said.

"We'll meet every other Wednesday after school, starting this week." She headed off through the crowd, looking for more volunteers.

As Emily and James walked on to the cafeteria, the door to the faculty room swung open, nearly clocking Emily. Mr. Quisling halted midstride, his palm pressed to the door. Both parties blurted apologies for almost colliding. Emily stared at their teacher, unable to think of anything but him fishing his hand in that purse at Hollister's bookstore.

"You're looking sharp today, Mr. Quisling," James said. "Is that a new shirt?"

"Oh . . ." Mr. Quisling looked down as if he needed a reminder of what he had on. "Yes, it is."

Mr. Quisling brushed an invisible speck from his shirt with the side of his hand, and the sheet of paper he held flapped with the movement. Emily saw scribbled handwriting on the page, a series of letters and scratched-out words. Her notebook was filled with writing like that from all her attempts to crack Book Scavenger codes. Could Mr. Quisling be working on the unbreakable code?

An uneasy worry washed over Emily. She and James were entirely stumped on what to do with the grid of letters they'd copied at the library. They had tried anagrams and substitution ciphers, they had treated the letters like a word search puzzle, but no luck. What if Mr. Quisling had already made a break-through?

Emily tilted her head, trying to get a better look at the page, but Mr. Quisling turned abruptly and walked away. "See you in class," he called over his shoulder.

CHAPTER 13

IN MR. QUISLING'S class that afternoon, their teacher
hunkered over a notebook at his desk as everyone filed
in, rather than standing in his usual spot at the front of
the room. Emily couldn't stop staring at him and worrying about what he was doing.

Sitting in the desk next to hers, James muttered,
"Brace yourself. The Royal Fungus returns."

Maddie Fernandez. It would be a little dramatic to
say Maddie was their archnemesis, but ever since Emily's
first day at Booker, she'd seemed to have a grudge
against Emily for no reason at all. James had explained
that Maddie was a competitive person and had been as
long as he'd known her—since second grade. Her com-
petitiveness was something they'd witnessed firsthand
when James and Maddie had engaged in a cipher challenge last fall. But after that had ended, Maddie acted
like she'd forgotten they knew each other. Emily didn't

miss Maddie's jabs and antagonizing comments, but she still found it unnerving to be around her. It was like approaching a light switch that had once shocked you.

Emily and James privately called her the Royal Fungus because her hair used to remind Emily of a mushroom cap, but now that Emily was seeing Maddie for the first time since school let out for winter break, she noticed that Maddie had changed her hair.

"Not much of a fungus anymore," James commented, observing the same thing. Instead of the bangs that cut straight across her forehead and smooth shell of hair that puffed out, her bangs were softened and combed to the side, her hair was wavy and cut in an angled bob.

"Your hair looks nice," Emily said as Maddie took her normal seat behind James. The words tumbled out before Emily gave them much thought, and she anticipated Maddie snapping a response along the lines of *Why would I care what you think?* Instead, Maddie raised her eyebrows, perhaps surprised at the compliment and possibly assessing her to see if she really meant it.

"Thanks," Maddie finally said, and dropped her backpack on the ground. After a minute of pulling out her binder and arranging her mechanical pencil and fruit-shaped eraser, she said, "My mom showed me the thing about you two in the paper. It's cool you guys found that book."

James was swinging his head back and forth between Maddie and Emily. "Have I entered an alternate universe?" he asked.

"Of course, you didn't have any competition," Maddie went on. "I probably would have found it, too. Maybe even faster."

"Annnnnd there she is. All is right with the world." James sighed contentedly and refocused on the circles he'd been drawing.

The bell rang, and the low mumble of conversation cut off almost instantly, as that was the routine, but Mr. Quisling still didn't stand. Someone coughed, and Mr. Quisling finally looked up from his work and frowned, like he was annoyed to see the class sitting there.

Emily and James raised their eyebrows at each other.

"We're going to try something different today," their teacher said. "Take out your world history book and a clean sheet of paper and read chapter twenty-four silently. Then write an outline noting the main topics and their supporting facts."

He resumed his seat and bowed his head over his notebook. Total silence hung in the room, the entire class either spellbound or confused that Mr. Quisling wasn't launching into his typical lecture.

Someone unzipped a backpack. A voice hissed, "We're supposed to do what?" Like a volume dial being eased up, more sounds filled the room. Whispers and murmured conversations. Notebook paper tearing.

Binder rings snapping open and shut. Sitting in the middle of the room, Emily and James swiveled their heads around, taking in the activity. Their eyes settled on Mr. Quisling, who didn't seem at all perturbed by the noise.

"What's wrong with him?" James whispered to Emily. The normal Mr. Quisling would have been calling out reminders to work silently.

Emily mouthed, *The unbreakable code.*

They stared at their teacher a minute more. Mr. Quisling intently wrote things down, then crossed them out.

"I dare you to go peek at what he's doing," James said.

"Right. He'll subtract points from this assignment for goofing off."

"The normal Mr. Quisling would, but this is like a Quisling cyborg. He's not paying any attention to the class. He probably won't even notice you."

"If you're so sure about that, why don't you try it, then?" Emily asked.

"I'm wearing my extra-squeaky shoes," James said with a grin.

Behind them, Maddie huffed loudly. "You two are pathetic. I'll do it, since you're both too chicken."

Emily hadn't realized they'd been having their conversation loud enough for others to hear. Before either one could say anything in response, Maddie was already halfway to their teacher's desk.

"Mr. Quisling?" Maddie's voice was a honey-soaked sugar cube. "Is this what you mean by an outline?"

Mr. Quisling looked up and assessed Maddie's open binder. "Yes, Maddie, that will do fine." Then he looked to the class, his eyes glassy, as if he'd woken from a dream. "Read the chapter first before you start your outline," he said. "The main topics of this chapter will be your headings. Supporting facts and important details are bulleted underneath."

Maddie made her way back to her seat. "He's working on a puzzle," she whispered.

"What puzzle?" Emily asked.

"One he printed from the Book Scavenger site. The logo was on the page."

"He's working on a Book Scavenger puzzle?" James asked.

Maddie nodded, now bored with the conversation, and flipped open her textbook to do the assignment.

James scratched at Steve. Emily wrinkled her nose. They both studied their teacher, confused. At least he wasn't racing ahead of them on the path to solving the unbreakable code as they had feared, but a Book Scavenger clue? During class? Really?

After school, Emily and James were still perplexed about Mr. Quisling's odd behavior when they saw him round the side of the building and jog to the line forming for the approaching city bus.

"He's sure in a rush," James said.

They watched their teacher tug on his neon green jacket as he ran, then throw his satchel across his shoulder.

"Let's follow him," Emily said.

"*Follow* him? Won't he be able to tell?" James asked.

"There are tons of kids getting on. He won't even notice us." Emily sprinted toward the bus, James right next to her. "We'll get off when he gets off, and if he sees us or says anything, we'll act totally uninterested in him and make up an excuse for what we're doing. We'll say we're meeting my parents somewhere nearby."

"I guess so," James conceded. "Even if he notices us—so what? It's not like anything bad could happen."

CHAPTER
14

THE BUS TOOK them to the Financial District, the crowd thinning along the way as more people got off than on. Emily and James sat in the front, where the seats faced sideways, while Mr. Quisling was all the way in the back. James slumped in his seat next to Emily, not wanting to be seen, while Emily kept an eye on their teacher. Mr. Quisling read a book the whole time, so Emily watched the gray-dusted, bristly top of his head jostle around with the lurches of the bus.

When they neared the pyramid-shaped Transamerica building, Mr. Quisling reached up and pulled the bell cord. Emily whipped her head down, her ponytail falling like a curtain that she hoped concealed her face. When they'd first boarded the bus, it had been so packed that people had to stand in the aisles. That wasn't the case now, and it would be tricky for James and Emily to exit at the same time as Mr. Quisling without drawing his attention. Fortunately, two other people also rose to get off, standing behind Mr. Quisling at the back doors. Emily and James trailed at the end of the line, and their teacher seemed none the wiser.

When they stepped off the bus, Mr. Quisling was already almost a half a block ahead of them. He stopped abruptly, so Emily and James did, too. Emily half expected their teacher to spin around and shout, *Caught you!* But instead he stared at his reflection in the tinted windows of a restaurant, swiping his fingers at his hairline before continuing on. The approaching people curved around him like he was a boulder and they were a stream. It was funny, Emily thought, how some people were the boulders and others the water. She wondered what would happen if a boulder met another boulder on the sidewalk—would both refuse to change their course of direction, forcing them to collide?

"Where did he go?" James asked.

"What?!" Emily was pulled back from her daydream to see their teacher was missing from the sidewalk. They stopped walking. "How could he . . ."

"I lost sight of him in a crowd of people, but he couldn't have just disappeared."

They started walking again, albeit a bit more hesitantly, and soon came to a metal fence with an open gate. Through the bars was a redwood grove in between office buildings. An actual pocket of redwoods formed a little public park, smack-dab in the middle of all the hustle and bustle of the city. The trees shaded a paved courtyard bordered by lush bushes and mounds of clover. There was a fountain designed to look like a pond, complete with bronze sculptures of frogs jumping off lily pads.

"In San Francisco?" Emily said, in awe. This was the citiest part of the city, with skyscrapers and glitzy business buildings and one-way streets packed with a variety of vehicles.

"I didn't even know this was here," James said. Then he grabbed Emily's arm and pulled her back behind the wall of the neighboring building. *Mr. Quisling*, he mouthed, and pointed around the corner.

Their teacher was in the park, pacing around the pond. Several fountains of water shot up from the middle, drowning out the city noise and briefly obscuring him from view as he circled. Mr. Quisling's eyes scanned the ground as if he was seeking a lost item.

As they watched their teacher, Emily realized that if they were near the Transamerica Pyramid, then they must be where the *Niantic* had been uncovered. Were they standing in a part of downtown that used to be water? Could there be an ancient ship underneath her feet?

Mr. Quisling now faced away from them, looking up at the towering redwoods. He crossed the courtyard and peered behind another bronze sculpture—this one of a group of children holding hands and jumping. There were a few other people in the courtyard, either walking through or seated on one of the many benches scattered around, but nobody else seemed interested in what Mr.

Quisling was doing. They were too focused on their phone screens or open books or conversations.

Their teacher stepped delicately onto a patch of clover, then disappeared behind a trio of redwoods. He reemerged holding a green zippered pouch.

"What is that?" James asked.

Emily pulled away from the wall, ready to move when Mr. Quisling walked in their direction, but then he stopped and sat on a bench. They watched as he unzipped the pouch and removed a paperback.

"A book!" Emily said, even though James could see for himself. "This must be from the Book Scavenger clue he had in school."

"Why was the book put in that pouch?" James asked.

Emily shrugged. "Because it's green? Maybe it's to help camouflage and protect it."

Mr. Quisling pulled a pencil and notebook from his school satchel and opened the found book. He spent some time flipping through the pages, running his pencil over the words and occasionally jotting something down. When he was done, he tucked his notebook and pencil back into his satchel, slid the paperback into its green bag, and placed it back in the shrubs where he had found it.

James nudged her. "He's hiding it again."

"Why would he do that?" Emily wondered.

Their teacher crossed to the exit on the opposite side of the park, leaving on the next street over. When he was gone, Emily tugged James's shirtsleeve. "Let's get that book."

While Mr. Quisling hadn't drawn much attention, a few heads turned as Emily and James walked into the redwood grove. She supposed it was more unusual to see two kids with backpacks wandering through a business area of the city than a grown man looking for a lost item.

"Let's sit on that bench near where Mr. Quisling left the book," Emily suggested. "We can pull out our binders, and people will assume we're doing homework and waiting for our parents. Then I'll get the book when people stop paying attention to us."

"Or I can just do this." Before Emily could say another word, James tromped under the redwoods, thrust his hand into the shrub where Mr. Quisling had hidden the book, and pulled out the green pouch.

"Would you come over here, please?" Emily hissed. Nobody seemed interested or alarmed by what James had done, but still. How would they get to the bottom of what their teacher had been up to if someone took the book away from them?

James unzipped the pouch as he crossed back to the bench. He removed a copy of *The Adventures of Tom Sawyer* by Mark Twain.

"Hey," James said as they sat together, "it's *Tom Sawyer*. That's awfully coincidental. Mr. Quisling's note mentioned the unbreakable code, which once belonged to Mark Twain and Tom Sawyer, and now he book hunts a copy of *Tom Sawyer*. . . ."

An old memory pushed its way to the front of Emily's mind. "Wait a minute," she said as she flipped through her Book Scavenger notebook, going back to the puzzles she'd solved when her family had first moved to San Francisco. "There!" She tapped a page. "That's what I thought! Do you remember when we first went book hunting together?"

"At the Ferry Building? Sure. But the book wasn't there. It had been poached."

"Poached by . . ." Emily prompted.

"By Mr. Quisling?" James's forehead wrinkled as he tried to connect the dots between that day and today.

"Do you remember what book I was hunting?" Emily asked.

James looked down at the book in his hands, then back to Emily. "This? You were looking for this book?"

"Maybe not that exact one, but it was a hidden copy of *Tom Sawyer*, yes."

"But . . . if Mr. Quisling has already found this book once through Book Scavenger, why would he be looking for another one? And why didn't he keep this one today after he found it?"

"Good questions." Emily whipped the pencil from her ponytail and gestured for James to hand her the *Tom Sawyer*. She flipped through the book, waving her pencil over the words as she scanned. Toward the end, she stopped on the opening page of a chapter where a sentence had been underlined.

Emily read it out loud, "There comes a time in every rightly constructed boy's life when he has a raging desire to go somewhere and dig for hidden treasure."

"Seriously?" James leaned close to read the sentence for himself. "This has to be about the unbreakable code, don't you think?" James said. "Tom Sawyer? Mark Twain? Dig for hidden treasure? But what would two books hidden through Book Scavenger have to do with a centuries-old code?"

Emily thumbed through the pages of the book one more time, but there was nothing else to find. "Let's go check out the Book Scavenger clue. Maybe that will help us understand what Mr. Quisling was doing."

CHAPTER 15

THE PHOENIX wasn't expecting the children to show up. He recognized them, of course, but he didn't let on that he'd observed. Standing just out of their line of sight, he watched as they removed the book from the shrub.

He couldn't get over how grown-ups had fawned over those two like they were geniuses for figuring out Mr. Griswold's scavenger hunt. And for what? Playing a game and being lucky. People were always getting rewarded for being lucky. You could be the most intelligent person in the room—in the world—and it got you nowhere. But luck? Hand the person a promotion, an award, respect, prestige.

The Phoenix watched as Emily slipped the green pouch into her backpack, instead of putting *Tom Sawyer* back where they found it. He clenched his fists. This wouldn't do at all. This wasn't how his plan was supposed to go. Now what was he supposed to do? His dominoes had been lined up perfectly, ready to tap each other down in a satisfying succession. Removing that book threw off the whole grand design.

He watched Emily and James turn and leave the park the way they'd come in. They were surely running home to mark their precious book "found" on Book Scavenger, which would ruin his plan even more. He needed to get to a computer first and hope this misstep didn't foil his plan for revenge.

CHAPTER 16

BACK IN HER ROOM, Emily sat crisscrossed on her bed and opened her laptop. James's socked foot dangled over the armrest of the secondhand chair her parents had recently added to her room. Ever since she had told them she wanted a normal kid experience for once, without all the moving, with a bedroom that felt like hers and not temporary, her parents had been buying her random things to decorate her room, like that chair or the globe that appeared one day when she got home from school, or the hotdog lamp. Not exactly what she had in mind for a "normal kid experience," and now that she knew they were worried about money, she wished they would stop. Even if it was a thrift store chair and not expensive, she'd been fine before, reading on her bed or flopped on the family room couch.

James held the retrieved copy of *Tom Sawyer* open

in front of him, but upside down. When Emily gave him a questioning look, he explained, "You already looked through it at the park, so I'm trying from a different perspective."

After logging into Book Scavenger, Emily typed in a search for copies of *Tom Sawyer* hidden in San Francisco. There was only the one they had found. Noting the name of the location, she asked, "Did you know that redwood park is in Mark Twain Plaza?"

"I'm sure that wasn't a coincidence," James said.

"Wait a second," Emily said. "The book's been marked found! Why would Mr. Quisling find a book, then re-hide it in the same place, and then mark it found? That makes no sense. And now we won't know what the clue said." She sighed.

"If he marked it found, then he must not want anyone else to find the book," James said.

"Right," Emily agreed. "But then why not just take the book with him? It's not like it's hard to carry a book. It makes no sense," she said again. "I wish there was a way we could find out what he was up to and what this has to do with solving the unbreakable code."

"What if . . . we hid our own copy?" James suggested. "Like setting out bait. We could pick a hiding spot that would be easy for us to keep an eye on. We'll hide a copy of *Tom Sawyer*, post a clue to Book Scavenger, and then watch and see what Mr. Quisling does."

"Genius!" Another idea sparked, and Emily typed

something quickly into her computer. "I'm also setting an alert for hidden copies of *Tom Sawyer*, so we'll know right away if someone else hides another copy."

"We can hide the book at school," James suggested. "All three of us are there all the time."

"Don't you think that might make Mr. Quisling suspicious? And speaking of, we should use my brother's old account—Mr. Quisling will recognize me as Surly Wombat. Matthew's had his account from when he and I first started playing the game years ago. He hasn't hidden or found any books since we lived in Colorado. I'm sure he hasn't updated his profile to say he lives in San Francisco. Mr. Quisling would never guess it's us."

"Where should we hide it, then?" James asked. "It needs to be somewhere easy for us to keep an eye on it."

Emily clapped her hands together as the perfect place occurred to her: "Hollister's," she said.

Mr. Quisling was back to his normal teaching routine the next day, but it was clear he was still distracted, although that could have been due to their class visitor. When Mr. Quisling introduced him as Mr. Sloan, an aspiring teacher who wanted to observe their class, Emily recognized the man from the book party. He was the one who'd told them about Mr. Quisling finishing the literary labyrinth in record time.

Mr. Sloan dragged a chair to the front corner, the

metal feet screeching along the linoleum. He smiled to the class and boomed, "Don't mind me!"

During work sheets, Emily kept an eye on Mr. Quisling, curious to see if he would be madly solving another puzzle. But if he had any plans to, she'd never know, because Mr. Sloan popped out of his chair and was talking to their teacher before he even reached his desk.

"Great lesson, Brian. Just great." Mr. Sloan made no effort to lower his voice, so it was easy to hear what he was saying. "But have you considered turning those work sheets into a small group exercise? I read a study that showed kids make more connections through conversation than—"

Mr. Quisling held up a hand to indicate *stop*. "This is a quiet time."

"Of course, of course. But that's really the point I was going to make—"

"Harry." Mr. Quisling's voice was low, but patient. "The students need to concentrate. Please lower your voice."

They continued speaking in muted tones. James gave Emily an amused look. "Mr. Quisling is enjoying having his friend visit our class, don't you think?"

Emily grinned and shook her head.

After school, they stopped by Hollister's. The door opened with the familiar *ting-a-ling* of bells looped through the handle, but an unfamiliar face greeted them at the counter. *Greeted* wasn't really the right word for it. The college-aged guy scowled, then went back to reading his book. His ears were pierced with nickel-sized disks, and his face was covered with what Emily assumed he'd call a beard, but it looked more like coffee grounds clinging to his cheeks and chin.

"Is Hollister here?" James asked.

Emily wasn't sure at first whether the guy heard James, because he didn't look up again, but then he said, "He's here."

Once they realized that was all the direction they were going to get, James said, "I guess we'll go find him."

They wandered to the back of the store and heard Hollister before they saw him, clomping down the metal staircase that led to the storage loft he had nicknamed the Treehouse.

"Hey, kids. Happy Tuesday!"

"Not for that new guy up front," James said.

"Who? Charlie?" Hollister waved dismissively. "He's a marshmallow inside. C'mon."

They followed Hollister back to the front counter. "Charlie is a jack-of-all-trades. Computer programmer, website designer, social media expert. Didn't you say you DJ, too?"

"Here and there," Charlie replied.

"All that, and a full-time college student." Hollister shook his head. "Don't know how you do it."

If Hollister's praise flattered him, Charlie wasn't

showing it. He drummed a pencil eraser on the open textbook and continued to study.

"I hired Charlie to help with tech stuff. Fix up my computer, set up some social media for the store. I had a serviceable website—"

Charlie grunted, and Hollister chuckled. "It did the job, provided the pertinent info. Anyway, Charlie is going to be sprucing that up—"

"More like setting it on fire and starting from scratch, but sure," Charlie said.

"And then getting the store up on Twitter and Instagrammatic—"

"Instagram," Charlie corrected him.

Emily thought it was ironic that someone as anti-social as Charlie was being put in charge of social media, but Hollister didn't seem to mind.

"See how I need him?" he said. "I can't be bothered with all this digital stuff. I live and breathe paper, but you can't be stubborn about the future. Not if you want to stay in business. Got to keep moving with the times."

Emily thought about the conversation she'd over-heard between her parents, about the publisher client of her dad's who went bankrupt. Her dad had other people he worked for, at least, but Hollister had only his store. She would be so sad if it had to close.

"Do you need help with anything else, Hollister? I was hoping to make some extra money." Emily cringed as the words came out of her mouth. She was *just* thinking about Hollister staying in business, and now she was asking him to pay her?

Hollister didn't seem concerned. "Too bad the holiday season just passed—I can always use gift wrappers that time of year." He tapped his nose, thinking.

"You need money?" James whispered, surprised.

Emily shrugged. "My allowance is small." She hadn't said anything about her parents' money problems to James because his grandmother was their landlord. She knew he wouldn't say anything unless he thought it could help, but if it got back to her parents that she'd overheard her dad was struggling to find work, that wouldn't be good.

"You're too young to hire officially," Hollister said, "but if you bring me a letter of permission from your parents, then I think we can make it work. It might not be much, or glamorous, but it will be something."

Emily leaped forward and hugged Hollister. Her parents didn't have to know she planned to save her money and turn it over to them. "Well, gee!" he said. "That was nice. Charlie, how come you didn't react that way when I offered you your job?"

Charlie turned a page in his book in response.

"Hey, Hollister," James said, "how is what he's doing right now helping with social media?"

Charlie replied in a bored monotone, "I'm updating his operating system. Should be finished soon."

Hollister tipped his head forward like he was saying *there
you go*. "So what brings you
kids in today?"

"Could we hide a book
in your store for Book
Scavenger?"

"Sure, go right ahead,"
Hollister said.

Emily and James bowed their heads together for a
brief conference on where to hide the green pouch holding *Tom Sawyer*. They ended up tucking it inside one of
the tote bags dangling near the front counter.

"Hey, Hollister," Emily said once they were finished.
"Have you heard about something called the unbreakable code? Our teacher Mr. Quisling is—"

Charlie groaned. "He's still at Booker? Mr. Quisling
is the worst."

"You went to Booker?" James asked.

Charlie nodded. "So he's still droning on about the
unbreakable code?"

Emily and James exchanged a look.

"Not really," Emily said cautiously. "But you've
heard of it?"

"Only because he wouldn't shut up about it. There
was a series of books that came out when I was in his
class—*The 39 Clues*. A bunch of students were into it and
this game that went along with the story. Mr. Quisling

would go on and on about real-life puzzles, like the unbreakable code."

Hollister whistled long and low. "The unbreakable code. Haven't thought about that in years!"

"You know it, too?" Emily said.

"Sure, sure. There was a big to-do about it decades ago. Way before your time. There was an old ship that was discovered buried under the city that made the news—"

"The *Niantic*?" Emily said.

Hollister nodded, eyebrows raised. "I'm impressed! Yes, that sounds right. When it made the news, so did a legend about that code. Apparently it survived a fire on the *Niantic*. . . . I can't really remember the details, but there was a revival of interest in trying to crack it back then."

Emily chewed her lip. They knew Mr. Quisling had been there when the *Niantic* was rediscovered, so he probably participated in that revival of interest.

"It didn't get solved, though, right?" Emily asked.

"No, I don't think so. If you already know about the *Niantic*, then you probably know as much as I do. Although"—Hollister snapped his fingers—"you *do* know somebody who led the charge for trying to solve it back in the eighties."

"Who?" Emily and James asked in unison. Emily was certain *Mr. Quisling* would be the name that came out of Hollister's mouth, but it wasn't.

CHAPTER 17

"M R. GRISWOLD," Hollister said.

"Mr. Griswold?!" Emily and James repeated, in unison once again.

"Are you sure?" Emily asked.

"I'm getting old, but I don't think my memory's failing me *that* badly yet." Hollister laughed. "Yes, I'm sure."

Emily and James exchanged a look.

"Well . . ." Emily began, thinking about their recent visit to Bayside Press. Why wouldn't Mr. Griswold have said more when they asked him about the unbreakable code? "Do you think Mr. Griswold's memory could be failing *him*?"

"We saw him last week and asked him about the unbreakable code," James explained.

"He barely seemed to know what we were talking about," Emily added.

"Did he, now?" Hollister harrumphed. "Well. Could be from his injury, I suppose." He looked concerned. "He most definitely knew about the code at one time. I witnessed his obsession firsthand—it was back when we were co-owners of this store. He was convinced there was a way to spin the renewed interest in the unbreakable code into traffic to our store, but beyond carrying books with an angle on treasure hunts and ciphers, we weren't able to capitalize on it."

"Weird," Emily said softly, more to herself than anyone else. She thought about how Mr. Griswold had seemed like a watered-down version of himself. "Have you seen him recently? Since he's been out of the hospital?"

Hollister rested a hand on her shoulder and held her gaze with his good eye. "He's been through a lot. But Gary always bounces back. Don't worry."

Emily wanted to feel uplifted and reassured by Hollister's words, but she couldn't help it: She was still worried.

At the start of Mr. Quisling's class on Wednesday, Emily dug through her backpack to find a paper she'd printed at home the night before, after their visit with Hollister. "I forgot to show you this on our walk to school," Emily said, and handed the paper to James.

"It's an old interview with Mr. Griswold. I found it

on Book Scavenger," she said. In the website forum, there was a section dedicated to everything Garrison Griswold. Several years ago, another Book Scavenger user had scanned and posted an old interview from a magazine.

James laughed looking at the photo that accompanied the interview. "Check out his hair! I didn't realize it was so curly."

"The striped pants are pretty sweet, too," Emily said. "But that's not the most interesting part. Read it."

The interview featured Mr. Griswold shortly after he'd launched Bayside Press, more than a dozen years before Book Scavenger existed.

INTERVIEWER: You have a reputation for being a treasure-hunt enthusiast. In 1980 you spearheaded interest in a cipher that dates back to the Gold Rush and is alleged to lead to a miner's lost fortune, and you also participated in the Masquerade treasure hunt in England. Why are you drawn to activities like that?

GRISWOLD: There is wonderful potential for a treasure hunt to bring people together in collaboration. I love that. A treasure hunt also forces you to slow down, but with all your senses engaged. Pay attention. Listen. What are your surroundings telling you? Is that rock just a rock? Or does it conceal something valuable? I love the idea of something precious being hidden in plain sight, of noticing the potential for something amazing in something bland.

It's not what's at the end of a treasure hunt that motivates me. It's really not. Some people talk about what they would do with sudden riches—I'm not interested in that. Anyone who focuses on the outcome instead of the journey is missing the point, not to mention setting themself up for disappointment.

INTERVIEWER: Why do you say that?

GRISWOLD: You can't control an outcome. To any endeavor, whether it be a treasure hunt or something else, a friendship or a business venture. The only thing you can control is yourself. Your actions and reactions determine the type of journey you will have. Will it be magical? Joyful? Fearful? Will you be the victim, or will you be the hero? That's up to you.

INTERVIEWER: Is a treasure hunt appealing because it provides a diversion from the struggles and stresses of the real world?

GRISWOLD: Not at all. It's not a diversion. It's a remedy. Anything we pursue with passion and

curiosity can heal us. It's not unlike my philoso-
phy behind starting a publishing company. I
want to populate the world with jewels. Finding
that book you connect with is a type of treasure
hunt. I want to create things for others and be a
force of good and fun and positivity in this
world.

"This is great," James said.

"Don't you think?" Emily took the paper back and folded it neatly into her notebook. "This part—*Anything we pursue with passion and curiosity can heal us*—made me think about how different he seems now. Sad and fearful."

"Broken," James said, understanding.

"I'm going to bring this article to our next advisory meeting to show him. Maybe reading his old words will help him feel better. I wish we didn't have to wait, though, and could show it to him this afternoon."

"Well, we could have." James leveled a gaze at her that had Steve pointing her way, like a finger. "But *you* wanted to be on the dance committee."

"You didn't have to volunteer, too," Emily said.

James shrugged in response.

"You two are on the dance committee?" Maddie piped up behind them.

"Mind your own business, Maddie," James said. "I don't want to hear it: We'll make the dance the most boring ever, blah blah blah."

Maddie opened her mouth for a retort, but the bell rang to start class. Emily and James swiveled in their seats to face forward as Mr. Quisling clapped his hands to get everyone's attention before launching into the day's lesson.

After school, Emily and James made their way to their first dance committee meeting. Emily wasn't sure why, but she'd pictured the meeting taking place in a room with couches and school spirit posters on the wall and a mini fridge stocked with sodas and a bowl of popcorn for a snack—maybe she'd gotten that idea from a TV show she'd once seen? In any case, she was disappointed to find the dance committee met in James's science classroom. The stark black tables, beakers clustered on the back counter, and a wall papered with student-illustrated periodic tables did not exude the cozy let's-make-new-friends atmosphere she'd envisioned.

James's science teacher, Mrs. Ortega, was the faculty advisor for the dance committee. He'd said Mrs. Ortega was very pregnant, and he wasn't kidding. Her belly popped out so much that it made a little shelf, which Mrs. Ortega rested her clasped hands on as she walked around the room.

James had roped his friends Kevin and Devin, the twins, into joining the committee so he wouldn't be the only boy, and they were already there, slapping down cards on a table in the middle of the room. Nisha sat next to them, writing in a notebook, and Vivian had her clipboard poised and her eye on the door to check people off as they walked in.

"Have a seat," Vivian said. Her pen scratched sharply: *check, check.* "One more will be joining us, but we can go ahead and—oh, hi, Maddie."

Emily turned to see Maddie walk into the room. The final member of their committee. James sighed. "Of course it's her. You're *sure* you want to do this?"

"It sounds like fun," Emily said, although she wasn't sure anymore. It had seemed like a good idea when she volunteered.

"Is everybody going on the Angel Island field trip in two weeks?" Mrs. Ortega asked.

"You're not going, are you?" Maddie asked, taking the seat opposite Emily. She looked pointedly at Mrs. Ortega's belly.

"Of course. I'm one of the teacher chaperones."

"I've been to Angel Island before," Maddie said. "It's a lot of walking."

"For heaven's sake, Maddie. I have more than two months until my due date."

Vivian tapped her pen on her clipboard. "Let's get started, please."

"So, what are the plans for the Valentine's Dance?" Maddie asked.

"First of all, it's a *Presidents'* Day Dance," Vivian said.

"We should make it a costume party," James said. "You'd look great in an Abraham Lincoln beard, Vivian."

Mrs. Ortega cleared her throat. "Why don't you guys start by making a list of to-do items and—"

"Do we really even need a theme?" Devin asked, slapping another card onto the table. His brother swiped it away and placed two cards from his hand instead.

"Or why not a cool theme?" Kevin added. "Like GameCon." He framed his hands around the invisible words.

"*GameCon?*" Vivian spluttered. "What does that even mean?"

"You know, like ComicCon but about games and stuff. It'll be original."

"A Presidents' Day theme is original," Vivian argued. "GameCon is juvenile. It would be silly."

"Now, now, let's not tear one another down in order to make our point," Mrs. Ortega said.

"Silly?" Kevin pressed a palm to his chest and gasped. "Did you hear that, Dev? Oh, golly gee, heaven forbid we have a dance that's *silly*. I forgot that Stanford is going to be judging us on our hoedown skills when we apply to college."

"No, no—it's Harvard that cares about hoedown skills," Devin said. "Stanford cares about how well we twerk."

"I still think it should be a Valentine's dance," Maddie interjected. "It's *on* Valentine's Day. Everyone will be treating it like it is anyway."

The conversation reminded Emily of debates her family had, like the time they had been driving from

Connecticut to live in Colorado and planned to stop near Chicago for the night. They'd been in the car for almost six hours straight, and everyone was tired and hungry and stir-crazy, and nobody could agree on what to do for dinner. Matthew wanted to find a place in the city where they could eat while watching a live band. Their dad wanted to drive up to Wisconsin to eat cheese curds because he couldn't believe they'd never done that in the previous year, when they'd lived in Illinois. Emily's mom wanted to eat in Naperville so she could revisit a favorite bookstore called Anderson's. And Emily wanted to eat at Hardee's because she missed their jalapeño poppers.

All the banter about the dance made Emily feel not so far out of her comfort zone.

"Why can't it be all of it?" she interjected.

It might have been her imagination, but Emily felt like all the arguments halted and every face was suddenly staring at her. She swallowed.

"A Presidential Valentine's GameCon?" Vivian sounded like she was spitting the words on the table.

James rested his head on a palm, massaging Steve with his fingers, but he looked contemplative, not judgmental.

"We'd dress up as presidents," Emily said. "People could come as presidential couples if they wanted to make it a Valentine's thing." She nodded to Maddie, who frowned. Emily supposed that might not be the kind of romantic dance she'd had in mind, but whatever. "And then we could do some games." Mr. Griswold had nixed her and James's ideas, but maybe they could repurpose them now.

"*Games?*" Vivian cried. "At a dance?"

"There would be dancing, too," Emily said. "Just more . . . variety for everyone else."

"It's not like anyone danced at the sixth-grade dance," James said.

Maddie rolled her eyes. "That was sixth grade."

"The costumes could be mash-ups of presidents and gaming," Kevin said. "Like Abraham Kong."

"Abraham Kong?" Devin scrunched his nose.

"An Abraham Lincoln and Donkey Kong mash-up. Or maybe Taft-Man, like Pac-Man and President Taft?" Kevin shrugged. "So we work on the ideas. Emily's got my vote."

Devin was back to scanning his cards. "Me too," he muttered.

"We weren't voting!" Vivian pressed her hands to the table and stood up.

"Me three," James said.

"Mrs. Ortega!" Vivian and Maddie said at the same time. Nisha continued to write things down in her notebook.

James smiled at Emily, and she realized that the majority was in her favor. She should have been thrilled. She should have been clapping gleefully. Not out of gloating but because she'd done it. She'd joined a school group and done more than sit in the background daydreaming about reading and book hunting. But what if a presidential GameCon slash Valentine's Day dance was the most ridiculous dance in the history of school dances? What had she done?

Mrs. Ortega clapped her hands. "Wonderful! A presidential GameCon sounds like a fantastic compromise, doesn't it?"

"Sure," Nisha said softly, continuing to scribble.

Maddie slumped back in her seat. "Whatever."

"Fine," Vivian said. She pointed her pen to Nisha. "You've been writing all this down?" Nisha nodded, and Vivian said, "Congratulations. You're our committee secretary." As she wrote on her clipboard, she zipped a line through her original theme and sounded out *Presidents' Day GameCon Dance*. "At least it's not an insipid lovey-dovey theme. All right. Now the real work begins. We're going to need to get the word out: posters, flyers, mentions in the morning announcements."

Maddie raised her hand. "I'll do posters. I love to paint."

"I can help," Nisha quietly added.

"We'll need refreshments—"

"Food!" Devin waved a hand wildly. "We love food!"

Vivian sighed and continued, "Decorations for the dance, people to man the welcome table, a DJ—"

"We know a DJ," Emily interjected. To James she said, "Right? Didn't Charlie say he DJs?"

"You really think he'd want to play music for a middle school dance?"

"We can pay him five hundred dollars," Vivian said.

James whistled. "Maybe I'll be our DJ, then. I can put together a playlist."

Vivian rolled her eyes and directed her question to Emily, "Can you talk to this Charlie person?"

Emily nodded. "Sure."

The dance was a top spinning in motion, and she'd opened her mouth—twice now—and changed its trajectory. There was no turning back.

CHAPTER 18

THE REST OF THE WEEK passed in a blur of school, unsuccessfully attempting to make sense of the unbreakable code letters, and brainstorming plans for the school dance. Before Emily knew it, it was Sunday. She and James were hanging out in his room, sketching ideas for turning the gym floor into a game board for some sort of presidential game, when Emily abruptly jumped up.

"I'm checking one more time."

James groaned. "You just checked an hour ago."

"Maybe the book's been found in the last hour," Emily said. She shook his mouse to wake up his computer.

When she had helped out at Hollister's the day before, she double-checked the tote bag and found the *Tom Sawyer* still there. It had remained there the whole day.

She logged into Book Scavenger and looked under Matthew's account. The *Tom Sawyer* they'd hidden and posted with his user name hadn't changed its status. Mr. Quisling wasn't taking their bait.

This frustrated her. It was similar to the feeling she got when she was faced with a puzzle that seemed like something she should be able to solve, but she still couldn't figure it out.

Not to mention, it drove her nuts wondering if Mr. Quisling had made any progress toward cracking the unbreakable code. Did he know what the letters meant? Could he have even already solved it? You'd think that would make the news, though, someone deciphering a legendary unsolved cipher. But Mr. Quisling seemed like the sort of guy who wouldn't want to solve it for the fame or notoriety; he would want to prove to himself that he could do it. The possibility of finding gold was probably motivating, too. Emily related. Those were pretty much her exact reasons as well.

Feeling restless to find out *something*, Emily searched for *Babbage*, Mr. Quisling's Book Scavenger identity, to check on his recent activity. There was nothing new other than the book she and James had watched him "find" a week ago in the redwood park. The user who had hidden that book was called Coolbrith.

Out of curiosity, Emily clicked on Coolbrith's account and was surprised to see Coolbrith had only ever hidden four books. When she pulled up the titles of those books, she straightened in her seat.

"James, the only books Coolbrith has hidden are copies of *Tom Sawyer*."

"That seems weird," James said.

"Very coincidental," Emily agreed.

"Ferry Building." James tapped one of the locations for Coolbrith's hidden books on the screen. "Didn't you say the book we hunted but never found last October was *Tom Sawyer*?"

Emily's neck prickled. She knew that Mr. Quisling had found multiple copies of *Tom Sawyer*, but she'd only been thinking about their teacher and the book, and whether there was a connection to him working on the unbreakable code. It hadn't occurred to her that the copies of *Tom Sawyer* might have all been hidden by one person. But, sure enough, Coolbrith had hidden copies of *Tom Sawyer* at the Ferry Building last October, the Mission in November, Washington Square in December, and Mark Twain Plaza in January. Babbage was the user who found them every time.

Emily entered both user names into the search bar on Book Scavenger: *Babbage* and *Coolbrith*. The top hit was a thread buried deep in the user forums titled "Quest For Babbage."

"A quest! I should have known," Emily said.

"What's a quest?" James asked.

"It's a game within the game. Book Scavenger players sometimes challenge others to a quest, or they might create an open quest for anyone to participate in. The quests can be anything people think of: You have to find books with titles that begin with every letter of the alphabet, you have to find books published in every year of a certain decade, that sort of thing. Sometimes there are prizes offered for finishing a quest the fastest, but usually it's just a pride thing. Or something to do with friends."

The forum thread was a back-and-forth between Coolbrith and Babbage, only Coolbrith's messages were written in numbers instead of words.

James smacked a palm to the side of his head, causing Steve to quiver. "I should have guessed this the day we watched Mr. Quisling."

"What? What? What?" Emily looked from the screen to James and back again, desperate to see the solution that had appeared for him.

"Two people hiding a book back and forth? It's a book cipher!"

"Of course," Emily whispered.

With a book cipher, the book itself was the key. You chose words found in the pages to make up your message. To encrypt your message, each word was identified by the page number, lines down, and words across, so three numbers equaled one word.

"When Mr. Quisling flipped through the book in the redwood grove, he was figuring out the message left for him," Emily said.

Emily and James scanned the forum thread between Babbage and Coolbrith.

Name of Quest: "For Old Times' Sake"

COOLBRITH has challenged BABBAGE to a quest.
Here are the rules set by COOLBRITH:

1) No outside help.
2) Find the book before anyone else.
3) Decipher the message.
4) Leave the book where you found it.
5) You'll know you've reached the end of the
   quest when you receive your reward.

COOLBRITH

Level: Encyclopedia Brown   Posted October 8—11:12 PM
Posts: 1

Let's revive an unfinished adventure from our past. You
will understand more when you complete the first
challenge in my quest:

www.bookscavenger.com/october/FerryBuilding_267

Your message to solve:
(193, 3, 1) (33, 21, 5) (85, 17, 9) (173, 19, 6) (21, 18, 3)

BABBAGE

Level: Sherlock   Posted October 9—8:23 AM
Posts: 74

Robbie?

COOLBRITH

Level: Encyclopedia Brown   Posted November 5—6:35 AM
Posts: 2

Well done for round one. Here is your second challenge:
www.bookscavenger.com/november/Mission_935

Your message to solve:
(75, 2, 1) (1, 11, 6) (179, 1, 4) (165, 24, 5)
(1, 7, 3) (63, 18, 1) (178, 1, 7)

BABBAGE

Level: Sherlock   Posted November 11—4:23 PM
Posts: 75

You aren't Robbie, are you?

COOLBRITH

Level: Encyclopedia Brown   Posted December 27—5:15 AM
Posts: 3

It's that time again. Here is a clue to who I am:

www.bookscavenger.com/december/WashSquare_094

Your message to solve:
(21, 9, 10) (209, 7, 6) (66, 27, 2) (43, 32, 8) (157, 2, 5)
(235, 6, 9)

BABBAGE

Level: Sherlock   Posted December 28—1:35 PM
Posts: 76

I lost the card, but I know it's you, Miranda. Do you
want to meet to talk about the new info you found?

"He calls Coolbrith *Miranda*." James pointed to the December post. "I wonder what he means by 'new info.' "

The name rang a bell from their visit to the Maritime Museum. "Miranda? As in Miranda Oleanda, the girl he was with at the *Niantic* dig?" It was hard to forget a name like that.

"He's doing a quest with someone he knew in high school or college?" James asked.

"I wish we still had the copy of *Tom Sawyer*," Emily said. "We could decode this and figure out what they were saying to each other."

"Well, why don't we go get it? It's Sunday—Hollister's is still open."

Emily and James entered the bookstore and found Charlie crouched in front of a small stack of books on a table that normally displayed literary-themed T-shirts. He snapped a picture with his cell phone.

"Hi, Charlie," Emily said to his back.

Charlie spun to face them.

"You're jumpy," James observed.

"You're chirpy." Charlie resumed his normal slouched posture. He nodded to the small tower of books. "It's spine poetry for Hollister's Instagram. You arrange book titles to make a poem."

Charlie's stack of books read:

One Flew Over the Cuckoo's Nest
Bird by Bird
Saving Fish from Drowning
Love in the Days of Rage

"Interesting." James posed like he was scrutinizing a piece of artwork. "So are you saying the birds love the fish? And they're crazy? Are they crazy *because* they love the fish?"

Emily nudged James—Charlie didn't seem so amused by his commentary, and she had just now remembered they needed to ask him a favor.

"Hey, Charlie, before we forget—didn't you say you DJ?"

Charlie slid the books this way and that, stepped back, and took another picture. "Yup," he said.

"Would you DJ our school dance? It's about a month from now, on Valentine's Day."

"I don't do kid functions," he replied, studying the photo he'd taken on his screen.

"We'd pay you five hundred bucks," James added.

That got Charlie's attention. He pulled a business card from his back pocket. "E-mail me the info. I'll see what I can do."

A short while later, Emily and James were camped out on the plush purple chair in the nook. Emily sat in the seat, and James perched on the armrest, a copy of *Tom Sawyer* in his hand. Hollister had copies of *Tom Sawyer* so they were using one of those. It was easier than digging out their hidden copy from the pile of tote bags. Plus Emily was a little superstitious and didn't want to remove the hidden book in case Mr. Quisling ended up looking for it after all.

"Okay," Emily said. "The first word in the October message is on page one ninety-three, three rows down, and one word across."

James flipped through the book. "*Do*," he recited.

Emily read the numbers to find the next two words and James read aloud, "*Do ghosts chaos*."

"That doesn't make sense." Emily frowned at what she'd written in her notebook. Had she made a mistake copying the numbers from the website?

"The words must not fall in the same place in this version of *Tom Sawyer*," James reasoned. "Maybe Coolbrith hid a different edition each month." When they'd pulled the book off the store shelf, they had noticed the cover wasn't the same as their hidden copy, but they didn't think that would matter.

"It makes sense, if you think about it," Emily said.

"If it was always the same edition, then you wouldn't need to go find a new book to solve the next message. Our hidden copy must solve the January code."

James tapped the copy on his lap. "Maybe this book was used for a different month. Let's try one of the other messages."

Emily recited the numbers for November next, but the correlating words were more gibberish. They tried December to be thorough, and this time had luck:

Flower bag will lead to me.

Emily gasped. "Flower bag! The one Mr. Quisling was stealing out of!"

"I told you he wasn't stealing. This lady told him to look in there."

"That card he dropped with the coded message must have been from her, then," Emily said.

James stood up from the armrest of the purple chair and paced in front of Emily. "So let me get this straight. Coolbrith is a woman named Miranda—we think Miranda Oleanda, who was in a picture with Mr. Quisling back when they were teenagers at the *Niantic* dig in San Francisco."

"Right," Emily agreed. "And the card she left for him at the book party said something about meeting in person after they've solved the unbreakable code."

"Don't forget the directions at the bottom—didn't

the note say something about leaving the solution in the *next book*? She must have meant the next *Tom Sawyer*."

"But he dropped the card with her puzzle and we took it—"

"And he posted a message in their quest thread asking to meet," James finished Emily's thought.

She jumped up. "Let's get other editions and see if we can figure out the rest of the messages." She ran to the tote bag display to recover the one they'd hidden—this was too exciting to worry about superstitions—while James pulled a different copy of *Tom Sawyer* from Hollister's shelf.

Emily pointed to James's. "Use yours first and see if we can solve the messages for October or November."

They sped through, reciting numbers and flipping pages, but the book didn't work for decoding the October message.

"Moving on to November," Emily said. "Page seventy-five, two rows down, one word across."

"I," James read aloud.

"Page one, eleven rows down, six words across."

"Have."

"Page one seventy-nine, one row down, four words across," Emily said.

"New." James's eyes flicked up and locked on Emily's. They were halfway through the sentence, and so far it was making sense. He nodded for her to go on.

"One sixty-five, twenty-four, five," she said.

"Information," James said.

Emily's pulse quickened. *I have new information.* Was this new information about the unbreakable code?

Emily bounced her knees as she recited the numbers for the last three words of the message. When James was counting down the lines to find the final word, she read aloud what they'd found so far: "I have new information about the . . ."

"*Map,*" James said.

CHAPTER 19

"MAP?" EMILY PULLED the book from James's hands to look for herself.

"There." He pointed to the word *map*.

Emily double-checked the numbers written in her notebook and re-counted the rows and words across. James was definitely right.

"Do you know what this means?" she asked.

James was already grinning when she looked up. "There is a map for the unbreakable code!"

The thought induced both despair and hope for Emily. Despair because in order to know a map existed, Mr. Quisling or his friend must have figured out the code, but hope because, well, there was a map!

"Let's see what the most recent message says." She hoped it would tell them how to find the map.

James picked up the copy of *Tom Sawyer* they'd found in the redwood park, and she called out the numbers from the January message. James read each word out loud as he found it: "Change . . . of . . . heart. . . . You're . . . on . . . your . . . own."

Emily and James were quiet for a beat, absorbing the words. Then Emily said, "Change of *heart*?"

"Did our . . . did our teacher just get dumped?" James asked.

"Dumped in code," Emily added.

"Through a Book Scavenger quest," James said. "Ouch."

And, amazingly, Emily felt for her teacher. He'd embarrassed her in class on her first day at Booker when he'd caught her passing a note, and he could definitely be strict, but he was universally strict. He treated all his students the same, and there was something to be said for that, even if he wasn't a warm and jolly person. It was kind of endearing that he had traded coded messages through a book-hunting game with an old girlfriend.

There was a clatter at the front of the store. Hollister yelped. Emily and James ran through the aisles and found the store owner holding a dolly stacked with cardboard boxes. The top box had fallen off, spilling the hardback books contained inside.

"Are you okay, Hollister?" Emily asked.

"Fine, I'm fine," Hollister said. He shook his head and squeezed around the dolly to start picking up the dropped books. Emily and James stooped down to help him.

"Just clumsy, I guess," Hollister said. "I swear this table's been moved over a few inches. I clipped it when I was rolling these boxes."

Charlie was at the front counter writing something down. Emily was pretty sure he must have moved the table when he was taking his photos earlier, so she wondered if he'd say anything or apologize, but he didn't. Maybe he hadn't heard Hollister. Perhaps because she'd been staring at him so long, or maybe because his guilt prompted him, Charlie looked up.

"Need any help?" he asked.

"Nah, I've got it," Hollister said.

The cardboard box that spilled had been filled with copies of the same book. There was an illustration of the San Francisco skyline on the cover. Emily picked one up and flipped through the pages. "This is a cool book," she said.

"Isn't it? It's brand-new—we just got them in. It's about the changing landscape of San Francisco over the years, but the book itself is truly a work of art. Go on. Look through it. I can clean up my own mess."

Emily and James carried the book to the front counter to get out of Hollister's way. They flipped to the first page, which had an illustration of a barely recognizable San Francisco with undeveloped hills and only a few low buildings close to the water.

"Look, that inlet is probably Yerba Buena Cove," Emily said, thinking of their talk with the docent at the

Maritime Museum. As they turned the pages in the book, detailed cutouts layered on top of the previous page so gradually the city developed and aged right before their eyes.

"It reminds me of a grille cipher," James said. "I would have never thought of using it with illustrations, though."

"What's a grille cipher?" Hollister asked as he stacked the scattered books back into the cardboard box.

"It's a way to conceal a message. I always thought of it for words hidden in a paragraph, but I suppose it could be a drawing, too. With words, you would take a secret message like *attack at midnight* and write out something that sounds boring but uses those words. Like *Gary the attack rooster was at it again, practicing his ninja skills at midnight.* The person who is decoding the message has the grille—it's like a piece of cardboard with holes cut in it. When you put the grille over the paper with the story about Gary the rooster, everything gets covered up except the message *attack at midnight.*"

"Fascinating," Hollister said. "What an interesting way to hide something in plain sight."

Before heading home, Emily and James put the copies of *Tom Sawyer* back where they'd found them, including re-hiding the one for Book Scavenger. Even if Mr. Quisling wasn't going to look for it, maybe another Book Scavenger user would.

Walking home, Emily felt a little down about how

much further along Mr. Quisling probably was toward figuring out the unbreakable code until she realized that Coolbrith had posted her breakup message after Mr. Quisling asked about meeting up. Which meant they probably never talked about the map, which meant Mr. Quisling might know only as much as Emily and James did: that a map existed.

The thought made her feel lighter. It also made her realize that if she wanted to get information about the map from someone, Coolbrith might be a better choice than Mr. Quisling.

And Emily had an idea for exactly how she could do that.

"Should I be worried about you doing this?" James asked. "I feel like I should be worried."

They were back in his room. He was sprawled on his floor with computer paper and scissors, testing out some grille cipher creations while Emily sat at the computer.

"No, you shouldn't be," she said.

Coolbrith didn't have private messaging enabled in Book Scavenger, so Emily had done an Internet search, hoping that the unusual name Miranda Oleanda would turn up some results. And she'd had good luck, because there, in the middle of a list of results that mostly had to do with the flower oleander, was a profile on a scrapbooking forum. The woman in the photo looked like she could be an older version of the teenager who had been buddy-buddy with Mr. Quisling at the *Niantic* dig many years ago, and there was an e-mail address in the profile, too.

Emily quickly typed out a message:

Dear Ms. Oleanda,
Our teacher is Mr. Quisling. We play Book Scavenger with him, which he tells us you like, too. Recently, he told us about the unbreakable code and how you are working on it with him. He showed us the map once, and we thought it would make an awesome gift to copy the map and frame it for him as a surprise. But we don't know where to find it. Could you tell us? Remember, this is a surprise.
Thank you,
Mr. Quisling's students

"You can't send that!" James cried. He'd left his paper cuttings and scissors on the floor to see what Emily was up to.

"Why not?" Emily asked.

"Because . . . because . . . are you kidding me? For starters, we don't know this lady. Second, what if she talks to Mr. Quisling?"

"That's why I kept it anonymous. My e-mail has a generic handle. She won't know it's me. All she can tell him is that some of his students like him enough to want to give him a gift—that's not so awful."

"And he'll know that whoever sent this e-mail is lying because he never told us about the unbreakable code. He'll know someone else is trying to solve it."

"Technically, he did tell us when he dropped that note at Hollister's party. And anyone can look at the unbreakable code in the library. It's not like it's top-secret information. Anyway, she probably won't even reply. Worst-case scenario is we hear nothing, but maybe this will give us the clue we need."

Emily pressed Send. James covered his face with his hands. "I can't believe you did that!" He peeked through his fingers.

Emily giggled. This revelation about the existence of a map had turned her into a giant, grinning balloon. Imagine being the person who proved that something that was considered impossible was actually possible?

CHAPTER 20

THE NEXT DAY Mr. Quisling stood in the dimly lit classroom, illuminated by the projector as he described slides about ancient Greece. Emily drew a palm tree on the margin of her notebook, glancing up every now and then, and jotting something down in her class notes. Next to her, James was using a sharp pencil to poke holes in a piece of binder paper in order to make a grille cipher. He poked a final hole in the paper and placed it on top of his notebook. Smiling at the results, he lifted the notebook up for Emily to see:

BRONZE

TURKEY

IS

KING

Emily smiled, then quickly redirected her attention to Mr. Quisling so he wouldn't notice they hadn't been listening to him talk about King Minos. She wrote down the next few things he said, then while his voice droned on, she outlined bubble letters across the top of her page.

Change of heart.

She filled in each letter with diagonal stripes and thought about the week before, when Mr. Quisling had been preoccupied solving the Book Scavenger code in class, and then they followed him to the redwood park. Now she realized they'd watched their teacher decipher a breakup message. Mr. Quisling was probably heart-broken.

Their teacher rubbed the dry eraser against the board, and it flipped out of his hand, bouncing off his chest. Mr. Quisling picked up the eraser and kept talking, brushing at the blue ink mark on the fabric. It was the same new shirt James had complimented him on last week, the day they followed him. He had probably worn it that day in hopes that he might see Miranda.

Emily sighed. She wouldn't have thought it was possible, but she felt sorry for Mr. Quisling.

Emily and James were in her room, hunched over their tracing of the unbreakable code. That was how they'd spent the majority of their free time that week, staring at the page as if they could summon the letters through the powers of eyesight to reveal their secrets and tell them where the dang map was already.

"We could ask Mr. Quisling," James said.

"You've said that before, but now we're in an even worse spot," Emily said. *"Um, Mr. Quisling? Not only did we decipher your secret message from the book party, but we followed you and decoded the messages you traded with your ex-girlfriend, and now we know about the unbreakable code and that a map exists somewhere, and could you tell us more about this map?"*

"Don't forget to mention you e-mailed his ex-girlfriend, too," James said. "He'll be sure to help us then."

Emily squirmed uncomfortably. "Oh, yeah. I did that, didn't I?" It had been several days since she sent the e-mail, and there had been no response.

"Okay, let's think like a gold miner." James stood up and stretched, shaking his hands, then arms and legs like he was getting ready to run a race. "I'm a grizzled old miner, and I've hidden some gold. I want to make sure I can find it again, so I write directions in a secret code and make a map. Where would I put the map?"

"It seems weird to have two different objects to keep track of," Emily said. "Like, what if the map got lost? Or the message? Why wouldn't you try to limit yourself to one piece of paper?"

"It's more secure if you double up," James pointed out. "If you need both the map and the cipher to figure out where the gold is, it makes it harder for someone else to solve. Think of it like this."

James flipped to a clean page in Emily's notebook and wrote the following key:

A	B	C	D	E	F	G	H	I	J	K	L	M
B	C	D	E	F	G	H	I	J	K	L	M	N

N	O	P	Q	R	S	T	U	V	W	X	Y	Z
O	P	Q	R	S	T	U	V	W	X	Y	Z	A

"This is a simple substitution cipher, right?" James wrote down a series of letters and handed the notebook back to Emily. "Now solve this message."

SPDLFU DBU DPNF GMZ BXBZ

It only took her a couple of minutes. "Rocket cat come fly away," she said.

"Right! But then what if you combined that substitution cipher with a rail fence cipher?"

In a rail fence cipher, you wrote the letters of your message up and down in a zigzag, so on the notebook page, James used the already encrypted message and wrote:

S   D   F   D   U   P   F   M   B   B
  P   L   U   B   D   N   G   Z   X   Z

After that, he grouped the letters into sets of five, which was the final step with a rail fence cipher:

SDFDU PFMBB PLUBD NGZXZ

"Doubling up your security tactics makes it more difficult to solve," James said. "Even if someone figured out the substitution cipher, they would end up with RCECT OELAA OKTAC MFYWY, and they probably wouldn't realize they'd deciphered the letters correctly because they're in a jumbled order."

"I know you're right, but if I was trying to remember where I left something valuable, I wouldn't want to keep track of two objects necessary for finding my way back. What if I lost one of them?"

Emily studied the tracing from the library, flipping the page over to see the doodles they had copied, and then back to the letters. Smoothing the paper, she noticed the doodles—four circles and some squiggle lines—showed through, faintly. She flipped the page over again.

The drawings looked like something she would do mindlessly in class, or like what her mom did when she was on the phone. But what if they weren't as mindless as they looked?

Emily folded the notebook paper in half.

"You're not giving up on it, are you?" James asked.

"No, I'm experimenting." She held up the page so the light shone through. The doodles and letters overlapped. Most of it was a muddle of lines and curves, except for one circle where an x landed perfectly in the center.

"Check that out," Emily said. She opened the paper and scanned the grid of letters. In all the letters, there was only one x. She folded the paper again, pressing a hand across the crease to make it flat and smooth. It wasn't a fluke—the x was the only letter that fell inside a circle.

"X marks the spot," Emily said. "The unbreakable code *is* the map."

"You might be right," James said, leaning close to the paper. "It's still doubling up on the security, but the miner wouldn't have needed to worry about keeping track of two papers, like you said. So what does the circle represent?"

"Maybe you find out when you decode the cipher," Emily said.

"Or . . ." James slid the paper away and turned the drawing to the side. "What if the squiggly lines mean water? Like the San Francisco Bay? And the circles are islands? These three are grouped together like Angel Island, Alcatraz, and Treasure Island. And the x marks the spot on . . ."

"Treasure Island," Emily said. "The treasure might really be there! Have you been before?"

James shook his head. "Not yet. But I think we need to make a trip."

CHAPTER 21

E MILY THOUGHT there might be a ferry they could take to Treasure Island, but it turned out you had to drive there, even though it was an island. To drive, they needed grown-ups, and James's mom and grand-mother had a big event they were preparing food for. Emily's parents, however, were always up for exploring new places. When Emily pitched the idea of a bike ride around Treasure Island, they immediately agreed. The only problem was her parents refused to drive during rush-hour traffic, which was the only option if they went after school, so it wasn't until Saturday that the Cranes and James piled into Sal, the Cranes' old minivan.

They drove halfway across the Bay Bridge, where they exited into the tunnel that bored through the rugged and craggy landmass in the middle of the bay. The van curved out of the tunnel like a gumball dispensed from a machine. The road sloped around the green-clad island

and then straightened out and became flatter than flat along a waterfront sparsely lined with palm trees.

As she took in the paved road and sidewalks, the Treasure Island Yacht Club, and an old horseshoe-shaped building, Emily realized how impossible this mission might be. What if the gold was on the island, but a building had been erected over its burial spot? They'd never find it.

Well, they were here. It couldn't hurt to scope the place out, she told herself. Emily had learned from both solving puzzles and book hunting that it was always good to keep your mind open to possibilities and to never stop observing. You might find the key to unlock a difficult problem in the most unlikely of spots.

They parked next to a small marina in front of the horseshoe building, which looked like it had seen better days, now that they were closer. The parking lot was practically empty. Emily wasn't used to going someplace in San Francisco so unpopulated. They rounded the building to find the bike rental shop tucked in the back. A jackhammer rattled the quiet, and Emily could see a construction site in the distance. It prompted a new worry: Maybe the gold would be found by a construction crew, similar to how the *Niantic* was rediscovered.

"Do you have the coupon?" Emily's dad asked.

Her mom dug through her purse, pulling out a printout from a website. "Two-for-one bike rentals!" She waved the paper and added, "We're covering yours, James. Don't worry about it."

Emily internally cringed with the realization that this outing was costing her parents more money. Even though they didn't seem worried about it, she knew they must be under the surface. She straightened her shoulders and tightened her ponytail. If it could help her stay in San Francisco, that was all the more reason to find this treasure.

Once the Cranes and James got set up with bikes and helmets, they pedaled to the sidewalk that ran along the water. The view of the San Francisco skyline from here was better than any postcard Emily had seen. But the island itself struck Emily as . . . dilapidated. Maybe she'd connected the name Treasure Island too closely with the book, which made her imagine something lush and tropical. She certainly hadn't anticipated the boarded-up buildings and rusted docks they cycled past.

Her parents slowed to a stop and straddled their bikes, facing the water and the city. Her mom pulled her camera from the bag slung across her body and began snapping photos. A rocky border separated the sidewalk from the water. Just beyond her brother's foot, Emily could see a watermelon-sized rock with the words *I got mugged* in blue spray paint.

"This is not what I was expecting," Emily said, adjusting the chinstrap of her bike helmet.

"With a view like this, you'd think Treasure Island would be the most desirable place to live, wouldn't you?" her mom said, twisting her focal lens.

"I read it was owned by the navy until recently," Emily's dad said.

"Is that so?" her mom replied. *Click. Click.* "Is that why the island was originally built? For the navy?"

Emily squinted at her mom, not sure she heard her right. "What do you mean, 'built'?"

Her mom lowered the camera. "This isn't natural. Can't you tell? See how flat everything is?"

"But you can't *build* an island . . . can you?" Emily stupidly scanned the ground, as if she'd actually see the seams and bolts of an island pieced together.

Emily's mother pointed the camera in her direction, taking a picture of the view beyond her shoulder. "That part is natural," she said.

"The part we drove in on from the bridge is a separate island," Mr. Crane added. "It's called Yerba Buena."

It seemed obvious to Emily now. The first part of the island had been an irregular, green-covered lump. It looked wild and rocky, whereas this half was mostly bald concrete.

"You didn't know about this?" Emily asked James.

He shrugged. "I'm not a San Francisco wiki page."

The towering buildings of downtown San Francisco taunted her across the bay. Where those buildings stood was once water. She shouldn't have been so surprised to learn that an entire island could be materialized.

"When was Treasure Island built?" Emily asked, with a sinking feeling that they were way off in their guess about the unbreakable code treasure being buried here.

"There was a World's Fair in the late 1930s," Emily's dad said. "My memory is telling me they made it for that."

The 1930s. That was well after the Gold Rush, well after Mark Twain had lived in San Francisco, and well after the San Francisco Tom Sawyer had been alive. This couldn't be the burial spot for the gold.

They continued their ride around the island, pedaling past warehouses that looked abandoned and apartment buildings with a few signs of life, like clothes draped over railings and potted plants that weren't dead. They cycled past an empty ball field, which struck Emily as a particularly lonely site on this Saturday morning. They'd lived by ball fields in Colorado, and the weekends were always a frenzy of noise and the traffic of parents coming and going. On their way back to the bike shop, they passed the construction site with banners advertising a big island transformation to come.

The more they pedaled, the dumber Emily felt for thinking treasure could be hidden there in the first place. As if the unbreakable code would lead to *Treasure* Island, and nobody else had guessed that for over one hundred sixty years. She might as well have believed there would be a giant black X painted on the ground to mark the hiding spot.

CHAPTER 22

EMILY, JAMES, and Matthew had their second Book Scavenger advisory meeting on the Tuesday after touring Treasure Island. Jack pushed open the doors to Mr. Griswold's office as before, but this time they anticipated the dogs that came rushing over. Once again, Claus greeted them with enthusiastic barks, then pranced to his pillow and paraded around with it in his mouth. Angel rolled onto her back and let Matthew rub her belly before trotting over to her basket and curling up with a satisfied sigh.

"Hello!" Mr. Griswold smiled and stood from papers he'd been reading at his desk. He still wasn't dressed as flamboyantly as Emily was accustomed to imagining for him, but at least today he wore a burgundy sweater with his slacks, which seemed to be a nudge back in the direction of the old Mr. Griswold. That made her hopeful enough to charge forward with her plan.

"Mr. Griswold," she said. "Look what we found online!"

She offered the printout of his old interview. Mr. Griswold's hand shook ever so slightly as he accepted the clipping. Emily wasn't sure if that was from the physical effort of holding the paper steady or if it was upsetting him to see the old interview.

"You looked pretty hip back then, Mr. Griswold," James said.

Mr. Griswold chortled, and Emily relaxed a bit. He didn't seem mad, at least.

"Can I see it?" Matthew asked. After looking at the photo, he exclaimed, "Dude! Your hair is curly! Is that a perm?"

"It was a long time ago," Mr. Griswold said softly. He let Matthew take over reading the interview and seated himself on the couch.

"I like where you talked about how we can control the kind of journey we're on," Emily said.

"This part?" Matthew asked. He read aloud from the interview, "*Your actions and reactions determine the type of journey you will have. Will it be magical? Joyful? Fearful? Will you be the victim, or will you be the hero?*"

"Yes, that part," Emily said. "It made me think about myself as the main character in my own story."

"Not just the main character," James chimed in. "The main character *and* the writer, too."

"Right," Emily said. "We're writing our own stories

with what we do and say every day. And if I find myself in a chapter where bad things happen, *I* get to decide what kind of story I'm in."

"I'm very glad my words had that effect on you," Mr. Griswold said. "It's important to be hopeful when you're young."

Emily wanted to reply, *It's important to be hopeful when you're old, too*, but she thought that might be rude. Instead she said, "It's important to be hopeful always."

"Yes, it is," Jack interjected. He'd been reading the interview over Matthew's shoulder. "You three are smart kids, you know that? No wonder you're so good at puzzles and scavenger hunts."

Emily wasn't sure how she'd expected Mr. Griswold to react to seeing his old interview again. She knew he wasn't going to jump up and down and shout, *Thank you for showing me this!* and then race into his secret bookcase room and hop out wearing a suit and top hat pinstriped in Bayside Press colors with a matching walking cane, but she thought she might at least see a small spark ignited.

She charged forward with the second half of her plan. If Mr. Griswold had tried to revive interest in solving the unbreakable code decades ago, then hearing about their map discovery—how the *x* fell perfectly in one of the circles when the paper was folded—would certainly excite him.

"The other thing we wanted to tell you has to do

with the unbreakable code," she said. "James was playing around with grille ciphers the other day—"

But before she could say anything more, Mr. Griswold snapped his attention to his watch. "Oh, dear," he said, and hoisted himself up from the couch, "I haven't been paying attention to the time. I have a vet appointment for the dogs."

"You . . . do?" James said. The three kids exchanged confused looks. Even Jack looked a little thrown.

"Oh," Jack said. "I didn't realize there was a time conflict with this today."

"Before you go, could we tell you—"

Mr. Griswold spoke over Emily, appearing not to hear her. "Claus, Angel, walk!" At the sound of *walk*, Mr. Griswold's office erupted into yips and whines and dancing doggy feet. It almost seemed to Emily that it flustered Mr. Griswold to hear the words *unbreakable code*, and he was trying to cause a distraction from the topic. Mr. Griswold attached their leashes to their collars, the chains jangling together. Over the racket, he called to Jack, "If you could run the show for this meeting, that would be great. Last time, we talked about setting you kids up as admins, so Jack will show you the ropes for that."

With a hasty wave, Mr. Griswold and the dogs were out the door. The *clack-clack-clack*ing of the constantly moving marble in the maze contraption seemed louder than ever after Mr. Griswold and the dogs had left.

Emily frowned. She had thought reminding Mr. Griswold of his own words would help him return to normal. But now Emily was starting to think maybe it wasn't that he had forgotten what he used to be like. Maybe the problem was that he remembered all too well and couldn't bear to face his old self anymore.

CHAPTER 23

LOCKER DOORS SLAMMED, creating an·uneven percussion as Emily and James walked to their next dance committee meeting. Between Treasure Island being a dead-end lead for the unbreakable code and Emily's flopped plan to cheer up Mr. Griswold, she felt a little down but hoped the distraction of planning a dance would help.

James pulled open the science classroom door. Mrs. Ortega paced the room with her hands pressed to her back, her pregnant belly leading the way. The twins were the only committee members who hadn't arrived yet.

"Hey, Vivian," Emily said, taking the seat next to her, "did you get the info about the DJ?"

"Yes." Vivian didn't look up from her homework. "He's confirmed for the dance."

James shook his head, bewildered. "I was sure Charlie would say no. I guess he needs the money."

Across the table, Nisha and Maddie were playing dots and boxes, a game Nisha had also taught James in their chemistry class. You make a four-by-four grid of dots and take turns drawing a line between two dots. Whoever makes a line that closes four dots into a box puts their initial inside the box and goes again. The person with the most boxes at the end of the game wins.

Vivian looked at the classroom clock and hopped up from her seat. "We need to get started."

Emily wondered if Kevin and Devin had decided to drop the committee—she wouldn't have been surprised. She knew they'd only been at the first meeting because James had asked them to come. Actually, she wouldn't have been surprised if James had dropped out, too.

The door to the science classroom banged open, and Emily turned to see Kevin and Devin carrying a large cardboard box between them.

"Look what we brought!" They tipped the contents onto one of the lab tables and dozens of white wigs, tiny round wire-frame glasses, and top hats spilled out.

"Team costumes!" Devin said.

"What teams? What costumes?" Vivian asked. She frowned at the assortment of items sprawled in front of her.

"For the presidential games," Kevin explained. "We came up with costumes for three teams of presidents. Part of the challenge can be putting on your costume as fast as possible, and then we all compete in some sort of game."

James strung the elastic bands of a long black beard around his ears. Emily picked up a pinafore. She couldn't believe the twins were actually latching onto this crazy idea she'd thrown out for the dance. Vivian sifted through the items with everyone else, and Emily tried to gauge if the way she petted the puffy white wig and gingerly lifted a tie was a positive thing or negative.

"Where did you get all this stuff?" Emily asked.

"Our mom volunteers at a costume bank. It's part of her charity organization. We'll have to return some of this stuff when we're done, but she's donating the rest to our class."

Devin handed James a black suit jacket and then dropped a top hat over Steve. The hat sank down over James's eyes, making his face mostly hat/nose/long beard. "Team Abraham Lincoln!" Devin declared.

"I'm swimming in this coat." James, with his hat still covering his eyes, raised his arms so the sleeves slouched to his elbows.

"It makes it funnier," Kevin said. He dressed himself in a blue coat, white wig, and pinafore. "Team George Washington," he explained.

"Or Thomas Jefferson," Devin added. "It's basically the same look."

"Stick with Washington," Vivian said, and pointed to Nisha. "Make a note of that." Vivian picked up the remaining items and put them on herself: a mustache, wire-rimmed glasses with a cord dangling from one side, and a tie. "Who am I supposed to be?"

"Teddy Roosevelt," Kevin and Devin said together.

Across the room Mrs. Ortega groaned.

"What's wrong with President Roosevelt?" Kevin asked.

Mrs. Ortega shook her head, her lips pressed into a thin line. "Not the costumes. The baby." She lowered herself into a chair, but didn't last long before she was back up and pacing. She waved a hand. "Go on. I'm fine."

Their eyes lingered on the teacher with hesitation before Vivian said to Kevin and Devin, "So you have enough of these costumes to divide everyone at the dance into three teams?"

"Definitely yes with the wigs and beards and hats and glasses. My mom can lend us some jackets and ties, but we might need to borrow more of those."

"That should be easy enough to organize," Vivian said, indicating for Nisha to make a note of that as well. "All right. So we have three presidential teams. This was your idea, Emily. What exactly will we *do* for the game?"

Nisha waited, pen poised to jot down whatever she said. Maddie cocked her head and smirked, as if she could smell Emily's insecurity. James removed the top hat from his eyes and gave her an encouraging nod. Only Devin and Kevin didn't seem that invested as they played hot potato with a George Washington wig.

"Well," Emily said, "with three teams we could . . ."

Hanging from the ceiling of the classroom were models of atoms made out of Hula-hoops with a cluster of balloons in the middle. "We could do a balloon stomp."

Nisha wrote this down.

"What's that?" Vivian asked.

"Each team member ties a balloon on a string to their ankle. We'd have different colors for each team—"

"Red, white, and blue would be presidential." Vivian tapped Nisha's notebook.

"Then the object is to stomp the balloons of the other teams. Last team with an unpopped balloon wins."

"Cool," Kevin and Devin said, attempting to stomp on each other's foot.

"We could turn it into a relay race, too," James volunteered. "The costumes for each team could be in a giant box at the start. Each player dresses up, runs through an obstacle course, then ties on a balloon. Once an entire team has balloons on, they can start popping the other teams' balloons."

The more they talked, the more Emily could actually visualize the game taking place at the dance. It sounded ridiculous, sure, but the kind of ridiculous that might be a lot of fun, like the sort of event Mr. Griswold would plan.

Mrs. Ortega gave a loud yelp.

"Sorry, kids," she wheezed. "We've got to end this meeting. I need to call my doctor."

Everybody inched back from Mrs. Ortega like she was a bomb set to explode, except Maddie, who crossed to a lab sink. "Have you been drinking water? My mom thought she was having my half sister early, but it turned out she hadn't been drinking enough water." Maddie pulled a Dixie cup from the stack on the counter. "Here, drink this."

Mrs. Ortega accepted the cup but said, "Really, you all, I'll be fine. You can head home now."

Maddie stayed by Mrs. Ortega's side while the rest of the students helped put the costumes back in the boxes for Kevin and Devin. When Emily and James left the room, Maddie was keeping an eye on their teacher and holding her purse as Mrs. Ortega spoke to someone on her cell phone.

CHAPTER 24

THE NEXT DAY was the annual seventh-grade trip to Angel Island. The wind whipped Emily's ponytail back and forth as she and James leaned against the railing on the top deck of the ferry. On a bench behind them sat the last-minute substitute teacher for Mrs. Ortega, who was on bed rest because of her contractions the day before. The substitute was Mr. Sloan, the same man who had told Mr. Quisling he was looking for sub work at the Poe book party, and then observed their social studies class a couple of weeks ago. He sat with his head clutched in his hands. Every so often, a moan would drift over to where Emily and James stood. He didn't handle being on water very well.

As they approached Angel Island, a blinding ribbon of sunlight unfurled across the water to a marina tucked in a cove. Trees transformed from a generic green mass into distinct broccoli shapes. This was a real island, a natural island, as opposed to that flat faker Treasure Island.

"Maybe we have the grille cipher wrong, and it's actually marking Angel Island," Emily said.

The thought was hopeful and disappointing at the same time. Hopeful because at least then they would have a location to focus on. But Angel Island looked pretty massive compared to Treasure Island. They had pedaled around Treasure Island in less than an hour, and it was flat and spare. Angel Island was hilly and heavily forested. It would take days or weeks to explore the whole thing.

The ferry docked, and Emily and James crossed the deck to join their classmates and parent and teacher chaperones filing down the stairs and off the boat. Mr. Sloan stood, a little shakily, his face the shade of pistachio ice cream. Another seventh grader, José, clapped Mr. Sloan on the back as he walked by, making the substitute grimace.

"Yo, Mr. New Guy, if you puke, don't face into the wind," José said.

Emily and James stepped around Mr. Sloan and joined the flow of people heading off the ferry. There were more than just Booker students on the ferry, so the shouts of various teachers instructing their students on where to stand was confusing when they walked up the ramp and stepped off the dock. Emily and James walked past a group of students wearing matching navy St. Raymond sweatshirts chanting a song about llamas, then crossed the pavement to stand with the Booker group of students, teachers, and parent chaperones waiting in front of a small pink building.

A light wind wafted the smell of sewage their way. James pinched his nose and said in a nasally voice, "You'd think we could pick a different meeting spot than in front of the bathrooms."

Mr. Sloan, with a slightly less green face, was the last to arrive. Their class climbed on an open-air shuttle and bumped along a path around the perimeter of the island until the immigration station came into view.

It was a long, two-story building dwarfed by the forested hillside that rose behind it. A rigid procession of cement stairs led up to the building. The cement planters on either side of the stairs were engraved with words like *dreams*, *hope*, and *fears*.

A tour guide welcomed their group and explained that immigrants came through Angel Island for a thirty-year period between 1910 and 1940. Emily scanned their surroundings, thinking about how the unbreakable code and the hidden treasure happened well before the island was used for immigration.

Emily raised her hand. "What was here in 1851?"

James snorted, knowing what she had on her mind when she asked the question.

"Let's see . . . 1851?" The guide looked around thoughtfully. "A Spanish explorer gave it the name Angel Island in 1775, and of course the Miwok Indians were in this area long before that, but in 1851, California was a brand-new state, only a year old. Angel Island was actually declared a military reserve that year, but I don't think it was utilized until the Civil War. There was a ship, however, used as a prison, that was anchored offshore."

Emily let this information sink in as they continued up the stairs and into the building. If the island was owned by the military in 1851, then she doubted a gold miner would choose it as a hiding spot for his treasure. She and James had struck out with Treasure Island, and now Angel Island didn't seem like a promising candidate for the treasure location, either.

The guide said, "At the time Angel Island operated as an immigration station, there was a lot of racial prejudice against the Chinese. There were exclusionary laws that restricted their travel here. Chinese travelers were often detained here for longer periods of time than other nationalities, sometimes as long as months or even years."

"Why? What were people afraid of?" someone asked.

"Even though the Chinese were among the first to arrive in San Francisco during the Gold Rush, gradually over time, some people began to feel threatened by the number of Chinese who were living here, how industrious they were, and their general willingness to take on menial and even dangerous jobs for little pay. It wasn't a proud time in our country's history, and when China became an ally during World War II, President FDR declared the exclusionary laws and prejudiced treatment a historic mistake."

They toured the dormitory designated for Chinese men. Metal cots stacked three high with barely enough room to sit up. The tour guide mentioned there had been guards and strict rules for what you could and couldn't do. In order to leave the island, you had to pass a series of interviews about minute details of your life to prove you were who you said you were. It all seemed too much like a prison to Emily, but it wasn't supposed to be. The people who came here weren't criminals. They were only people moving from one place to another, something Emily had had a lot of experience with. It had never occurred to Emily that her family's ability to move whenever and wherever they wanted might make them *lucky*.

Next to her, James studied a placard with a picture of a group of Chinese men and boys standing in a horseshoe, no shirts on, being inspected by a man in uniform. Emily was shocked to see the majority of the people in the photo looked their age, or not much older. She wondered how those boys felt in the picture. She would have been embarrassed if she'd had to stand in a group of people like that, being looked over like an object. But then she would have been scared if she was alone with that inspector guy, so maybe it was comforting to have the other people in the same situation there. If she had to choose between being embarrassed or being scared, she'd choose embarrassed, but those didn't seem like fair choices.

"My great-grandfather had to stay here," James said to Emily.

"He did?" She looked again to the picture, wondering

if his great-grandfather was in that group. "How long did he have to stay?"

"I don't know," James said with a shrug. "My grandmother said he never talked about it. She's only mentioned it a few times herself."

The walls of the immigration station were covered almost completely with poems written by the detained immigrants, the majority of which were written in columns of Chinese. Many of these poems were carved into the walls, and then in an attempt to conceal the words the carvings had been filled in with putty and painted over. Over time, the putty shrank, which almost made the poetry stand out more. Emily traced a finger over one of the characters, admiring the persistence of words refusing to be censored.

"Do you think your great-grandfather wrote any of these?"

"I don't know," James said softly, thoughtfully, as he wandered off to scrutinize the poetry.

The tour guide said many of the poems expressed anger or despair from the inhabitants over how they'd been treated, and some expressed hope for what their future would hold.

Emily slowly moved around the room, stepping behind Mr. Sloan, who was sketching in a notebook. Looking at what he was drawing, she saw he was copying down some of the characters.

"Amazing, isn't it?" Mr. Sloan said, without looking over to her.

"It—it is," she stammered, embarrassed that she was caught peeking. "Do you know Chinese?"

Now he looked at her, but uncertainly. She nodded to what he'd been drawing. "Yours look exactly like what's on the wall."

"Ah, that, yes." He smiled. "I'm a good mimic. One of my unusual talents. Some people solve crosswords; I practice my penmanship."

She left the substitute teacher to his copying, and moved over to where James was reading a translation of one of the poems. He said the last line out loud: "Even if it is built of jade, it has turned into a cage."

"It's so sad to imagine the people who had to stay here," Emily said. She pictured someone carefully carving those words, taking breaks to look through the chain-link-covered window.

"It's only sad if you assume that's the end of their story," James said. "If you imagine the person's next chapter, living over there"—James nodded out the window to the city across the bay—"then it's heroic. They refused to be broken just because someone tried to hold them back."

CHAPTER 25

EXACTLY ONE WEEK after the school trip to Angel Island, Emily received an e-mail with the subject "Old Friends." She read the sender's name, "M. Oleanda," and sucked in her breath. Miranda Oleanda. Coolbrith.

Emily and James had continued to study the unbreakable code, even though the letters refused to reveal their secret, but they had assumed Coolbrith's Book Scavenger quest for their teacher had come to a conclusion when they decoded the breakup message. There hadn't been any alerts for more hidden copies of *Tom Sawyer*, and the one they'd placed in Hollister's store had sat ignored for weeks.

Emily hesitantly clicked her mouse to open the new e-mail. Miranda Oleanda wrote:

I appreciate you reaching out to me, but I believe there has been a mistake. While Brian Quisling is indeed an old friend and colleague, it has been over ten years since we have been in contact. I am also not familiar with the game you mentioned—Book Scavenger—and I no longer live in California. I have been living in Ohio with my husband and children for the past fifteen years. The unbreakable code rings a distant bell, but not well enough to remember anything about a map. I'm sorry I can't be of more help. I'm sure Mr. Quisling would be tickled to know his students care enough about him to want to give him a special gift.

Wishing you the best,
Miranda Oleanda

Emily released her held breath with a confused puff. Mr. Quisling's ex-girlfriend was married with kids? She didn't live in California? She'd never heard of Book Scavenger? She thought Mr. Quisling would be *tickled* to know something?

So this woman *wasn't* Coolbrith?

Emily had to let James know about this. She retrieved the broom she kept handy for knocking on the ceiling. *Thud. Thud-thud-thud. Thud.* That was the pattern that alerted James to an incoming bucket message. On a slip of scrap paper she scrawled:

EKUEO DXLP UNTBW.
(Check your email.)

She dropped the note in the bucket and hoisted it up

to James's window, then returned to her laptop to forward the e-mail from Miranda Oleanda to James.

The knock signaling James's reply came soon after, followed by the bucket returning to her window with this note:

BI SKU'S FXV EXXWHPBVK, VKUF ZKX BS???
(If she's not Coolbrith, then who is???)

Exactly. Mr. Quisling certainly thought Coolbrith was Miranda Oleanda. Why else would he have called her Miranda? James's note continued:

SKXLWQ ZU VUWW KBN?
(Should we tell him?)

Again, Emily wrestled over whether or not they should say something to their teacher. What would they even say? It would have been easier if they'd brought up the code from the beginning, but she'd been suspicious of Mr. Quisling then, and now she didn't even know where to start. How do you tell your teacher that the girlfriend they think they're trading notes with—the one who maybe broke up with him in code—is totally not who he thinks? Talk about embarrassing, both for Mr. Quisling and for them having to tell him about it. And then what if they were wrong? They needed to find out more before they said anything to him, if they said anything at all.

Mr. Quisling and Coolbrith obviously didn't care about just any old copy of *Tom Sawyer* hidden through Book Scavenger. But what if Emily and James reposted the clue for the book under a different user name? Would Quisling go look for it then?

Emily scribbled a note to James:

ZU FUUQ VX IBFQ XLV NXPU.
B KTAU T JWTF.
(We need to find out more.
I have a plan.)

On Friday, Emily and James uploaded their new clue to the Book Scavenger site for the copy of *Tom Sawyer* hidden at Hollister's. The difference this time was that they made a dummy account that looked almost exactly like Coolbrith's: They used the same avatar, and they copied her profile information. The website wouldn't let them replicate the same user name, but they used *Coolbirth* and hoped Mr. Quisling wouldn't look closely enough to notice the typo. Actually, if Mr. Quisling took any time at all to investigate this user—clicked on her book-hunting history, for example, he would find it blank and most likely realize this was an imitation account, but Emily and James hoped that if they mimicked the pattern of Mr. Quisling and Coolbrith's communication, then he wouldn't be given any reason to second-guess this latest post.

"And you never know," Emily said. "Maybe the plan will still work even if he *does* realize this is someone imitating his friend. I mean, wouldn't you be curious? If it were me, I'd still go find the book."

"But is there ever a hidden book you wouldn't be tempted to find?" James teased.

Emily nudged him. "Just click Submit."

James's finger hovered above the Enter button. "This isn't a bad thing for us to do, is it? Impersonating Coolbrith?"

"Not any worse than Coolbrith impersonating Miranda Oleanda. Something weird is going on with this Coolbrith person, and I don't think Mr. Quisling has a clue. We're helping him by doing this. We just need to find out more before we talk to him."

James nodded in agreement and tapped the key.

SATURDAY MORNING, the Phoenix discovered the
Coolbrith copycat post. It had been uploaded to
Book Scavenger the night before. He stared at it for a
very long time.

Someone was sending him a message.

Someone was boasting they were onto him.

Someone needed to be taught a lesson.

Removing his black gloves from the top drawer of
his dresser, the Phoenix tugged them onto his hands
before sifting through his collection of vials and glass
bottles. He selected the brown jar with the
liquid-covered lump inside.

This wasn't part of his plan. He
wasn't even sure what he was going to do,
his rage had taken over the driver's seat.

He needed to show this someone he
wasn't to be trifled with.

CHAPTER 27

EMILY GOT TO HOLLISTER'S right at ten, when he opened. She actually arrived a little bit early and was leaning against the cool glass of the front window when Hollister walked up, tossing his keys and catching them with one hand. The bookstore owner grinned when he saw Emily. He tossed his keys again but missed catching them, and they clattered to the sidewalk. Emily bent to pick them up.

"Look who's bright eyed and bushy tailed!" Hollister said.

"James is coming by later, too," Emily said.

"Then it's my lucky Saturday." Hollister rattled the key in the lock. The doorknob bells cheered as Emily followed him inside. She went straight to the display of totes and squeezed the bottom bag to make sure another Book Scavenger player hadn't found the *Tom Sawyer* and neglected to update the website. It was still there.

Hollister flicked on the lights, then went to the CD player behind the counter. He kept a collection of instrumental CDs piled next to it. He selected one and popped the disc into the tray, adjusting the volume as sprightly piano music came out of the ceiling speakers.

"Feels like a Miles Davis kind of morning, don't you think?" he said. He finished fiddling with the stereo, then stood at the counter, drumming his fingers as he took in the space.

"Anything you need me to do today, Hollister?" Emily asked.

"I've been meaning to update the window display with more items for Chinese New Year. You said James is coming by later?"

Emily nodded.

"Then you two might enjoy making paper lanterns. We can string them above the books—that might look nice. There's an old box with decorations up in the Treehouse." Hollister tossed his head to the back of the store, where the rounding metal stairs led to the storage loft.

The bells jingled, and Emily turned to the front door—probably too eagerly—in hopes that it would be Mr. Quisling, but instead Charlie walked in.

"Oh," she said.

"*Oh* to you, too." Charlie pulled off his newsboy cap and gloves and tossed them onto the counter.

"I didn't know you were coming in today," Hollister said.

Charlie shrugged. "There's some content I need to

add to the website, and my roommates were driving me nuts. Figured I could work on the website here."

Hollister looked at his watch. "This might help me out a great deal. I didn't have time to pick up a prescription this morning. Maybe I can run out and get that now. You okay holding down the fort?"

Charlie nodded without looking up. He pulled his laptop out of a limp backpack.

Hollister reached under the counter where he kept a notebook and removed a handwritten list. He slid the paper over to Emily. "Here are the books I wanted to add to the front display, if you want to get started pulling them."

"Sure," Emily said. *The Year of the Dog* by Grace Lin was the first title. "Can I use the computer?" Emily asked Charlie, meaning the store computer, not his laptop. He grunted in response and slid aside. Emily typed in the title and found where it was shelved. She left the front of the store and wound her way through bookshelves and under the winding staircase to the back corner that was lined with picture books, children's novels, and various stuffed animals and puzzles and games.

"Lin, Lin, Lin." She bumped her finger along the spines. The door jingled—a customer, unless Hollister had forgotten something and come back in.

Eager to see if it was Mr. Quisling, Emily bumped her finger along the spines more quickly, found the book she was looking for, then hurried back to the front. Sure enough, her teacher stood at the counter talking with Charlie.

"Hi, Mr. Quisling!" Emily said with too much perkiness. She was horrible at playing it cool. She wished James was here already.

"Emily! Two of my students in one day," Mr. Quisling said. "What a surprise."

Two? Emily looked around, wondering if James had showed up early. Then she remembered Charlie had also been his student, years ago.

"So this is where you work now, Charlie?" Mr. Quisling said.

All Charlie said in response was "Yup."

"Well. Good for you."

"James is supposed to be here soon," Emily said. "We live nearby." She wasn't really sure why she was offering him this information. It was just nervous chatter as she became increasingly aware that she had more or less tricked her teacher into coming to find this book.

"You'll be pleased to know I'm on a book hunt," Mr. Quisling said, and raised the printout of her and James's clue. Well, Coolbirth's clue. Mr. Quisling pointed a finger at Emily. "No poaching," he said, then laughed good-naturedly. Emily felt a pang of regret as she watched her teacher slip between two bookcases, scanning the shelves like he was browsing. Mr. Quisling seemed extra chipper, and she couldn't help but think anticipating a new message from his "girlfriend" might have something to do with that.

Turning away, she caught Charlie looking after Mr. Quisling, too.

"He's the worst," Charlie muttered.

Emily looked over her shoulder, worried Mr. Quisling might have heard. "He's not so bad," she said.

"He gave me my only D ever," Charlie added.

"Oh. Yeah, he can be tough."

The phone rang, and Charlie answered. Emily inched toward the path of her teacher, eager to spy on him and see if and when he found the hidden *Tom Sawyer*, but Charlie called her name, prompting her to spin around like she'd been caught.

"It's Hollister," he said, shaking the cordless phone. "He wants you to check the decoration boxes to see if we have a paper dragon for the window display."

Hollister's voice came through the receiver, and Charlie tilted his head, his eyes on the flickering bulb above the local authors section. Charlie recited to Emily, "He says we had one, but it might have gotten damaged and then thrown out. He can't remember. He can pick up another one by his pharmacy, but doesn't want to buy it if it would be a duplicate." To Hollister on the phone, Charlie said, "Okay, she'll look. We'll call you back if we don't have one."

Emily looked toward the aisle Mr. Quisling had disappeared down. "Can't you check, Charlie? I was in the middle of doing something else."

"I'm in the middle of something, too." Charlie nodded to his laptop. "You're already working on the window display."

Emily sighed and took a route past Mr. Quisling on her way, so she could at least get a peek at what he was doing. He was browsing the poetry section, so she guessed he was checking to see if there was a collection by Bret Harte. She hoped it would take her teacher a while to realize their clue, *Did you leave your Harte in San Francisco?* led to the tote bag featuring an illustration of the writer and his quote, "The only sure thing about luck is that it will change."

Emily scurried to the back, up the metal stairs, and over to the stacks of boxes labeled for decorations. Several were labeled CHRISTMAS/HANUKKAH, and there were THANKSGIVING and BACK TO SCHOOL. Finally she spotted one labeled NEW YEAR/CHINESE, just as the entrance bells chimed again. Or was that a sound in the store music? The jazz Hollister played through the speaker system was louder up here, but she was pretty sure that far-off tinkling was from the door. Mr. Quisling couldn't be leaving already, could he? Emily moved to the half wall that bordered the storage area, but most of the store was obscured from her view.

Emily hurried back to the bins. Of course the one she needed was underneath three others. She lifted off the first one and placed it on the ground. The bells chimed for sure this time, and Emily hoped it was just a busy morning with customers arriving. As quickly as she could, she moved the rest of the boxes and finally unsnapped the lid of the New Year/Chinese decorations. She shifted through the contents, pulling bagged items out to read Hollister's handwriting on the masking tape labels. No paper dragon. The doors chimed *again*. She snapped the lid back on but left the bins in disarray. She'd restack them later. She was about to head down the stairs when she heard the pop of a balloon. At least that's what it sounded like. But there weren't any balloons in the store.

At the top of the stairs, she called haltingly, "Charlie?"

As if in response, she heard the door chimes again, loud and clear, the way they sounded when the door got opened or shut forcefully. Then Emily heard something like the hiss of an enormous snake, and she froze. What could *that* be? From her vantage point, the store looked empty, but that was impossible. Charlie, at least, was somewhere. She gripped the railing and hesitantly placed her feet step by step down the stairs. Every movement was an argument between her body wanting her to cower in the Treehouse and her mind urging her forward.

At the bottom, a switch flipped in her nose and the dusty smells of paper and books were tainted by something that reminded her of burnt popcorn. She dashed to the front of the store. Even before she got there, she could see a hazy cloud at the end of the bookcases, twisting and turning around itself into a dark plume.

Emily's throat tightened, and she coughed, maybe more from the suggestion of smoke than the actual smoke. The front of the store was completely empty.

"Charlie?" Her voice came out in a whisper.

Flames licked against the tote bag display, the bottom bags blackening from a fire. Her breath zipped up inside. Her limbs were sandbags. Where did Hollister keep an extinguisher? What did you throw on the fire if you didn't have an extinguisher? Water? Should she run all the way to the bathroom in the back to get that? How quickly did a fire get out of control? Should she stay in the store and pick up the phone so help could get there as soon as possible, or should she run outside and find another phone?

Why wasn't somebody here to help her?

Emily pressed the crook of her elbow to her mouth and nose, one cough turning into a succession. She remembered hearing you could smother a fire with a blanket, so with her free hand, she grabbed a folded Great Gatsby T-shirt from a display and hurled it toward the blaze, hoping to smother it, but the fire's flickering arms only snapped around it.

She stepped forward and hurled another shirt, then retreated, coughing into her elbow. The fire crackled, laughing at her, and pulled itself up the side of the bookcase, then leaped from the tote bags to the greeting cards.

Her eyes stung. Smoke streamed upward, like a reverse waterfall flowing to the ceiling. She couldn't believe how rapidly it filled the front of the store. She had to leave. With her nose still pressed to her elbow, Emily ran bent over, because the air was less smoky down low. She hit the door with her shoulder and pushed it open, the bells jangling wildly.

She expected relief when she stumbled outside, but the day was warm and breezeless. It was like stepping from a hot shower into a humid room. Her coughs battled with each other. A deliveryman raised the back door of his truck with a thunderous rumble and dropped the ramp with a clank. He was lifting a crate onto a handcart when Emily lunged forward, slapping her hand on the floor of the cargo area to get his attention.

Her voice came out in a rasp—"Fire." The man squinted at her, uncertain, and she jabbed her finger toward Hollister's large front window.

He leaned out the truck, looking to the bookstore, swore, and dropped the crate with a boom. Clear liquid leaked through the cracks, drip-dripping over the lip of the van. The man swore again and tugged a phone from his pocket. Emily didn't wait for him to dial. She ran into the café, elbow folded over her mouth as she erupted in another coughing attack. She dropped her arm and forced the words to scratch their way out of her throat: "Fire! The bookstore is on fire!"

CHAPTER

28

EMILY STOOD in the middle of a crowd of onlookers who had gathered outside Hollister's store, but she'd never felt more alone. She shivered, even in the warmth of the sunshine. Someone draped a blanket over her shoulders.

Hollister's main window cracked, and Emily watched numbly as a triangular pane of glass dropped. The group around her collectively jumped back, but she didn't move. She didn't even feel like she was actually there on the street anymore.

The in-store sprinkler system had kicked on, and through the broken gap of window she could hear water hiss in its battle with fire. There were sirens, and emergency responders got there quickly. Or was it slowly? Her perspective of time wasn't working right.

A paramedic looked Emily over. A man with the fire department spoke with her. She felt useless not being able to give any sort of insight into why the fire began.

"I heard a sound," she said.

"Could you describe it?" the detective asked.

She tried to remember, but it was difficult to recall amid the hum of idling vehicles, the background medley of excited and agitated and hushed voices, and the crunch of firefighters' boots stepping on shards of glass from the piece that had splintered on the sidewalk.

"There was a pop, I think, and then a kind of . . . sizzling sound."

"Sizzling?"

"Or crinkling. With a sizzle. Like paper when you toss it in a fireplace."

The detective nodded succinctly, and Emily realized how unhelpful her answer must be. Of course a bookstore fire would sound like paper burning.

"It was more than that, though—it was . . ." Emily studied her clasped hands. "I can't remember," she said.

The detective placed a firm hand on her shoulder. "You did just fine. You've been a great help."

Emily spotted Hollister walking up the street from more than a block away, and her heart felt like it had been plunged in ice water. His brown skin shone with sweat, and his familiar side-to-side sway looked so upbeat it made her eyes tear up. He tilted his head in a wondering kind of way, focused on the flashing lights and double-parked vehicles. They would have passed him as he came back to the bookstore. She imagined how he might have been curious about them at first in that distant sort of way where you feel bad for the strangers who must be on the end of the emergency call, and then when he saw they were parked in the street right by his store, his concern probably tightened to worry that a friend was in trouble. When Hollister stopped abruptly in the middle of the sidewalk, Emily knew he had realized it was his store that was the emergency. She would never forget that moment.

The second thing Emily would never forget was noticing the door next to the bookstore. She must have walked by it a hundred times on her way to and from school without giving it a second glance. After the fire, it was propped open and revealed a staircase. Emily realized it was the entrance to the apartments overhead. She didn't know what that said about her that she'd been worried about the books and Hollister, who hadn't even been there, but hadn't given any thought to the people who lived upstairs.

The authorities wanted to talk to her parent or guardian before she left, so Emily sat next door in the café waiting for her family to arrive. Her parents had been across the city with Matthew at the beach. Now that she was sitting in a tranquil café with a woman complaining about the pickles on her sandwich and an old doo-wop song on the radio, she could clearly picture Hollister's fire extinguisher around the corner from the front counter, feet from where she'd been standing if she had looked in the right direction.

It twisted Emily's insides to relive everything.

Maybe if she had done something different, the fire wouldn't have happened.

She thought about the lightbulb near the front of the store that always flickered. Every time she'd been in Hollister's store, she'd noticed that lightbulb, but never once pointed it out to him. He didn't have the best vision—maybe he'd never noticed. Could the flickering lightbulb have sent off a spark that started the fire?

Emily had overheard a firefighter say the fire had been contained before it spread all the way to the back, which sounded like a good thing, but then he also said something about damage from smoke and the in-store sprinklers. She wished she'd grabbed something for Hollister, maybe his notebook from under the front counter or the framed photo from the day he and Mr. Griswold first opened the store back in the '70s.

Someone placed a glass of water in front of Emily, breaking her from her reverie. She looked up to see Charlie. Her eyes narrowed. "Why did you leave the store?" she demanded.

He kept his eyes on the glass. "I . . . I'm sorry," he said. "I left because . . ." Charlie looked out the window. Hollister paced by, a cell phone pressed to his ear.

"I had to feed my meter," Charlie said meekly. "I didn't think I would be gone long. And I didn't expect . . ." Charlie wiped droplets of condensation from the side of the glass and left his sentence unfinished. "Anyway." He slid the glass closer to Emily and said, "In case you're thirsty," before walking away.

Emily stood up from the table and went outside. Maybe it wasn't fair to be mad at Charlie, but she shouldn't have had to face that fire alone.

Hollister was off his phone, sitting on the curb between two parked cars, his head in his hands. She was simultaneously compelled to go sit next to him and afraid to. She worried she had let him down, even though the first thing he had done after he ran to his store was find her and make sure she was okay.

All Emily could think about as she looked at Hollister's bent form were her favorite things in his shop. The purple chair that curved perfectly around her when she sank into it to read a book. The cat-shaped pillow that Hollister perched on top of a bookshelf, which occasionally tricked people into thinking it was a real cat. The guest book signed by visiting authors. The bookmark shaped like Herb Caen that she and James moved around the store to surprise browsers. Where had they last hidden Herb?

She wanted to say something to make Hollister feel better, but it was hard to offer hope when you felt hopeless.

Someone said her name, and she jumped to see James standing beside her, his face slack with shock. Normally, the sight of Steve standing at attention filled her with comfort and smiles, but now it made her want to crumple up and cry. She and James should be making paper lanterns to hang in Hollister's window display, not watching firefighters stomp in and out the front door.

"There was a fire?" James said when she reached him. "What happened?"

"I don't know," Emily said.

A van double-parked behind one of the emergency vehicles with the letters *KSAN* on the side. Out jumped the woman reporter who had been at the Poe book

launch party and her cameraman. A few of the people lingering in the crowd outside the barricade recognized the reporter and greeted her. It was jarring to hear people coo praise and the reporter reply, "Thank you! You look great in person, too!"

The reporter talked conversationally with some of the bystanders. *Were you here when it happened? Did you see anything?*

A fireman walked out of Hollister's store holding a clear bag with a blackened lump inside.

"This one might be evidence," he called to the detective who had talked to Emily earlier.

The reporter stood on her tiptoes, not at all shy about trying to see. "What is that?" she called over to the fireman. "Is it what I think it is?" But he went back inside without answering.

"What did he mean by *evidence*?" Emily said to James. "Isn't that something you need to prove a crime?"

The reporter overheard her and replied, "How else would you categorize arson if not a crime?"

"Arson?" Emily felt a little dizzy. "You think someone set this fire on purpose?"

"If what's in that bag is what I think it is, then I most definitely think this was arson."

James asked in a low and halting voice, "What . . . what do you think is in the bag?"

"I think it's a fireproof pouch holding a copy of *Tom Sawyer* by Mark Twain," the reporter replied.

CHAPTER 29

I T'S FIREPROOF?" James said. Emily knew he was picturing the green pouch they had found at the redwood park. Well, that Mr. Quisling had found. They had kept the book in the pouch in case it was something that their teacher and Coolbrith always included in their book trading. They hadn't known it was fireproof.

The reporter didn't understand James was familiar with the pouch, of course, so she said, "Amazing what they can make nowadays, isn't it? This will be the fourth one to survive an otherwise random"—she used air quotes when she said *random*—"fire in the last several months."

Emily was too stunned to say anything.

"*Four* fires?" James asked.

"That I'm aware of." The reporter ticked names off her fingers. "The pier at the Ferry Building, one in the

Mission, one at Washington Square, and now here at Hollister's. This is the first indoor fire, though. The others didn't cause personal damage. I wonder if that means the arsonist is getting bolder . . . or more desperate." The reporter chewed on her pen, mulling this over.

"The pier at the Ferry Building?" Emily repeated. "A copy of *Tom Sawyer* survived a fire there? In October?"

The reporter looked surprised. "How did you know it was in October? None of the media outlets picked up the story. At least I didn't think any did." She frowned, surveying the crowd loitering outside Hollister's bookstore as if a traitor were among them.

Last October, Mr. Quisling had poached the copy of *Tom Sawyer* Emily had hunted at the Ferry Building. At least she'd assumed he'd poached it, because it wasn't there when Emily and James had arrived. She remembered that she had also flagged that post in order to make it worth more points, so Mr. Quisling had known someone else was on the hunt for it. Which, now that she knew he needed to find that particular edition in order to decipher the message from Coolbrith, she could imagine her flagging the book would prompt him to seek it out as soon as possible.

Emily assumed one of the door jingles she'd heard while up in the Treehouse had been Mr. Quisling leaving the store. She figured he'd found their hidden copy of *Tom Sawyer*, decoded the fake Coolbirth message, and then left. Did he have any idea about the fire? Had the same sequence of events happened with the earlier copies of *Tom Sawyer* that he had found?

When she got home, Emily was going to check Book Scavenger to see if the hiding places for Coolbrith and Babbage's books matched the fires the reporter had just listed. She mentally recited the locations to herself so she wouldn't forget: Ferry Building, Mission, Washington Square, and Hollister's.

"What about the redwood park? Downtown?" Emily asked. "Was there a fire there?"

The reporter looked at her very oddly. "No. Why would you ask that?"

Emily felt as if she were toeing the edge of a trap. To her relief, she heard her mother calling her. She turned to see her family rushing down the sidewalk from wherever they had parked the minivan. Her parents grouped her into a hug; Matthew stood back and offered a good-natured eye roll at their over-the-top affection. Her dad went to talk to an officer while her mother stood behind Emily, arms wrapped firmly across her shoulders.

Matthew dropped next to Hollister on the curb. Her brother put a hand on Hollister's shoulder and said something. Hollister nodded, patted Matthew's knee. Matthew said something else that made Hollister tip his head back and laugh. Emily smiled at the sound of it and marveled at how her brother could do that: jump into a situation and do or say something without any second-guessing. So often his impulsive actions provoked positive responses. If her brother had been the one in Hollister's store when the fire started, he would have run to the front at the first thought of anything being wrong. Emily had hung back, not sure of what to do.

As the Cranes and James drove back to their home, Emily was lost in thought. Did someone really start that fire on purpose? Who would do that to Hollister's store? Were there really copies of *Tom Sawyer* recovered in four different fires? If so, and if they were the same ones Mr. Quisling had found, then how and why was their teacher involved?

Staring out the window as the minivan climbed a hill, she spotted Charlie getting into his car. He didn't recognize her parents' van, and she wasn't about to wave or call hello. Now that she saw how far away he had to park, she could understand why he'd been gone from the store for so long, but she was still mad at him for leaving her alone in the first place.

When the van reached the top of the hill, Emily saw a two-hour parking sign that made her twist around to look out the rear window. Charlie's car was at the bottom with its blinker on, waiting to turn left.

"What is it?" James asked.

"This whole block is two-hour parking," Emily said.

"Yes . . ." James said.

"No parking meters," Emily said.

James looked concerned. They didn't drive, after all, so she could see how this line of thinking might perplex him.

"When I asked Charlie why he left the store, he said he had to feed a meter. But I just saw him get into a car parked on this block."

James stared down the hill with Emily, understanding now.

"He lied. Why would he do that?" he asked.

"Good question," Emily said.

James came over to Emily's when they got back to their building. His dad was out of town again on a business trip, and his mother and grandmother were at the flower fair on Grant, shopping for Chinese New Year.

In Emily's room, she opened her laptop and pulled up the Book Scavenger website. She and James sat with their backs to the wall under her window, where their message bucket dangled outside. A set of reindeer antlers James had given her and a photo of the two of them on Emily's first day of school were propped on the sill. The color blobs Emily had painted on her bleak walls before New Year's Eve were still there, waiting to see which of them would be chosen. She'd kind of forgotten about them—gotten used to them, really—but today they were jarring, like crushed soda cans in a field of snow.

"The history matches up." Emily couldn't quite believe what she was seeing on the computer screen. "Mr. Quisling hunted a copy of *Tom Sawyer* at the Ferry Building in October, in the Mission in November, and Washington Square in December. The reporter said there was no fire at Mark Twain Plaza, but we took that book after Mr. Quisling found it and re-hid it as Coolbirth at Hollister's."

"So maybe there would have been a fire at the plaza that day, if we hadn't taken the book," James said.

They stared silently at the Book Scavenger screen.

"Remember what Ms. Linden told us about the unbreakable code?" Emily fiddled with the cuff of her jeans. "About the legend that anyone who tries to solve it will suffer a fire? The curse couldn't be . . . That couldn't be a real thing, right?"

Hearing Ms. Linden tell the story of the fire curse that day in the main library had been like listening to a ghost story around a bonfire, the kind that gives you shivery arm prickles, but you know deep down it's all pretend. But today, with the bitter burnt smell of Hollister's fire smoldering in her memory, the idea of a curse made Emily's stomach turn.

"No." James's voice had the firmness of a period at the end of a sentence. "A curse can't post as Coolbrith. A curse can't hide books on Book Scavenger. This isn't a legend come to life to haunt us. Something weird is going on with Coolbrith and Mr. Quisling and the fires. If we can figure out why fires are happening in the same places where Mr. Quisling is finding these books, then we'll probably have our answer."

"You don't think Mr. Quisling could be an . . ." Emily couldn't even finish her sentence—it seemed so ludicrous to suggest their teacher might be an arsonist.

"I don't think so, but there has to be an explanation," James said. "If it's not Mr. Quisling, then maybe it's Coolbrith? Whoever Coolbrith is."

"What if it's Charlie?" Emily asked.

"Who started the fire?" James frowned, skeptical of her suggestion. "Why would he do that?"

Emily couldn't imagine why anyone would do something as malicious as starting a fire in Hollister's store. "He did lie about what he was doing when he left the store, and he's known about the unbreakable code since he was Mr. Quisling's student. He could be Coolbrith."

James waved for the laptop.

"What are you going to do?" Emily asked, handing it over.

"I'm logging in as a Book Scavenger admin to find out more about Coolbrith."

Emily raised her eyebrows. "Are we . . . can we do that?"

"Part of what Mr. Griswold and Jack asked us to do is help monitor the community to make sure it stays a safe and positive environment. I'm going to check Coolbrith's account registration info."

"To see if they list 'arsonist' as their occupation?" Emily said wryly.

"People have been known to do stupider things," James said. "But if the account shows Charlie's name, then the mystery is solved." He typed for a minute more until he found the results he was looking for. He squinted at the screen and chewed on a thumbnail. "This doesn't make sense," he finally said. "Coolbrith's account lists an e-mail for Mr. Quisling."

"It says what?" Emily leaned toward the screen.

"When you register for Book Scavenger, you provide an e-mail and password, right? Admins can't see the password, but we can see the e-mail that goes with the account. Coolbrith's is brian.quisling@email.com."

"But if Mr. Quisling is both Babbage *and* Coolbrith, then he would have been trading book cipher messages with himself. That's . . . that's ridiculous," Emily said.

James switched over to Mr. Quisling's Babbage account. "Interesting. The e-mail listed here is different. It's brquisling@email.com."

"He has two e-mail accounts?" Emily asked.

"He could. He could have fifteen different e-mails, if he wanted to. The question would be why? And why multiple Book Scavenger accounts?"

"And why have a forum conversation with yourself? Is he trying to make someone else think Coolbrith is real?"

James drummed his fingertips on the keyboard,

thinking. "Or maybe someone else is Coolbrith, but wants it to look like Mr. Quisling, so they registered with an e-mail that uses his name."

"But . . . why?" Emily finally asked.

"If we knew the answer to that question," James said, "we'd know who Coolbrith is."

CHAPTER

30

THE EVENING after the fire, Emily collapsed on her bed, wanting to close her eyes for a few seconds before dinner, but the next thing she knew, church bells were waking her up late Sunday morning. She didn't want to think about anything related to the day before. She didn't even want to work on solving the unbreakable code, because that made her think of Mr. Quisling, so Emily walked with her parents and Matthew to Pier 39 to watch the sea lions and eat clam chowder in sourdough bowls. Normally a bookstore or library would be her ideal comfort spot to escape to, but on the day after Hollister's fire, she shuddered at the thought of being closed in by walls of books.

On Monday before school, James tottered down their stairs under the weight of two bulging trash bags.

"What is all that?" Emily asked.

"Every year at this time, Po-Po goes into a

house-cleaning frenzy. She wants the New Year to start on the right foot, without old baggage around."

"A fresh start." Emily remembered standing at the *Wave Organ* and wanting the same thing, a little over a month ago. For a moment, she wished she could rewind to that day, that perfect first day of the New Year.

James hurled the bags into the can for pickup, but they piled so high the lid wouldn't close. He put his hands on top of them and jumped, trying to use his body weight to squash the bags down, and when that didn't work, he slammed the lid once, then again when it rebounded up. He finally left it hinged open, gaping like a mouth full of food. Emily watched James stomp away and hurried to catch up with him.

"Are you okay?" she asked. It didn't seem like James to get so frustrated with trash.

"Yeah," James said, but his word felt like *no*. They walked in silence until James said, "Remember when we were talking about what we'd do with the treasure if we found it?"

Emily nodded.

"I'm changing my answer. I wouldn't get a computer. I'd give the money to my dad. He laughed at me this morning when I told him he should get a different job so he doesn't have to travel so much, and he said, *Let me run down to the corner where they're handing them out.* Anyway, it's stupid. But I'd give him the money so he could quit his job and find a new one. I know that's boring, but that's what I'd do." He gripped his backpack straps and held his head high with determination, like they were on their way to retrieve treasure that very second.

"It's not stupid. And it might be boring, but I get it. I'd give the money to my parents, too. So we could stay in San Francisco."

James stopped walking. "You're not moving! Are you?"

"No, no," Emily said hastily. "I don't think so, at least. The extra money would make sure of that, though."

"Good," James said. His mood seemed more upbeat now than when he'd been attacking the trash bags. He started to talk about a show he'd watched the night before about an artist named Aowen Jin who had hand-drawn invisible ink murals depicting scenes from ancient Chinese mythology.

"If you visit this gallery, you have to carry an ultra-violet torch in order to reveal the pictures," James explained.

"What a cool idea! It's like secret art."

They continued to talk about creating invisible art until they rounded the corner onto Hollister's street and lapsed into silence.

The bookstore window was boarded up where the glass had cracked and fallen out. The inside looked darker than it normally did in the early morning. The closed sign wasn't even propped in the door window. Emily hadn't realized how reassuring a CLOSED sign could be.

"What if Hollister can't reopen his store?" Emily asked as they continued on toward school. Her parents had said structural damage to the store would need to be repaired before he reopened, and Emily knew many— if not all—of the books had been damaged from smoke and water. She and James had been talking about fresh starts earlier, and that's what Hollister would need to do. But *fresh start* had a different meaning, she realized, when you were coming from a place of loss.

"It's not fair, this happening to Hollister," James said.

"I know. It's bad enough if the fire was an accident, but if someone did that on purpose? They can't get away with that."

At school that day, some kids were talking about the nearby bookstore that had suffered a fire over the weekend, but nobody seemed to realize Emily had been there, and she didn't volunteer the information. She didn't want to talk about it. Mr. Quisling must have sensed this when she entered his classroom, because all he did was pat her shoulder and say, "It's good to see you, Emily." He didn't normally single students out for a greeting, so she read between the lines of his actions and understood this was his way of saying he was glad she was okay.

She couldn't concentrate once he began class. Watching her teacher made her think about how the only reason Mr. Quisling had been in Hollister's store Saturday morning was to find a book she and James had set up to lure him there, and if there was some connection between him and Coolbrith and these fires that happened in the locations of their hidden *Tom Sawyer*s, then she was partly to blame for what happened. She swallowed guilt the size of a peach pit.

Emily managed to get through almost half the week pretending things were normal, until the dance committee meeting on Wednesday. Mrs. Ortega was on bed rest indefinitely, so Mr. Sloan had taken over as the club advisor and for Mrs. Ortega's classes.

"Emily," he said, his voice soft, "I'm sorry to hear about what happened to Hollister's bookstore. I understand you were there. That must have been frightening."

"Oh." Emily swallowed, still feeling that lump of guilt stuck in her throat. So word had gotten out that she'd been in the store after all. "It was. But I'm okay."

Mr. Sloan patted her back. "It's okay to not be okay, you know."

Emily knew he was trying to be reassuring, so she smiled lightly and took a seat, but his words were a reminder that she couldn't pretend this hadn't happened. As much as she hated to think about it, Hollister's store had suffered a fire and she'd been there. She couldn't imagine that away. The only way to make things better would be to get to the bottom of the Coolbrith mystery, but she didn't know how to go about doing that.

She and James hadn't been sure if they should tell Mr. Quisling about Coolbrith's account being registered with an e-mail in their teacher's name. Now that they knew arson fires were somehow involved, she was even more confused about what to say. She didn't *think* her teacher had any clue about these fires, but what if she was wrong? What if talking to him about everything somehow made it all worse?

All she could think to do for now was keep an eye on the Book Scavenger quest thread between Mr. Quisling and Coolbrith. There hadn't been any activity there since the breakup message, even with her and James's attempt to hide a decoy book.

Once the dance committee had assembled, Vivian clapped her hands and said, "All right. We've got a lot to get done, and there's only one week left until Valentine's Day!"

"A week and a half, actually," James corrected.

Vivian continued, "First things first, let's finalize the details of the game."

After they hashed out their ideas, Nisha read aloud her notes to review what they'd decided. "Three teams will compete—George Washington, Abraham Lincoln, and Theodore Roosevelt. We are planning for ten people on each team based off ticket sales so far—"

James interjected, "If there's a jump in ticket sales right before the dance, then we can have two heats so more people can play."

"And maybe we won't even have ten people per team

because not every student at the dance is going to want to play a childish game," Maddie added, her arms crossed.

"If we agree to put hearts all over the decorations, will you stop being such a whiner?" Devin asked.

Maddie dropped her arms to her sides and straightened in her seat. "I'm not whining. I stated a fact. Not everyone will want to play."

Mr. Sloan raised his hands. "Okay, okay. Maddie and James have both made valid points. It's good to have contingency plans for all scenarios—too few participants, too many, and just right. Nisha, you want to continue?"

Nisha cleared her throat. "Kevin and Devin have the costumes their mother lent and donated, and they will borrow more jackets and accessories from classmates so we have enough."

The twins both gave a thumbs-up to show they were onboard.

"The game will work as follows," Nisha said. "One at a time, each team member will dress up as their president, then race through an obstacle course that consists of hopping from Hula-hoop to Hula-hoop, crawling over and under a crepe-paper web, and finally rolling on a skateboard to the end, where they tie a ribbon attached to a balloon around their ankle. Once they have the balloon on their ankle, the next team member puts on the costume and does the obstacle course. The first two teams to get their balloons on compete in the balloon stomp. The last team standing with inflated balloons wins."

"Everyone in agreement?" Vivian asked. The group responded in head nods and muttered yeses. "Okay, let's get moving."

Vivian sorted everyone into different workstations. Nisha and Maddie painted a WELCOME banner. Emily and James cut giant red, white, and blue hearts out of poster board, to be dangled from the gym ceiling. Kevin and Devin experimented with making red, white, and blue lemonade. Vivian marched from station to station, yelling at random intervals, "Valentine's Day is only a week away, people!" As if her panic and loud voice could help them paint and cut and mix any faster.

"A week and a half," James repeated.

Vivian threw her hands in the air. "This dance is going to be a disaster."

Mr. Sloan perched on the edge of the teacher's desk and looked bewildered by all the noise and activity. "Let's not throw in the towel yet, Vivian. We can meet next Wednesday as well. This will all come together. Why don't you help Emily and James with the cutting?"

Emily offered a pencil in one hand and scissors in the other. "Do you want to trace the template or cut?"

Vivian plucked up the scissors and flopped into a chair. "I'll cut out hearts."

Mr. Sloan clapped his hands and rubbed them together. "Great! That will help speed things along. Nisha and Maddie . . ." He opened and closed drawers to the science lab until he found what he was looking for. "This heat gun can be used to dry the paint. That way you can get through the posters more quickly without worrying about your colors getting muddy."

Nisha accepted the heat gun and plugged it into the nearby outlet. She turned it on to test it out. The tool wasn't much different than a travel-sized hair dryer, but a little smaller and quieter.

"And, Kevin and Devin," Mr. Sloan continued, "maybe the lemonade experiments aren't the most crucial thing on the to-do list."

The brothers stared at the sub through safety goggles, which they'd insisted on wearing even though Vivian had said they were unnecessary and ridiculous. Both boys also wore thick rubber gloves and held chemistry beakers filled with red and blue liquid. Rows of Dixie cups were spread in front of them.

"Did he just say food and beverages are not important?" Kevin said to his brother.

"Blasphemy," Devin whispered.

"How can we discover the formula for the perfect shade of patriotic blue without experimentation?" Kevin said.

Devin whipped off a glove and held up a Dixie cup. "Or make sure this lemonade tastes like freedom?" He took a sip and immediately spit it back in the cup. He grabbed a paper towel and rubbed it on his tongue.

"Not there yet?" Kevin asked.

"It tasted like being grounded in a one-room house while your little sister watches a *Yo Gabba Gabba* marathon. That is NOT the taste of freedom," Devin said.

"Blech." Kevin shuddered. "Vivian's right—this dance is going to be a disaster."

Everyone laughed except Vivian, who pursed her lips and sawed her scissor blades more fiercely against the poster board. "Mental note," she muttered. "No weirdos allowed on the committee next time."

After a few minutes of concentrated silence, Maddie piped up. "Did anyone else hear about the fire over the weekend?"

Nisha said, "I heard it was at your friend's store, James. The same place where the party was for the Poe book you and Emily found."

Emily suddenly became very focused on making her cuts fall exactly on the traced outline of her heart. She didn't have to look up to feel all the attention on her and James.

Kevin or Devin—Emily couldn't really tell the difference in their voices when she wasn't looking—said, "I heard about that. My dad said the bookstore owner probably needed money."

That got Emily to look up. "Why would your dad say that?"

Kevin nudged Devin, trying to give his brother the hint to be quiet. "He's their friend," he said.

Devin went on, "I'm not saying that's what happened.

It's just a theory our dad had. He said most cases of arson are started by the business owner to get money from their insurance. It's called insurance fraud."

Emily fixed her glare on Devin, hoping her eyes could make him feel like a handful of pebbles were being flung at him. She normally liked Devin, but sometimes even nice people said dumb things. "Spreading a rumor like that isn't any better than being the one to make the accusation in the first place. It's worse, if you ask me."

Devin looked startled. She could tell he felt bad for saying anything and hadn't been trying to get under her skin. But she was still mad.

"Hollister wasn't even—" Emily had been about to say that Hollister wasn't even there when the fire happened, but then someone would ask how she knew that. She didn't want to talk about being there.

"He would never do something like that," James finished for her.

"Right," Emily agreed, and returned her concentration to cutting the poster board. Her hand was a little bit shaky with the scissors. The dance committee meeting had distracted her from thinking about the fire and wondering why it had happened and what it had to do with Mr. Quisling's and Coolbrith's messages about the unbreakable code. But now that was all she could think about again.

"So." Mr. Sloan filled the awkward silence. "Fill me

in on the rest of your dance plans. It sounds like you've got the fun-and-games part figured out, but what about the dance part of your dance?"

Vivian stood up from her seat, her clipboard ready and pen poised. "What about it?" she asked.

"Relax, Vivian." Mr. Sloan held up both hands in surrender. "I'm not interrogating you. I'm just wondering if you hired a DJ—"

"Of course. He's their friend," Vivian said, nodding to indicate Emily and James.

"I wouldn't call him a *friend*," James said. "But we know him."

Emily and James exchanged a look, and she knew he was thinking about Charlie's lie. But one lie didn't mean he was an arsonist.

"Have you all come up with a list of song suggestions?" Mr. Sloan asked. "That can be helpful. And see if he has a fog machine and those spinning lights. Those are always cool."

Vivian scribbled on her clipboard. "We hadn't thought about a song list," she muttered.

"You've got to have a song list," Mr. Sloan said. "Otherwise the DJ will end up playing the 'Macarena' on repeat."

Everyone laughed and groaned. Emily felt lighter now that the conversation had moved away from Hollister's fire. Kevin and Devin chanted the "Macarena" with their safety goggles on. They extended one gloved hand, then the other, flipped their hands over, then folded them onto each elbow and wiggled their hips. "Heeeeeey, Macarena!" they cried.

James shook his head. "I can't believe they know that."

"This should be part of the presidential challenge!" Kevin cried.

"*No* with a capital *N-O*," Vivian said.

Kevin and Devin jumped to the side to do the dance moves facing another direction, but they bumped their table covered in Dixie cup samples of lemonade. Several cups tipped over; one fell off the table and onto the poster Maddie was painting below. Maddie yelped. More liquid came racing down the lab counter and began dripping onto her work. Mr. Sloan raced to the wall and spun the roll of paper towels, grabbing several, before hurrying back to mop up the watery blue and red mess. Nisha aimed the heat gun at the liquid to dry it.

"It's turning brown!" Maddie cried. "You're burning it!"

Nisha snapped off the heat gun.

"No," Emily said. "It's turning brown because it's lemon juice. Acidic liquids can be used as an invisible ink and change color with heat."

Mr. Sloan looked up from his mopping, impressed. "Very good!"

She had learned about invisible inks and how they react with heat when she was hunting down Mr. Griswold's lost Poe book last fall. In fact . . .

Emily got down on her hands and knees under the guise of helping with the mess, but really she wanted a better look at the browned lemonade spots. They reminded her of the mark on the unbreakable code parchment that had looked like someone had carelessly set a coffee mug on it and left a ring, but what if that mark wasn't from someone's mug? They had already discovered the paper could be folded in a way that marked an X on an island. Could there be even more?

CHAPTER 31

EXCITED BY THE PROSPECT of there being more to the unbreakable code than they realized, Emily bumbled picking up the spilled cup of lemonade and more juice poured out.

"Watch it," Maddie snapped.

Holding a cluster of paper towels, Emily helped blot up the mess, but the liquid and paint smeared together and the poster puckered with wet spots.

"Ruined." Maddie harrumphed. "And my lettering was perfect."

"Sorry, Maddie," Emily said, even though she hadn't been the one to knock the cup off the table in the first place.

"Time's up for today," Mr. Sloan called.

"Of course it is," Vivian said. "We'll never be ready in time."

"Don't worry," Mr. Sloan reassured her. "There's still

next week. And remember, the important thing is students have fun. That can happen whether or not every last detail is perfect."

Emily jumped to her feet, eager to tell James her idea as soon as they left the committee meeting. The second they stepped outside the science classroom, she grabbed his arm and pulled him around a corner in the opposite direction from where everyone else headed.

"What—where are we going?" James spluttered.

"I have to tell you something. It's important." After making sure nobody was nearby, Emily said, "You know how the heat turned the lemon juice brown on Maddie's poster?"

"Boy, was she mad." James shook his head.

Emily waved away thoughts of Maddie. "The unbreakable code supposedly survived fires, right? What if that brown mark on the old parchment isn't random but part of a message written in invisible ink that got revealed with heat?"

Emily's idea hit James with enough force that he dropped his hands from their grip on his backpack straps. They dangled slack at his sides. "Whoa," he said. "Maybe that grid of letters that everyone has always assumed is the unbreakable code isn't even the code. It could be a decoy!"

They started walking down the hallway, an excited skip in James's step. "I read once that George Washington had his Revolutionary spies write secret messages in invisible ink between the lines of normal-looking letters.

If George Washington used invisible ink, then we know it existed during the Gold Rush."

"And don't forget *The Gold-Bug* by Edgar Allan Poe," Emily said, reminding him of a story they'd read last fall. "Invisible ink is mentioned in there, too, and Poe wrote that in the eighteen hundreds."

The hallway leading to the front doors was being mopped, so they turned a corner and headed for a side exit.

"There's one problem with my idea, though," Emily said. "How are we going to heat the paper in the library? Ms. Linden seems cool and all, but I can't imagine she'd be okay with us bringing in a hair dryer and blasting it on a historical document."

"No, probably not," James agreed. He pushed on the side door to open it, but the door resisted. "Is this locked already?" He tried the door more forcefully, then slammed his shoulder against it for extra oomph, and it gave way. Blackened chewing gum had been ground into the lock, making it catch before opening.

"Ugh, people can be so disgusting," Emily said.

They stepped into the sunshine, and James snapped his fingers. "I know—what about a black light?"

"A black light?"

"Yeah, remember that artist I was telling you about the other day? You needed a black light torch in order to see her paintings."

"A black light." Emily nodded. "That's a great idea. It sounds like something Matthew might have."

They found her brother in his room arranging

LEGOs for another stop-motion video he was making as a tribute to his favorite band, Flush. He didn't have a black light, but he pulled out his phone. "Maybe there's an app for that!"

It turned out there was, but it cost five dollars. Emily gnawed on her lip. "That's a lot of money for something we'd only use once." Why did everything have to be so expensive?

"Could we make one?" James mused.

One Internet search later, they discovered a simple hack that would temporarily turn Matthew's phone into a black light.

"All we need is clear tape, and blue and purple Sharpies," Matthew said.

Emily raided their mom's graphic design supplies and found the necessary Sharpies. Following the instructions, they colored two pieces of tape with blue Sharpie and placed them over Matthew's phone light, then placed one piece of tape colored with purple Sharpie over the blue one. Matthew turned on the flashlight feature, and a violet light beamed from his phone.

It was too late to go to the History Center where the unbreakable code was kept, so they would have to test their theory the next day after school. Emily couldn't wait.

When school finally ended Thursday afternoon, Emily and James raced home to meet Matthew before heading to the Main Library.

"Did I really have to come?" Matthew asked when they were all seated together on the bus.

"No, you didn't," Emily said. "I told you that three times already. I need your phone, not you. But you won't let that stupid thing out of your sight."

Matthew hugged his phone to his chest and patted the backside. "Don't listen to her," he said in mock baby talk. "You're not stupid. No, you aren't!"

When they reached the History Center on the sixth floor, Ms. Linden greeted them as before.

"Hello, you three! It's been a while." She flipped her long braid, threaded with green hair, behind her shoulder. "You make a break in the case?"

"Well." Emily shifted her feet and exchanged a look with James. They *had* made a break in the case when they discovered how the parchment could be folded to

overlay the X directly onto one of the circles. And of course there was her new theory about the beige blemish on the old paper. But she didn't want to say anything until she knew for sure whether her hunch was right.

"Could we look at the unbreakable code again?"

"Of course. I'll get it for you." If Ms. Linden suspected they were up to anything, she didn't let on.

They left their backpacks at the front desk as before, taking Emily's notebook, a pen, and Matthew's phone with them to the long table, where they waited for Ms. Linden to bring out the folder.

Once Ms. Linden left them, they stared at the manila cover. Emily had so many expectations tied up in the simple act of shining a light on a piece of paper.

"So," James said.

"So," Emily agreed.

"What are you guys afraid of?" Matthew flipped open the folder and pulled out his phone. "Let's do this."

Emily concentrated her attention on the mark that looked like a coffee stain. If that mark wasn't an accidental blemish and really was part of the unbreakable code, who knew what might be revealed by the black light? Maybe the paper would be covered in words, or maybe there was a more detailed map?

Matthew fiddled with his phone, turning on the flashlight setting. He held the phone up, bathing the paper in violet light. Emily squinted and leaned closer to the table. Under the colorful glow, it looked like a brush had painted light onto the page extending from the brown mark in a pattern of swoops and lines. Her breath caught. Was something really there? The variation in tone the light revealed was subtle, and Emily wasn't sure if she wanted to see something so badly her imagination was making this up, or if there really was an image there.

"Do you see that?" Emily asked her brother and James.

"I think I see something," James said.

"It looks like a drawing," Matthew added.

From behind them, Ms. Linden's voice made them jump. "What are we looking at?"

CHAPTER 32

MATTHEW SNAPPED his phone light off, and the three looked anywhere but at Ms. Linden, until Emily realized it was silly to pretend like they hadn't been doing anything when Ms. Linden had clearly observed them to some degree.

"I . . . I had the idea that there might be a message written on this paper in invisible ink. We rigged up Matthew's phone so it worked like a black light, and—"

"It looks like Emily was right," James jumped in.

"But my phone hack doesn't work well enough to get a great look," Matthew said.

Ms. Linden had one eyebrow cocked. "Invisible ink? Let me see." She tipped her head in Matthew's direction, indicating he should turn his phone light back on. She bent over the paper, her braid dropping forward over her shoulder. Matthew's phone glowed once more, like moonlight falling across the page, and again Emily could see the ghost of a pattern. She hadn't been imagining it.

"I don't believe it," Ms. Linden said in a hushed voice. She snapped upright, her spine very straight, and declared, "I have something that might help us get a better look. Hold on."

She nearly ran to the door and disappeared into the next room. When the librarian reappeared, she held a slim, black, ruler-shaped object in her hand. "Professional-grade black light," she said. "It's sometimes used for archival work, although you have to be careful with UV light. It can degrade paper and ink over time. But this could be a historical discovery you've made, so I think the situation calls for using it."

The four of them huddled over the parchment. Ms. Linden snapped on the light. The beam it emitted was bolder and brighter than their homemade version and clearly illuminated two symbols:

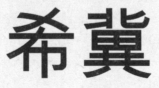

James stared, his eyes wide. "I think that's Chinese!"

Emily could see it now. The lines weren't making a drawing as they had first thought. They formed characters in another language.

"Amazing," Ms. Linden said.

"Do you know what it says?" Emily asked James.

"I can only read Chinese well enough to order dim sum. But my grandmother will know. I'll ask her tonight."

Matthew snapped a photo, and Emily and James copied the symbols onto paper.

"This is amazing," Ms. Linden said again. "I can't believe this." She turned the black light off, and then back on again, as if she was making sure the Chinese characters hadn't disappeared.

"So, why do you think the miner guy did this?" Matthew asked. "Did he just grab this piece of paper thinking it was blank and didn't know this was on it?"

"I don't think it's a coincidence," Emily said.

"Yeah," James agreed. "Maybe he was a Chinese miner and this reminds him where he hid his gold. The visible letters are meant to trick anyone who goes looking for it."

"Or maybe both parts are necessary to find the treasure," Emily said. "Maybe a Chinese miner and an English-speaking miner worked together to make this, and so they used both their languages to guarantee they would find their gold again as a team, so one wouldn't steal from the other—"

"Or kill the other," Matthew interjected.

"Ew. Morbid, but yeah, they would need each other to interpret the map and find where they'd hidden their gold on the island," Emily said.

"Island?" Ms. Linden asked. "How do you know they hid it on an island?"

Emily and James exchanged a look. James shrugged, and honestly, Emily was so excited about this new development she was itching to share their other discovery about the map. She showed Ms. Linden how the x marked one of the four circles on the back when the paper was folded.

"Amazing," the librarian said, folding the paper again to try it for herself.

"But we're stumped on what the island could be," Emily added. "We thought these three circles that are closer together are Angel Island, Alcatraz, and Treasure Island. No matter how you turn the page, the X doesn't look like it could be Alcatraz. Angel Island belonged to the military when the code was supposedly created. And Treasure Island didn't exist, so—"

"Yerba Buena has always been there," Ms. Linden said, referring to the natural island connected to Treasure Island.

"Yeah," Emily agreed. "That must be where it is." The theory didn't excite her, though, because Yerba Buena had gone through a lot of development over the years. A tunnel had been bored through it for the Bay Bridge, for one thing, and then the military and coast guard had used it for decades. Plus there was the new construction she and James saw when they had ridden bikes around Treasure Island with her family. Just like how the *Niantic* had been uncovered by construction workers digging to build a parking garage, she couldn't help but think it was more likely the treasure would be uncovered by someone with an excavator, and not a couple of kids.

"There's also Gull Island," Ms. Linden said. "I imagine that's what the fourth circle is supposed to represent."

"Gull Island? Did you know about Gull Island?" Emily asked James.

He grimaced in response. "I need a shirt that says *Not a San Francisco Wiki.*"

"It's very small, much smaller than any of the others," Ms. Linden explained. "It's definitely not a tourist spot like Angel Island or Alcatraz, and it's not accessible like Yerba Buena and Treasure Island. It's also a private island—the only one in the bay—so a lot of people don't know about it."

"Private? Like, someone lives on it?" Matthew asked. "That's pretty rock star to have your own island in the San Francisco Bay."

"Somebody owns it—a billionaire tech investor who now lives in another country, I believe. But nobody lives there. The island's never been developed. There's no running water, no electricity. A little-known secret—but common knowledge among the boating community—is that the owner has granted permission for the grounds to be used for picnics or birding."

"Birding?" James asked.

"Without any development or human interference,

it's become quite a bird sanctuary over time," Ms. Linden explained. "But there's no hunting, fireworks, or over-night camping allowed."

The librarian studied the paper with the circles again. "If you turned the map this way, then it would look like this group of three is Angel Island, Alcatraz, and Gull Island with the X, with Yerba Buena as the one on the outside of the triangle."

"Gull Island," Emily repeated. Between revealing the Chinese characters and learning about this island, they might finally be on the verge of solving this puzzle. It was a hopeful feeling that was quickly squashed when Ms. Linden said, "Your theories are all great. Historians are going to be so eager to jump on this and figure out the answers."

Emily fumbled her pen, then picked it up. "Historians?" She looked down at the unbreakable code, which had returned to its regular appearance now that Ms. Linden had turned the light off. Of course there would be a surge of interest in the unbreakable code once this dis-covery became known. The code would probably become a craze again, like what Hollister said had happened when the *Niantic* was uncovered in 1978. Emily imag-ined a team of historians barging into the room right that very second and ripping the paper away from her to crack the code themselves.

When Emily looked up from the parchment, Ms. Linden was staring at her, head tilted and a deliberating look on her face. "You know," the librarian said with slow and equal weight on each word, "I'll need to file paperwork for this, and that can take a while. I hope you all won't be too disappointed if the public doesn't find out about it just yet."

Emily couldn't help it—a huge grin spread across her face. She knew Ms. Linden wouldn't be able to hold off on letting the wider public know about these hidden Chinese characters indefinitely, but at least they would have a little more time to try and figure out the mystery on their own.

That night Emily sat in her room trying to concentrate on her homework, but really she was daydreaming about the unbreakable code and listening for James's knock. He planned to talk to his grandmother after their dinner, and Emily couldn't wait to hear what she had to say.

Finally, the knock came. Emily went to the already-open window and waited for the bucket. She removed James's slip of paper to read:

SKU STBQ BV NUTFS KXJU.
(She said it means HOPE.)

"Hope," Emily said softly. A pebble of disappointment plunked into her stomach. She didn't see how one word could lead them to find the treasure.

She wrote down a response and slipped it into the bucket.

ZKD QX DXL VKBFO BV'S VKUPU?
(Why do you think it's there?)

James replied,

B QXF'V OFXZ. NTDHU IXP WLEO?
(I don't know. Maybe for luck?)

Emily frowned, considering this suggestion. Whoever had written these characters went to the trouble of thinking up their plan in the first place, finding invisible ink, and then painting them onto the paper before writing the unbreakable code and map over the top. That was a lot of effort and steps to take in order to do something that was only a gesture of good luck.

Emily didn't know how it worked, but she was certain the invisible characters were part of the greater puzzle, and she was determined to be the one who figured out the solution.

CHAPTER 33

THAT WEEKEND, James was busy with his family celebrating Chinese New Year, so Emily flopped around her house, alternating between reading, picking at her homework, and mentally willing the letters of the unbreakable code to assemble themselves into some sort of useful message.

She wished she could go to Hollister's, but the store was closed indefinitely. Emily hadn't seen Hollister since the fire. She hoped he was doing okay. Devin's words about business owners setting fires on purpose for money floated back to her. She knew that Hollister worried about his business, but there was no way he'd destroy something he loved for money.

And it still bothered Emily that Charlie had lied about feeding a meter for his car. Why hadn't he told the truth about what he had been doing when the fire happened? What *had* he been doing when the fire started? Could he have lied because *he* was the arsonist? Could Charlie be Coolbrith? She knew he didn't like Mr. Quisling, but was his grudge deep enough to do something so hateful?

The only thing Emily knew for sure was nobody else knew about the hidden Chinese characters. Emily imagined herself and James digging up gold treasure. How amazing would that be? She'd been fantasizing about finding the gold in order to give it to her parents so they could afford to stay here in San Francisco, but that daydream changed a week ago. Now she fantasized about giving the gold to Hollister. He and his store deserved the second chance.

The following Tuesday at the Book Scavenger advisory meeting, Mr. Griswold said, "How *are* you?" in a tone that made it clear he'd heard about Hollister's fire. Emily felt tears spring to her eyes. She blinked them back, not wanting to cry in front of Mr. Griswold. "I'm so sorry you were there during the fire, Emily," he said, placing a hand on her shoulder.

Emily blinked again and looked to the floor. "I feel awful for Hollister."

"I know." Mr. Griswold patted her back, and their whole group sat down in his office. Mr. Griswold settled on the couch with Claus stretched out beside him. Emily sat on the other side of the dog, with Jack perched next to her on the armrest. Matthew and James sat in the two chairs.

Angel left her basket and sniffed Matthew's ankles. He patted his lap, and the dog jumped up, huddled into a ball, and snorted as she closed her eyes. Matthew petted her wiry white fur and smiled.

"Knowing Hollister," Mr. Griswold said, "he will view this as a challenge to come back stronger, kinder, and even more caring than before. Some people let a difficult loss or hardship warp them, but not Hollister."

Mr. Griswold and Hollister had known each other for a very long time—half a century, although they hadn't always maintained their friendship. Emily wondered if Mr. Griswold's words meant the two old friends had finally reconnected and mended their differences, but Emily thought it would be too personal to ask.

"You'll see. Hollister can bounce back from anything," Mr. Griswold mused, petting Claus's neck. "It's how we act in the face of adversity that defines us, and Hollister is a good man and a fighter."

"He said the same thing about you," Emily said. "That you can bounce back from anything."

"Did he?" Mr. Griswold had seemed perfectly at ease talking about the bookstore owner, but now that the topic was on himself, he shifted uncomfortably. "Well. See what I said about him being a good man?" Mr. Griswold cleared his throat and said, "Let's talk about Book Scavenger, shall we? Jack, do you want to tell them your idea?"

Jack nodded, and his hair bobbed enthusiastically. "Sure. This is what we're thinking: a monthly illustration puzzle on the website for Book Scavenger players to solve. You guys can help us brainstorm ideas." He pulled a piece of paper from the folder he held on his lap and extended it for Emily, James, and Matthew to look at. "Here's one example we thought up. We're calling this puzzle 'Snakes and Hedgehogs.' The answer is the title of a book we'll give away as a prize to a randomly drawn winner."

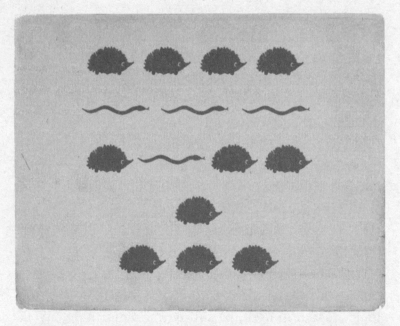

"The animals represent a code. Can you guess which one?"

The snakes and hedgehogs were arranged in groups. randomly. Emily didn't really see a rhyme or reason to it until she realized that the hedgehogs were drawn in a ball-shape and the snakes were long lines.

"Is this Morse Code?" she asked.

"Exactly!" Jack said. "Here's the key to solve it."

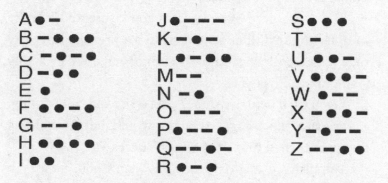

Emily's eyes darted back and forth between the drawing and the key. "H . . . O—"

"*Holes!*" Matthew shouted, startling Angel on his lap. "I love that book."

"Correct!" Jack said. "I have another one here, too." He rummaged through the papers in his folder but didn't find what he was looking for. "I must have left it in the printer. Let me go grab it."

Emily liked the idea of illustrated puzzles on the Book Scavenger site and was happy they were being included in brainstorming for them, but she couldn't help feeling that tug of sadness that Mr. Griswold was reluctant to plan events and real-life games like he used to.

"Mr. Griswold, did James and I tell you we're on the dance committee at our school?" she asked.

"Emily roped me into doing it," James added.

"That's wonderful." Mr. Griswold smiled. "Are you enjoying it?"

"Actually, yes," James said. "Emily came up with this crazy idea for a game, and it's been fun to plan."

"I was inspired by the games you've created," Emily said, feeling shy all of a sudden. "It's a presidential relay race with a balloon stomp—it sounds nuts. It's probably going to be a disaster."

"Don't sell yourself short," Mr. Griswold said. "In my experience, the ideas I thought would be the nuttiest disasters turned into the greatest successes."

Impulsively, she asked, "Why don't you come? To our dance this Saturday?"

Mr. Griswold coughed. "Me?"

"Yes." Emily looked to James and Matthew for encouragement.

"You wouldn't have to stay the whole time," James said. "We're doing the game in the beginning. And it will have you laughing, I promise."

"You could be a celebrity judge for their game," Matthew added.

"Oh, I don't know about that. I'm hardly a celebrity."

"You are to these nerds," Matthew replied.

Emily kicked her brother's foot, and Angel looked up, perturbed again with having her nap interrupted. "What Matthew means is Book Scavenger fans love you."

"Well, I'm flattered that you would want me there."

Mr. Griswold tugged at the collar of his sweater. "I know I've done events with schools in the past, but that was . . . before everything happened last year. The only places I'm really comfortable now are my home and this office." Mr. Griswold lifted his shoulders in a small, hopeless shrug.

Mr. Griswold, Emily realized, was like she had been on the stairs in Hollister's bookstore: unsure if it was better to go forward or back. She had stood there, stuck with fear, not wanting to make the wrong decision. But not doing anything didn't help. If she had continued to stand there on the stairs, the fire would have made the decision for her. You make your choices, or the world makes them for you.

"You know what someone wise told me once?" Emily asked.

"What?" Mr. Griswold angled his head curiously, petting Claus's neck.

"It's how you act in the face of adversity that defines you," she said. "I think you should define yourself by accepting our invitation to watch our game."

Mr. Griswold's mustache lifted into a smile. He wagged a finger at her. "I see what you did there. I'll think about it. Okay? How about that?"

Emily and James grinned at each other. "We'll take it," Emily said.

CHAPTER 34

THE REST OF THE WEEK, Emily continued to study the unbreakable code, certain both the Chinese characters and the English letters were necessary for solving it; otherwise, why would the miner have included them? It was clever to make it so you had to know two languages in order to solve the message, like two different locks wrapped around a treasure chest.

Thursday night, Emily got the idea that maybe the translation for the Chinese characters—*hope*—was the keyword for a cipher, similar to the "remember the *Niantic*" cipher in the note Mr. Quisling dropped at the Poe book party. If that were the case, then the key for the unbreakable code would look like this:

A	B	C	D	E	F	G	H	I	J	K	L	M
H	O	P	E	A	B	C	D	F	G	I	J	K

N	O	P	Q	R	S	T	U	V	W	X	Y	Z
L	M	N	Q	R	S	T	U	V	W	X	Y	Z

It seemed like the perfect solution. But when she lined up the letters of the unbreakable code:

RESARXMUTAETPPMATDIIBHRF

and translated them using that key, the result was still nonsensical:

RDSERXOUTEDTCCOETHKKFARI

Emily had been so sure she was onto something, but the fact that she wasn't made her feel like she was falling behind in a race. It had been a whole week since they'd found the Chinese characters with Ms. Linden. The librarian wasn't going to be able to stall for too much longer before the general public knew about their discovery. Who knew how quickly someone else would figure out the code? And then Emily's shot at finding the treasure would be gone.

On Friday morning, Emily was sliding her books into her backpack, about to head downstairs to walk with James to school, when her computer dinged. A notification from the Book Scavenger site. She'd left her laptop open on her bed and leaned forward to read the message.

It was an alert for a hidden copy of *Tom Sawyer*.

Emily hesitated before tapping a key to find out more about who had hidden the book and where. "It's just another book hidden through Book Scavenger," she chided herself. "Don't be such a chicken."

She pressed Enter.

It wasn't just another book. Coolbrith had hidden another copy of *Tom Sawyer*, this time at Coit Tower. Emily had to tell James. She scribbled down the clue and raced down her stairs.

When she flung open the front door, James was waiting on the stoop. A clear plastic poncho covered his head and backpack on this gray and drizzly day. He had one palm extended up into the water dripping over the eave of their porch.

"Are we late?" he asked, noting her panting.

Emily took a deep breath, trying to calm her charged-up feeling. There was a new challenge for Mr. Quisling in his quest. Did that mean there would be another fire after he found the book? She opened her umbrella and filled James in as they began walking.

"I wish we had time to go before school," she said.

"At least Mr. Quisling can't go right now, either," James pointed out.

"Maybe if we go to Coit Tower right after school, we could find the book before anyone else and remove it, so the arsonist won't set another fire."

"That might stop him today, but we took the book hidden in the redwood park, and now Coolbrith's hiding another one," James reasoned. "We should say something to Mr. Quisling."

James was probably right. They should talk to Mr. Quisling and tell him what they knew. But they didn't have anything concrete to show him. They could tell him fires had been set after he'd found copies of *Tom Sawyer* through Book Scavenger, but would he believe them? They could tell him Coolbrith was using an e-mail in his name, but maybe he already knew that. Maybe Coolbrith was someone Mr. Quisling knew, and there was a logical reason for the e-mail that didn't have anything to do with an arsonist. Not to mention how angry their teacher might be if he found out they'd been eavesdropping on his quest.

"What we need is proof," Emily said. "Starting with finding out who Coolbrith is."

"And we do that by . . ."

"Let's go to Coit Tower after school, find where the book is hidden, and then stake it out. If Mr. Quisling looks for the book, maybe Coolbrith will also make an appearance."

James nodded. "Do you have the Book Scavenger clue?"

"I copied it into my notebook. I'll show you when we get to school."

Once inside the halls of Booker and out of the rain, Emily and James huddled together in a stairwell before the first bell, her umbrella dripping dry on the landing in front of them. Emily's notebook was open to the page where she'd written down the Book Scavenger clue:

```
D  O  K  E  R  U  B  O  L
O  U  O  T  E  S  M  W  L
O  T  O  H  H  T  U  C  O
T  S  L  E  W  O  L  O  F
```

"Great," James said sarcastically. "Another grid of letters, just like the unbreakable code. Because we've had so much luck figuring that out."

"I'm sure we can get this," Emily said. Thinking maybe it was a substitution cipher, she started making a frequency chart, listing every letter that was in the message and how many times it appeared. She was only halfway through when James noted, "There aren't any word breaks."

"Maybe they'll be obvious when we decode what the letters stand for." Emily continued marking hatch marks underneath each letter that appeared.

"Hold on. Can I see this?" James took the notebook and scrutinized the grid. "It reminds me of a word search—an even rectangle, every letter perfectly spaced. And look—" With a finger, he drew a circle around a column with the letters *t-h-e*. "I found the word *the*."

"And next to it," Emily said, circling the next column over. "If you read it from the bottom it says *l-o-o-k*, *look*."

"I don't think this is a substitution cipher. If you go down the next column, there's the word *out*. If you read up and down those three columns, it says *the lookout*. It's like a letter maze."

"What happens if we read it starting from the side?" Emily asked.

Together they read out loud, *"Follow Columbus to where the lookout stood."*

In Mr. Quisling's class that afternoon, Emily and James scrutinized their teacher's behavior for signs that he'd seen Coolbrith's latest quest challenge, but he gave nothing away. Emily certainly wasn't going to ask him about it. She assumed he had set a notification for Coolbrith's posts, since he'd found the previous books so quickly, and she hoped this latest one would follow the same pattern.

Emily and James agreed to meet after school by the side door with the gummed-over lock, since that was the closest exit to where they had to catch the bus up to Coit Tower. Emily was eager to get there and find the hidden book, and she assumed James felt the same way, but it surprised her to see him tearing around the corner with a huge smile on his face, Steve flopping every which way as he ran.

"GUESS WHAT?!" he shouted, still twenty-five lockers away. A young teacher popped her head out a classroom door and said, "Who's yelling like a deranged monkey? Slow down, slow down!"

James reduced his speed to a fast-paced walk. When he reached Emily, he looked back to where the teacher had been and said, "I wonder if it would have been okay if I'd yelled like a deranged rooster."

"Why *were* you yelling like a deranged monkey?" Emily asked.

James smiled so big, you'd think someone had gifted him with a new computer. "I figured it out," he said.

"Figured what out?" They'd solved the Book Scavenger clue together, so Emily knew that wasn't what he was talking about.

"The unbreakable code!"

CHAPTER 35

*S*HUT UP," Emily said.

"I did!"

"Shut. Up."

"I'm totally serious! Want to see?"

"But I just saw you in Mr. Quisling's class sixth period," Emily said. "You hadn't solved it then, right?"

"Nope." James couldn't stop grinning. "We watched a movie during health."

"People have been trying to figure out this code for one hundred and sixty years, and you solved it during seventh-period health?"

James shrugged. "It was a boring movie."

"How . . . what . . . I . . ."

Emily didn't even know where to begin. She'd been daydreaming about figuring out a puzzle that had long been considered impossible to solve. Of course, in these daydreams *she* was the one who saw how the final pieces fit into place. If she was very honest with herself, underneath the smile she flashed James, there was a kernel of disappointment. Maybe a full-blown popcorn-sized piece of disappointment. She was tempted to say, *Why couldn't you wait for me?* But then she remembered all the hours she'd studied the grid of letters by herself, scribbling different cipher possibilities in her notebook. If the solution had started to materialize for her during one of those moments, she doubted that she would have been able to put on her puzzle-solving brakes and wait for James. They *had* worked together, she reminded herself. James only did the last little bit on his own.

James was her best friend. Emily flicked the popcorn of disappointment into her mental trash can. "So what does it say? How did you solve it? I'm dying to know."

James tugged his balled-up poncho from his backpack and shook it out. "We don't want to miss the bus to Coit Tower. I'll tell you on the way."

The bus curved around the ivy-covered side of Telegraph Hill, taking them to the tippy top where Coit Tower gleamed white against the stormy sky. Emily bent over her notebook and watched James re-create how he'd solved the unbreakable code.

"In health class, I was thinking about how when we first tried the keyword cipher as a solution, we assumed the letters had been written in order from left to right, top to bottom, the way we normally read. But in the

Book Scavenger clue we solved this morning, the message read from right to left going up and down the columns. That made me think about reading Chinese—you read in columns from right to left—and if this map was made by a Chinese man in 1850, then maybe he would have put the letters in the order he was most used to reading. If you write the letters as they appear in the grid columns from right to left, you have this."

He wrote the letters in her notebook.

X T D F R E T R A A A H S T M B E U P I R M P I

James flipped back through the pages of Emily's notebook to where she'd written out a cipher using *hope* as a keyword:

A	B	C	D	E	F	G	H	I	J	K	L	M
H	O	P	E	A	B	C	D	F	G	I	J	K

N	O	P	Q	R	S	T	U	V	W	X	Y	Z
L	M	N	Q	R	S	T	U	V	W	X	Y	Z

"If you use this as your key to decipher the letters in this order, it reads:

X T H I R D T R E E E A S T O F D U C K R O C K.

"*x* third tree east of duck rock?" Emily read aloud.

James nodded. "We almost had it before; we just weren't deciphering the letters in the right order."

"So these are directions," Emily said. "The X is the treasure, and we must have to go to the third tree east of duck rock, whatever that means." Emily leaned back in her seat. "I can't believe this."

James had really done it: The unbreakable code had been broken. And what was more, if they could figure out what the directions meant, then maybe they would find the treasure, too.

The bus slowed to the stop in front of Coit Tower. Emily held her umbrella outside the bus first to open it, then exited underneath. With his poncho on, James jumped off the step and landed in a puddle with a splash.

The tower itself was set back from the parking lot and up several flights of stairs. Cypress trees flanked the monument on either side. In the middle of the parking lot was a round planting bed with a large statue of a man wearing a cape.

Emily shook away thoughts of duck-shaped rocks and Gull Island. This might be their only chance to uncover Coolbrith's identity.

There were a few cars parked in the lot, but not many, and because of the rain nobody else was standing around like they were. The two other people who had gotten off the bus had already crossed the parking lot and were trudging up the stairs to the entrance of the tower.

"Do you think Mr. Quisling's been here yet?" Emily

asked. She had to shout a little to be heard over the rain.

James shrugged. "I can't imagine he would have been able to leave school before we did."

"Let's try to find the book before he shows up so we know what area to stake out. Coolbrith's clue said, *Follow Columbus to where the lookout stood.* Do you think Columbus is inside the tower?"

"I think he's right here," James said, shielding his face from the rain as he pointed up.

It turned out the giant statue was of Christopher Columbus.

"Okay, well, that was easy. So if we follow him, what does that mean? Stand behind him?"

A circular sidewalk surrounded the planting bed that held the statue. They walked around the ring until they stood behind Columbus, but there wasn't anything there.

"Maybe *follow* means to go where he's looking," James said.

They slapped through the wet parking lot to the outer edge, where a sidewalk and fence bordered the steep hillside that dropped down below. Every few feet along the sidewalk, there were posts that looked like oddly shaped parking meters, but Emily realized they were viewfinders. If this had been a clear day, there were probably spectacular views of the city below and the water beyond. As it was now, it was hard to make out anything through the curtain of gray rain other than the rooftops, trees, and bushes downhill. Directly in front of them on the ground in between the sidewalk and fence was a large plaque. Emily bent down to read it. It said this had been the point where a lookout had stood during the Gold Rush to raise signals for incoming ships.

"The clue said *where the lookout stood*. This must be it, James," she said.

They started hunting nearby, looking for the green pouch.

"There it is." James had spotted the bag tucked next to a bush.

Emily looked around the parking lot—they were still the only ones there. "Okay, so we don't want to take it. But we need to find a place to hide where we can keep an eye on the pouch."

There weren't any crowds of people loitering around that they could blend in with. The parking lot in general was a wide-open space. The only viable option was to cross back toward Coit Tower and stand next to the public restroom at the base of the long flight of stairs that led to the entrance. The restroom was its own little building, a futuristic dark green, oval-shaped toilet pod with a door that slid open to the side.

James tried to wipe away the water streaming down his face, but he only smeared the wetness around because his plastic poncho was soaked. "To the toilet pod."

They stood silently behind the restroom. Trees

sheltered them from the pattering rain, so Emily closed her umbrella and hugged her arms around herself in an attempt to keep warm. She couldn't believe how chilly San Francisco could be when it set its mind to it.

Minutes ticked by, and Emily wondered if this was pointless. Maybe nobody would come. They could be in their dry apartments studying the unbreakable code directions and plotting how to find the long-lost treasure.

James nudged her and nodded toward a set of stairs on the hillside closest to them. Mr. Quisling's distinctive neon-green rain slicker was making its way to the top. His hood dripped water past his nose as he looked down at the steps he climbed.

Emily and James retreated farther behind the bathroom. When he reached the top of the stairs, Mr. Quisling turned toward the plaque, not looking once in Emily and James's direction, much to their relief. Obviously he'd solved the Book Scavenger clue before coming and knew exactly where to go. When he reached the plaque, he began scanning the area around it.

"He spotted it," James said.

They watched their teacher pick up the pouch, then turn and cross the parking lot, headed in their direction. They concealed themselves completely behind the bathroom, peeking out after a minute to see Mr. Quisling's back as he climbed the stairs up to the Coit Tower entrance.

"I bet he's taking it inside to solve the book cipher where it's dry," Emily said.

"The inside of the tower is pretty small. It would be hard to follow him without being noticed," James said. "If he's doing this for Coolbrith, then he'll return the pouch when he's done, like at the redwood park. That was one of the rules of the quest. Let's wait here until he comes back."

As much as Emily wanted to get out of the rain, James's suggestion made sense. She bounced her knees off each other, and they waited. It felt like an hour, but probably less than ten minutes passed before Mr. Quisling came back down the main stairs, crossed to the outer edge of the parking lot, and replaced the pouch where he'd found it. Emily wondered what Coolbrith's message had said this time. With the rain and distance between them, she couldn't make out Mr. Quisling's expression. Their teacher left down the stairs he'd come up.

And now: more waiting. Would Coolbrith come? Had this all been meaningless?

"There are staircases all around Telegraph Hill," James said. "So Coolbrith could come from any direction. If he comes."

They continued to wait silently. The rain danced a staccato tune around them. Emily was on the verge of saying *maybe we should leave* when a man in a hooded black rain slicker stepped out from the top of a staircase across the parking lot from where Mr. Quisling had left.

"James," Emily whispered.

"I see him."

Like Mr. Quisling, the man walked straight to the plaque, but he didn't hesitate in locating the green pouch.

"It's Coolbrith!" Emily said.

CHAPTER 36

"CAN YOU SEE HIS FACE?" Emily asked.

James shook his head. "The hood makes it hard, and all this rain."

"At least we don't have to worry about a fire today," Emily said. "Good thing water isn't flammable."

The man bent into a crouch near the hidden book. He reached into his pocket and pulled out a black cylindrical object.

"What's he doing?" Emily asked. "What is that?"

The cylinder opened into an umbrella. "Oh," Emily said.

"A little late for that, Coolbrith," James muttered. "You're already drenched."

The man held the handle to the open umbrella in the crook of his elbow as he busied himself with something they couldn't see. Tying a shoe? Then he stood and headed back to the stairs he'd come up, closing his umbrella as he walked. Emily squinted, trying to make out his profile or any distinguishing detail, but he was too far away, and the hood and rain obscured too much of his face.

"We need to follow him," Emily said. "We've got to see who that is."

Emily and James were halfway across the parking lot to the stairs Coolbrith went down when there was a loud pop behind them. They spun around. A white cloud rose from where the green pouch had been hidden.

"Something exploded!" James said.

Flames flashed bright against the foliage.

"In the rain? How is that possible?" Emily asked.

"Maybe water can be flammable after all," James mused.

Emily stared at the small blaze. The rain was winning the battle of fire versus water. If Coolbrith had started another fire, then he obviously didn't care about what he had done to Hollister and his store. Emily pressed her lips into a firm line of determination.

"Hurry, before he gets away." She ran to the path Coolbrith had taken.

The staircase zigzagged down a hill. The already gray day darkened under trees. Large-leafed plants leaned in, enveloping them in a jungle-like world that seemed so different than the rest of the city. Pathways jutted off on either side, leading to the private entrances of homes planted into the steep hillside.

Rain pattered above them on branches and leaves, whispering, *Hurry, Hurry,* as they scurried from cement steps to dirt path to brick steps. Emily tried not to lose sight of Coolbrith, but they had to be careful, too. The steps were narrow and slick.

She could see the black hood flights below. Coolbrith wasn't running—he must not have realized they were following him, even though their wet steps sounded like shouts to Emily. Every so often water burst through gaps in the treetops, like a faucet.

Coolbrith reached the bottom, where a road interrupted the staircase before it continued down the next stretch of hill. He stopped and looked left and right for cars. They were so close. A few more stairs and Emily would have a good look at his face.

But then her foot shot forward. She grabbed the railing to slow her fall, crying, "WHOA!" before she realized what she was doing. Her bottom hit the ground, and a thunderbolt shot up her spine.

James helped her up. Coolbrith ran across the street.

"He heard me," Emily said.

"We can still catch him."

They took the steps faster and crossed the road, then down the next staircase. Emily concentrated on planting her feet solidly so she wouldn't fall again and kept one hand on the guardrail.

Coolbrith was about to dart across the next road down the hill when a passing car blared its horn. He jumped back and ran down the street a ways before crossing. When Emily and James reached the bottom of the stairs, Coolbrith was a dark shadow in the folds of rain, disappearing behind a building on the other side of the street.

Water splashed their legs as they stomped through puddle-filled potholes. They went down the next staircase and found it soon diverged. One direction led down cement stairs, and another down a dirt path that looked like a detour through gardens. Both ways turned so you couldn't see what was ahead—or below, as the case may be—which meant they couldn't tell which way Coolbrith had gone.

"Footprint," James panted, pointing to the mud on the side of the dirt path. So that was the way they went.

Soon, they turned a corner and found themselves in a small clearing with a bench and a graffitied parking meter randomly stuck in a mound of shrubs. It was a dead end, and Coolbrith was nowhere in sight. They'd picked the wrong path.

James side-kicked the trunk of a tree. The branches erupted in a flurry of colorful feathers as parrots took flight, their jewel tones bright against the dreary sky.

CHAPTER 37

THE PHOENIX panted under the awning of a corner market at the bottom of Telegraph Hill, his back pressed against the brick wall. Rain pelted the street. He looked down at his sopping wet shoes.

Being chased by children brought back a memory of running through muddy cornfields when he was a kid. The words *fire freak* floated out of the past, circling him now. Even though it was pouring, he could have sworn he smelled hot straw and dirt. He squeezed his eyes shut, trying to push it all away. He couldn't stand this bruising weight of being overlooked, judged as inferior or, worse, incompetent. Struggling to gain control of his ragged breathing, he closed his eyes and imagined each inhale like air from a bicycle pump, inflating him to his fullest height.

His breathing calmed. The plan was to right old

wrongs, and he was going to see it through. He couldn't let kids get to him, divert him from his intended course. He would end this tomorrow.

The Phoenix stepped into the rain and raised an arm to hail a cab.

CHAPTER 38

EMILY AND JAMES rode the bus home, quiet and drenched. Emily racked her memory for details that would identify Coolbrith. He hadn't seemed especially tall or short or heavy or thin. There'd been nothing distinctive about him at all.

"It has to be Charlie," Emily said. "That man looked about his size. And you should have seen Charlie's face when he talked about Mr. Quisling before the fire at Hollister's. He can't stand him."

James's plastic poncho crinkled as he adjusted in his seat. "But Charlie doesn't seem to like much of anything. And there are lots of guys who are about Charlie's size and who own black windbreakers. That guy at Coit Tower could have been anyone."

"But, James, Charlie *lied* about where he was during Hollister's fire. Why else would he do that if he wasn't trying to hide something?"

"Charlie's shady, that's for sure, but you can't go around accusing someone of being an arsonist because they have a bad attitude or told a lie. We need to tell Mr. Quisling what we know and let him take care of it. They're both going to be at the dance tomorrow. We can talk to Mr. Quisling then."

"Okay," Emily agreed. She knew it was the right thing to do, even though she still felt uneasy about talking to their teacher. "Tomorrow night we'll find Mr. Quisling, and we'll say we need to tell him something," Emily declared, trying to make herself feel more confident about the proposition.

"Yes," James agreed.

"We'll say we came across his Book Scavenger quest . . . but leave out the part about spying on him."

James nodded encouragingly.

"And we'll say we noticed he had found an awful lot of *Tom Sawyers* . . ."

"Sure . . ." James said.

"I guess we should leave out the part about planting a copy for him to find, to see what he would do?"

"And the part about e-mailing his old girlfriend because we thought she was Coolbrith," James added.

Emily sighed. Every action had seemed small and innocent on its own, just part of a game, but now all those small things had rolled into a giant snowball, and she didn't know where to begin with explaining everything.

"The important thing is that we find a way to tell him that Coolbrith isn't who he thinks," Emily said.

It wasn't going to be easy to come clean, but Charlie—or whoever was responsible for Hollister's fire—had to be stopped.

At home, Emily changed into dry clothes and plopped onto her bed with her laptop. She opened a web browser and typed *fire Coit Tower* in the search field. The only results told the history of Coit Tower and how it was a memorial to a woman named Lillie Hitchcock Coit, a wealthy patron of the city's firefighters.

There were no reports of a fire happening that day. Emily took a deep breath and exhaled. The rain must have extinguished Coolbrith's fire before it could become newsworthy. So many questions raced through Emily's mind. Who *was* Coolbrith? Why was he setting fires? Why was he trying to link their teacher to the locations of these fires? What did Mr. Quisling know about Coolbrith?

Emily typed in the Book Scavenger URL and searched for Coolbrith and Babbage's quest thread so she could see their latest exchange about the found *Tom Sawyer*, but when she logged into the forum, the conversation thread wasn't there. She typed *Babbage* and *Coolbrith* into the search bar again: no results. She went to the Quest directory and scanned the list of different quests launched by Book Scavenger players, but Coolbrith's "For Old Times' Sake" thread wasn't there.

It had been deleted.

Only an admin or the quest originator could delete a thread. Emily knew she and James hadn't deleted it. She couldn't imagine why Jack or Mr. Griswold would.

Coolbrith must have deleted his own thread. What did that mean? Without the back-and-forth between Coolbrith and Babbage, there was nothing left to show that Mr. Quisling had been participating in a quest. All that remained was the chain of books hidden and found by the two users—accounts that were both registered in their teacher's name. Maybe chasing Coolbrith had been enough to make him stop whatever it was he was doing with the quest and the fires. Or maybe he was trying to distance himself from them so the only person who would look responsible would be Mr. Quisling. Emily's stomach twisted with guilt. James was right—they should have talked to their teacher long ago.

Her Book Scavenger notebook lay next to her on her bed. She flipped through it, stopping on the page where James had written out the unbreakable code solution. In the beginning that's what Emily had thought Mr. Quisling's quest was all about, but now she wasn't sure.

"Third tree east of duck rock," Emily read out loud.

She didn't understand how that led to buried gold, but maybe, if she and James were standing on Gull Island, it would make more sense. Not that it would be easy for them to get to Gull Island. What they needed was someone with a boat.

And then Emily realized that they did, in fact, have a friend with a boat.

She dug through her backpack and found Ms. Linden's business card, then ran to the phone to dial her number. After hearing Ms. Linden's voice tell her to leave a message, she said, "Hi, this is Emily, um, Crane. Me and my friend James are the ones who are interested in the unbreakable code and we . . ." Emily paused. Announcing you'd broken a historical code was really the sort of news you should deliver in person. "We, um, want to ask you some questions about your boat. If you don't mind."

Emily left her phone number and hung up, feeling uncertain about having reached out to the librarian in the first place.

Saturday afternoon found Emily preparing for the school dance. At least that's what she was doing if "preparing" meant pacing her room while deliberating how to confess to Mr. Quisling that she'd spied on him and discovered an arsonist was impersonating him online, and simultaneously feeling anxious about the presidential relay race she had spearheaded, which could make her the laughingstock of the school if everyone thought it was ridiculous.

Her footsteps fell in rhythm with the beat of the Flush song permeating the wall between her room and Matthew's. Impulsively, she turned on her heel and went to knock on her brother's door. He was never at a loss for words. Maybe he could coach her on what to say to Mr. Quisling.

She knocked a second time, and his door swung open. Matthew was stretched out on his bed with his eyes closed and his hands behind his head. He clearly hadn't heard her come into the room. She gently scratched the tip of his nose to get his attention, and bit back laughter when Matthew twitched and batted the air above his face. She did it again, tickling his nose, and this time his hand swatted hers. Matthew opened his eyes and shrieked when he saw Emily bending over him. She laughed, and the laughter felt good, cracking her anxiety into more manageable pieces.

Matthew wasn't amused. He picked up his pillow and thwapped her.

"You ever hear of knocking?" he shouted between pillow swats.

She held up her hands to ward off more hits from the pillow. "I did knock! Twice." Emily laughed again. "I couldn't resist. Sorry!"

Matthew flopped on top of his pillow and used the remote to lower the volume of his music. "Shouldn't you be setting up for your dance?" he asked.

"I'm leaving with James in a minute. But I wanted to ask you something." Emily sat on the edge of Matthew's bed and picked at his comforter. "You always know the right thing to say to people. How do you do that?"

"Uh-oh. Who do you need to talk to?"

"Nobody," Emily said reflexively. "I mean, somebody but . . ." She sighed. "I've been putting it off because it's going to be awkward."

"Has it gotten less awkward the longer you put it off?" Matthew asked.

"No, it's gotten worse."

"So think of it that way. It might be awkward to say something today, but it will be *more* awkward if you wait until tomorrow."

"But how do you know what to say?"

Matthew readjusted his pillow behind his head. "It's not anything I plan out. Things pop into my head, and I say them. But I say stupid stuff all the time. You know that better than anyone. Go up to this person and start talking. Worrying about what to say is just another way of procrastinating."

There was a knock on the open door. "Hey," James said. He wore a Pac-Man hoodie for the GameCon theme. "Your mom let me in. Ready to go?"

"Yeah, let me grab my costume." She'd made herself a Scrabble tile by decorating cardboard for her front and back connected by two pieces of string that hung over her shoulders.

Matthew turned his music back up as Emily and James left his room.

Her brother made it sound like it should be so easy, like all she had to do was open her mouth, and the right words would tumble out—or any words for that matter.

She didn't even know where to begin with Mr. Quisling. At least James would be with her.

Emily's laptop, sitting open on her bed, was chiming a Book Scavenger alert when she returned to her room. She slid her Scrabble tile costume over her head.

"Did you pick the letter *x* because it marks the spot?" James asked.

"That, and it's worth eight points." She grinned and bent down to skim the Book Scavenger notice.

"James!" She grabbed the laptop to make sure she'd read the words correctly. "Another *Tom Sawyer* was hidden."

"Another one? By who?"

Emily swallowed before clicking the notification box so it would show more information.

"Coolbrith?" James asked.

She nodded grimly. "But that's not all." She angled the screen so James would have a better look. "The book's hidden at our school."

CHAPTER 39

EMILY AND JAMES hurried to their school, nearly tripping over their feet down the steep hill. After the gloomy rain the day before, the city looked freshly painted in crystal blue sunshine, but it felt fake, like they were speed walking through a movie set.

Emily felt sick to her stomach at the thought that they might have invited an arsonist to their dance.

"You can't jump to conclusions," James said, reading her mind. "We don't know if Charlie is Coolbrith."

"But what if I'm right?"

"And what if you're wrong? Look," James said, nearly panting with how quickly they moved. "The fires always happen *after* the book is found, right? Mr. Quisling isn't going to have time to go book hunting during the dance. We'll talk to him as soon as we see him."

Emily nodded, but the anxious knot in her stomach wasn't loosened by James's words, and it only tightened when they stepped inside the multipurpose room. It was already bustling with pre-dance activity. Mr. Sloan and Principal Montoya stood on the small stage hanging a banner that read HAPPY PRESIDENTS' DAY! with dozens of hearts painted around the letters. Dangling from the ceiling were the cardboard hearts Emily and James had cut out. The twins, dressed as Minecraft characters with pixelated boxes on their heads, were preparing for the presidential games, which at the moment meant spinning Hula-hoops across the floor. Vivian dashed by with one hand on her head, holding down a floppy hat, and the other wagging her clipboard at the twins in a menacing get-to-work way. She wore a baggy old-fashioned dress.

James watched her run by, tripping every so often on her long skirt, and said, "Is she supposed to be Martha Washington? Or Eleanor Roosevelt?"

Emily spotted Charlie on the stage untangling cords and wires from the speakers, fog machine, and colored lights that were part of his DJ equipment. She nudged James, and he nodded that he saw. A teacher pinned red, white, and blue bunting along the music table for decoration. Emily studied Charlie's movements, trying to detect some sort of suspicious behavior, but he acted uninterested in everything except setting up the DJ booth.

"Do you see Mr. Quisling?" James asked.

Two different chaperones passed by carrying bags of ice and flats of soda cans. Maddie balanced on a ladder while Nisha handed her strips of metallic red, white, and blue streamers to hang across the folded-up bleacher wall. Maddie appeared to be wearing a red party dress and not a costume, and Emily wasn't sure what Nisha was dressed up as. Her shirt had pointy black shoulders with a bright pink chest plate that matched her pink boots, and her black hair was pulled back in a ponytail.

"No sign of him yet," she replied.

Charlie freed one of the speaker wires and bent down to plug it in. When he stood, he scanned the room and locked eyes on Emily. She raised a hand, haltingly, not wanting to make him suspect that she might be onto him but also not wanting to be too chummy with a potential arsonist. He nodded in return.

Vivian appeared next to them with a trash bag in either hand. The rubber bands on her braces were red, white, and blue to match the patriotic theme of the dance. "I need you to hand out these Uncle Sam hats to the chaperones and DJ." Vivian thrust the bags into their hands and swished away.

"Have you seen Mr. Quisling?" Emily called after her, but she was already too far away to hear.

"Don't worry," James said. "He'll be here. We'll talk to him. If you're right about Charlie, he can't do anything now anyway. He's literally on a stage in front of everyone."

Emily nodded, but she couldn't shake the feeling that they needed to speak with their teacher as soon as possible.

They split up to hand out the hats on either side of the gym. James took the stage side, and Emily the other half. She couldn't help but be distracted watching James walk up the stairs to the DJ booth and hand a hat to Charlie.

"Just so you know, you don't have to worry," someone said next to her.

Maddie was standing there with her arms crossed, watching the stage with Emily.

Emily looked from Maddie to the stage and back. Did she somehow know about the fires, too? Could Maddie know something Emily didn't? Like that the arsonist had already been caught?

"Worry about what?" Emily asked tentatively.

"I don't like him anymore."

Now Emily was really confused. Maddie didn't like the arsonist? Charlie?

"Like who?"

Maddie rolled her eyes. "Right. As if you don't know." When Emily continued to stare, her mind trying to recollect when her classmate had ever met Charlie before, Maddie sighed and said, "*James*, if you're going to make me say it."

"You like James?" Emily asked. Maddie was looking at her like she was struggling to solve 1 + 1, but Emily couldn't help it. She didn't know what compelled Maddie to confide in her right now, and it took her totally by surprise. Somebody's crush was about the furthest thing from her mind.

"*Liked*," Maddie said. "It's in the past. He's all yours."

"All mine?" Emily's voice squeaked.

"What are you, a parrot?"

"I'm sorry, I just—I don't like James. I mean, I *do*, of course. He's my best friend. But I don't *like* him, like him."

Maddie scowled at her. "You don't?"

Emily shook her head.

"Not ever?"

"No," Emily said. To be honest, she wasn't sure she'd *like* liked anybody yet.

"Oh." Maddie looked disappointed. "Well, I still don't like him."

"Okay." Emily switched the trash bag of Uncle Sam hats from one hand to the other, not exactly sure what to do with this confession. "Good to know."

Maddie stalked off to the registration table to help check people in. Emily continued to distribute her hats, keeping an eye out for Mr. Quisling and making sure Charlie didn't disappear from the room. He fiddled with something on his DJ setup, and an upbeat song started

to play as more kids trickled inside. The star-spotted hat James had passed out to Charlie sat on a large speaker.

Students began to arrive. Emily recognized a few of the costumes— Mario, Luigi, and a knight chess piece. Vivian hurried up to Emily. "The fog machine and colored lights are for after the game, when the dancing starts. Does the DJ know that? He's not going to turn them on now, is he?" Before Emily could reply, Vivian answered her own question and said, "I'll go tell him," then ran over to the stage.

Emily finally spotted Mr. Quisling entering the gym from the school-side door, closest to the stage. She turned to find James so they could talk to him together, but bumped into a chair that was part of the obstacle course the twins were finishing setting up. Lines of chairs formed three aisles—one for each team—and Kevin and Devin were running crepe paper back and forth between the chairs to create a web for participants to crawl over and under.

James was blowing up balloons for the balloon stomp, but thoughts of grabbing him to talk to their teacher flew away when a very tall and familiar silhouette appeared in the main entrance to the gym.

"James!" Emily called to get his attention, then pointed to Mr. Griswold standing in the doorway looking very understated in jeans, a fleece, and a Giants cap. They both ran to him, meeting up in front of the publisher.

"You came!" Emily exclaimed.

"You could tell it was me?" Mr. Griswold tugged his baseball cap lower on his forehead. "I was trying not to be recognizable."

"Oh . . ." Emily and James exchanged a look. "You're not *too* recognizable." And it was true—most of the kids were paying more attention to each other than to any adults entering the gym. But Emily did see a couple of teachers look over, including Mr. Quisling, who did a double take before approaching.

"Excuse me," Mr. Quisling said. "Are you—"

"This is my uncle," Emily jumped in, knowing Mr. Griswold didn't want to be recognized. "My great-uncle . . ." Her eyes fell on James's hair. "Steve. We invited him to watch the game we planned."

Mr. Quisling raised his eyebrows. "Your great-uncle Steve looks an awful lot like Garrison Griswold," he said.

Mr. Griswold stepped forward. "You've got me, yes, and I apologize. Emily was only trying to help, as she knows I'm reluctant to make public appearances right now. But she is right—I am here in hopes of watching their game. I know they have been working very hard on it."

Mr. Quisling accepted Mr. Griswold's extended hand and shook it. "Well, *Steve*, it's an honor to have you here." Mr. Quisling, who was normally stoic, smiled in a way Emily had never seen before. For a fleeting second, her teacher looked boyish, and almost shy.

"I'm not sure when I'll have this opportunity again, so I have to tell you how meaningful Book Scavenger has been to me," their teacher said. "It's something I did with my son. We went through a rough patch when his mom and I divorced, and Book Scavenger gave us something to build a new relationship around. He's in college now and has no time for the game, but we still talk about old hunts and share book recommendations."

Mr. Griswold smiled. "That's wonderful to hear. Thank you for sharing that."

"I can't seem to let the game go yet, even though my son's moved on," Mr. Quisling confessed. "You'd be surprised at the people I've reconnected with while playing."

Emily realized her teacher might be thinking of Miranda Oleanda. This was her opportunity to speak up about Coolbrith. She swallowed repeatedly, closed her eyes, and said, "About that."

She opened her eyes expecting Mr. Quisling, Mr. Griswold, and James to all be staring at her, but instead they were staring at Vivian, who had joined their circle.

"It's time to start the game," Vivian said.

The gym had filled up. The lights were still bright—they'd lower them after their obstacle course, when the dancing started. Kids were clustered around the room in circled groups and staggered lines. One dressed as something that looked like a warrior squid and another dressed as a Pikachu kept trying to mess with the game setup, but Devin and Kevin guarded the obstacle course vigilantly, chasing them away by charging at them with their cardboard box heads lowered.

Vivian cleared her throat and stared pointedly at Emily, as if she was waiting for her to say or do something.

"What?" Emily finally said.

"It was your idea," Vivian said. "You explain it. The DJ has a microphone."

"In front of everybody?" Emily squeaked.

Vivian was so take-charge about everything, it had never occurred to Emily that she wouldn't take charge of this, too. That feeling of being zipped up too tight in her clothes came back, the same way she'd felt at Hollister's party. Emily looked at James. Maybe he'd volunteer to lead it.

"The game is great," he said. "And it was your idea. You deserve the credit."

Mr. Griswold set a hand on her shoulder. "Did I ever tell you how much I hate speaking in front of crowds?"

He had to be pulling her leg to make her feel better. Garrison Griswold, the Willy Wonka of book publishing, creator of Book Scavenger, and planner of outlandish games and activities couldn't ever feel the same way she did now.

"Ponder this," he continued. "Everybody is thinking about themselves right now, not you. Many of your fellow students might be feeling anxious for their own reasons. Games can be wonderful for shaking the seriousness out of people and bringing them together. Look at all these students eyeing your game contraptions."

The twins had fended off the squid warrior and Pikachu, but there were more curious observers pointing at the crepe paper or trying to peek in the large cardboard boxes that sat at the starting line.

Mr. Griswold continued, "Think of it like you're passing on information. That's it. You don't have to be a zany game show host or a comedian. Just be you, explaining how to play a game. If you need a friendly face to focus on, look for me."

"Or me," James chimed in.

"I fully support you as well," Vivian said. Her clipboard was pressed to her chin, and she gripped it so tightly her knuckles were white. Her unblinking eyes looked worried, and Emily realized that *Vivian*, of all people, was also anxious about talking in front of the crowd. What did you know? Take-charge, no-nonsense Vivian, who didn't have any qualms about approaching students in the hallway to sign up for the dance committee, did not want to stand in front of the gym with a microphone.

"Are we starting the game?" Kevin and Devin joined their group, with Nisha and Maddie following behind.

"You'll do fine, Emily," Mr. Quisling said.

Her stage fright must have overridden her worries

about coming clean to Mr. Quisling because she blurted out, "You haven't been book hunting tonight, have you?"

"Excuse me?"

"Before you came into the gym? You haven't found any books hidden on campus tonight, have you?"

Mr. Quisling frowned. "I'm here to chaperone the dance, not book hunt, Emily."

"Right. That's what I thought."

"You can get the mic from *Charlie*, Em," James said. His way of reminding her that even if her suspicion about him was right, nothing could happen while Charlie was on display in front of the whole room.

"Okay. But, Mr. Quisling, I need to talk to you about something after the game."

Her teacher looked bemused but nodded.

Emily took a deep breath. "Let's do this."

Vivian accompanied Emily up to the stage, half guiding and half pushing. Charlie handed Emily the mic. "Push the switch to turn it on," he said.

Classmates and grown-ups were scattered around the room. Some were already facing her, but most were still involved in conversations or goof-off dancing. Off to the side were James and Vivian, Kevin and Devin, Maddie and Nisha. Mr. Griswold stood behind them and gave her a thumbs-up. *Those are my friends*, she thought to herself, marveling for a moment that in a matter of months she had transformed from someone too shy to talk to anyone at the new schools she moved to, into a dance committee member leading her classmates in a ridiculous and hopefully fun game.

Charlie softened the music, and Emily spoke into the microphone.

"Hi, everyone." Her mouth bumped the mic as she spoke, muffling her words. She pulled back and tried again. "Welcome to the Presidential Valentine's GameCon Dance." She waved to the banner over her head, and people in the room cheered.

CHAPTER 40

THE FACES STARING at her became a blur as Emily explained the game just as Mr. Griswold had coached. Before she knew it, she was done talking. The sudden buzzing of conversation made her realize the gym had been fairly quiet as she spoke. There had been no heckling or laughs as she explained the game, and now that she was done people were starting to volunteer for teams or standing off to the side looking indifferent. Nobody seemed to think this proposed game was ridiculous. Emily stepped down from the stage feeling buoyant with relief.

There ended up being three teams of ten people. The rest of the seventh graders at the dance crowded on either side of the gym to watch.

Emily stood with her Teddy Roosevelt team members, who included Maddie and Kevin. James had been sorted onto Team Abraham Lincoln with Nisha. Devin and Vivian were on Team George Washington. Charlie played the sound of a loud clown horn to start the race, and they were off, the first member of each team digging through their cardboard box to find the three costume items they had to put on before proceeding through the obstacle course. Silly fast-paced music played in the background but was quickly drowned out by the shouts and claps of students.

When it was Emily's turn, she dug through the box to grab a tie to loop around her neck, slapped a mustache under her nose, and held the spectacles over her eyes as she began hopping from Hula-hoop to Hula-hoop. The crepe-paper maze was tricky to climb over and crawl under with the tie that hung down and her stiff Scrabble costume, but at least her team didn't have to wear a top hat. She ran to the skateboard and could sense someone in the next aisle coming up behind her. Before she knew it, the tails of James's too-large suit jacket were flying past.

Emily's Teddy Roosevelt team came in second in the obstacle course and faced off against Team Abraham Lincoln in the balloon stomp. As Emily ran, she caught a glimpse of Mr. Griswold on the sidelines throwing his head back in laughter. Mr. Sloan wore an Uncle Sam hat and clapped along. Mr. Quisling stood with his arms crossed over his chest but a smirk on his face, and she even saw him laugh once.

It was a wonderfully ridiculous moment, all these kids scrambling around with mustaches hanging off their lips or top hats angled over an ear, the loud pops as

balloons were stomped, the happy shrieks. Even Maddie was smiling, which made Emily feel oddly proud. She and Maddie teamed up to chase James, trying to stomp his balloon. Just when they'd cornered him, Emily felt a tug on her ankle and her balloon burst. Nisha flashed a grin and said, "Sorry!" before racing away.

Emily didn't even care that she was out of the game. She stood next to Mr. Griswold on the sidelines and cheered with him, "Go, Teddy Roosevelt!" But it was team Lincoln that ended up being victorious.

After the game, James jogged over to Emily and Mr. Griswold, his Abraham Lincoln beard pulled down around his neck and surviving balloon still tied to his ankle.

"What a game!" Mr. Griswold said. "What inspiration!" He looked up to the gym rafters with a daydreaming smile on his face. His eyes twitched side-to-side, like he was watching action on a movie screen, and his face lit up in a way Emily had only seen before in his Book Scavenger videos. "Oh, yes, I can see it now." Mr. Griswold stepped between Emily and James, squeezing them to his sides. "Thank you both. Truly. I have to go now—I hope you understand. Ideas are like bubbles; there's a limited amount of time before they pop."

Lifting his ball cap in good-bye, Mr. Griswold walked to the exit, turning back to wave once. "I can't wait to share this with you!" he called.

"We can't wait, either," James called back.

Emily couldn't stop waving her hand, even after Mr. Griswold turned away. The exhilaration of the relay race going over well combined with seeing Mr. Griswold so joyful overpowered her. It wasn't until one side of the banner hanging over the DJ table dropped onto the floor and her thoughts turned back to Charlie that she finally stopped moving her hand.

Charlie acted like he hadn't noticed the fallen sign, fiddling with a dial on his equipment. Mr. Quisling jumped onstage to fix the banner.

Emily drew in a deep breath. "Let's go talk to him," she said.

"Hold on." James bent down to pull the balloon from his ankle. He held the string as they walked, the balloon hopping behind him like an eager puppy.

They stood at the base of the stage waiting for Mr. Quisling to finish pressing down the poster tape. When he was done, he jumped to the floor and looked surprised to see Emily and James standing there. Shouting over the music and a group of girls squealing about the song that had begun to play, their teacher said, "I haven't forgotten you two! The fog machine solution was left in the break room. I need to grab that for the DJ so he can turn on the machine, and then you can tell me what you wanted to say."

Mr. Quisling walked off without waiting for their reply.

James tugged Emily's sleeve. "C'mon, let's just have fun for a little bit. Mr. Quisling isn't going to look for the book during the dance. Charlie clearly isn't up to anything evil right now." He gestured to the DJ, who was in the middle of an enormous yawn.

It was hard to feel worried when laughing kids and peppy music surrounded you. The more time that passed after their visit to Coit Tower, the more Emily questioned if they'd really seen what they thought they saw. It had been raining so much, after all. Maybe the fire had been some kind of trick of light—a reflection of lightning in a puddle that they mistook for sparking. And while Charlie's excuses for what he'd been doing during Hollister's fire didn't add up, James was right in that she couldn't conclusively say he started the fire in the bookstore, either.

"C'mon." James waved for her to follow him as he

joined the rest of their committee on the dance floor. The twins had removed their Minecraft heads and layered on every presidential costume piece and were doing goofy dance moves that looked like they were trying to get gum off the bottom of their shoes. Nisha, Maddie, and even Vivian were Hula-hooping.

Mr. Quisling returned carrying a large jug, but Emily decided James was right. What difference would it make telling him what they knew right this very second? This could wait.

James picked up a fallen Hula-hoop and balanced it on its side, twisting it into a rotating blur.

Through the spinning Hula-hoop orb, Emily watched Mr. Quisling crouch next to the fog machine, twist off the jug lid, and pour the liquid. That was the last thing she remembered seeing before the fog machine exploded.

CHAPTER 41

AT FIRST, EMILY couldn't make sense of what she was watching. The fog machine jumped, and Mr. Quisling did this weird backward crablike hop away from it. A piece of the fog machine launched into the banner, which ripped and wavered unsteadily. There was a sound, like a really large balloon had popped, but everyone for the most part kept dancing and goofing off. Emily didn't know if that was because the repetitive beats of dance music muffled it, or because they'd just played a game that involved popping balloons so the sound didn't stand out as bizarre.

The fog machine rattled with a succession of smaller pops, like a firework was trapped inside. People nearby started to take notice, gawking like Emily and James were.

Mr. Quisling stayed where he'd fallen, sitting up but

slouched, staring at the fog machine like he'd been stunned.

The pops became more insistent, and the machine jerked around more violently. Steam hissed up at an unnatural rate, immersing the DJ booth in its cloud. The people closest to the stage dropped to the floor and covered their heads or ran away.

From the opening where Mr. Quisling had poured the solution, an orange flame rose like a hand waving for attention. The banner overhead became unstuck once again and the paper swooped down. It made a perfect bridge for the flame to jump to.

"Fire!" Emily cried.

Understanding spread like a growing wave. Shrieks reverberated, but not playful like the ones that had filled the gym only minutes earlier during the game. Drifts of students and chaperones on the far side of the room surged toward the commotion, not understanding what had prompted the sudden distress, while those who understood were pushing them back or racing toward the exit.

Mr. Quisling broke from the spell he'd been under. He propelled himself to the wall, where he pulled a fire alarm. The bleating siren overrode the music. Teachers began corralling students and aiming them toward the exit. Their voices rose above the fray, "Remember our drills! Everybody stay calm! File outside!"

At the smell of smoke, Emily's body seized up. She

coughed reflexively, even though the gym was much larger and more open than Hollister's bookstore, but the memories of the previous fire triggered her reaction. A teacher retrieved a fire extinguisher and began dousing the banner and fog machine. James grabbed Emily's arm, pulling her away from the stage.

Outside, the evening buzzed. Everyone was supposed to gather in an organized fashion on the front lawn, like they had practiced a couple of months ago in a drill, but the students were a spilled bag of marbles that the adults frantically and unsuccessfully tried to gather up. A teacher marched by and yelled, "We need the attendance chart! Who has the attendance list for the dance? Nobody go anywhere until we make sure everyone is accounted for!" But some kids had already started walking home, either not hearing her or just blatantly ignoring the instructions. Others were on phones calling their parents.

A fire truck arrived, along with an ambulance and police cars.

"Why is there an ambulance?" Emily asked, worried that Mr. Quisling was injured.

"I don't know," James said.

Men and women jumped out of the emergency vehicles and ran into the gym. "Why is there an ambulance?" James called as they passed by, but they charged inside without answering.

Overheard conversations made it clear that nobody

really understood what had gone wrong. The stories ranged from the DJ booth catching fire to Mr. Quisling defusing a bomb.

"This was Coolbrith," Emily whispered.

James pulled off the Abraham Lincoln beard and threw it on the ground.

"Charlie brought the fog machine." He shook his head. "I didn't think he would do this."

"We have to warn Mr. Quisling," Emily said. "What if Charlie has more planned?"

James didn't argue with her. They ran together back toward the gym, but Mr. Sloan stepped in their path, hands up like a traffic cop.

"Can't go in there, kids. We've got to let the fire department do their job," he said. "You'll be able to collect anything you left inside later."

"We need to talk to Mr. Quisling," James said. "It's important."

Emily scanned the gathered crowds outside. The gym had been evacuated, but their teacher was nowhere to be seen, or Charlie, for that matter. "Why hasn't he come outside yet? Is he okay?" Emily asked.

"I'm sure he's fine." Mr. Sloan steered them away from the building and toward the mass of kids.

Emily and James walked through the crowded lawn, trying to spot their teacher or the DJ.

"We didn't see every single person exiting the gym," James reasoned. "They must be here somewhere."

On the fringe of a group, they overheard José telling

others, "Dude, a cop took Mr. Quisling into the school, like, for questioning."

"Did they arrest him?" someone asked.

"He was so uptight. He was bound to crack," another kid chimed in.

"You're lying, José," a girl retorted. "There's an evacuation. They're not letting anyone in the school."

"The fire was only in the *gym*, Ms. Know-It-All, and it's out. Not to mention it's a separate building. I'm telling you," José said, "I heard an officer tell Mr. Quisling they had an anonymous tip and they needed to look in his classroom."

James stepped up to the group. "Are you sure?"

José nodded.

"Where's the DJ? Have you seen him?" Emily asked.

José frowned. "Odd time for a song request," he said.

Another kid pointed to the street. "He booked it out of here. The fire freaked him out."

The students continued to buzz. Emily and James stepped back to the outskirts of the crowd.

"Mr. Quisling is going to be blamed for all of this," James whispered.

It had certainly *looked* like Mr. Quisling was responsible; Emily couldn't argue with that. She'd watched him fill the fog machine herself, and he scooted back a second before it exploded, almost as if he'd anticipated it. And what was the anonymous tip the police were questioning Mr. Quisling about, and who had called it in? Coolbrith?

"Charlie took off," Emily said.

James sighed, but nodded. "If he's been trying to frame Mr. Quisling to look like an arsonist, we let him walk right into our school and do it."

"We invited him, even," Emily added. "And now that the quest thread has been deleted from Book Scavenger, Mr. Quisling is the only person connected to the hidden copies of *Tom Sawyer* and the locations of the fires. We need to get in that school and talk to him. Right now."

"There's no way they're letting us inside," James said.

A police officer tied off yellow tape in front of the gym entrance to keep people from reentering. A group of girls were wailing about their purses being left behind with their phones inside, but the officer wasn't swayed.

The front of the school was still disorganized, with teachers trying but failing to get kids to sit on the lawn. Parents had started arriving in cars. One dad left his engine humming in the middle of the street with the door flung open when he ran over to hug his daughter. The parent started chewing out Principal Montoya.

James tapped Emily's arm. "I have an idea."

CHAPTER 42

WHILE EVERYONE ELSE was paying attention to the principal attempting to calm the outraged parent, Emily and James slipped away to the sidewalk and rounded the corner to a side street, like they were heading home, even though this wasn't the route they would normally take.

A chain-link fence enclosed the school blacktop and faculty parking lot, both dimly lit and devoid of people. This was the opposite side of the school from the gym, so there were no emergency responders here. James pointed to the school building, darkened other than the lit windows of Mr. Quisling's classroom on the ground floor, and said, "The side door with the gummed-up lock."

Of course! Emily remembered the door that hadn't opened or closed properly yesterday. They squeezed through the gate left ajar for the faculty parking and then climbed over the half fence that bordered the lot and blacktop. When Emily jumped to the ground, the fence rattled and clanged, sounding like it was amplified through a megaphone. The two crouched in the shadows to make sure nobody came running outside or around the building, looking for who made the noise. After several minutes passed, they ran, bent low, across the blacktop to the side door.

James pulled the handle, and it didn't budge at first, like before. He grimaced and tried again; Emily crossed her fingers the janitor hadn't taken the time to scrape out the old gum and actually lock the door tonight. Finally it gave slightly, then gasped open.

Once inside, they quickly pulled the door shut to snuff out the moonlight cast on the floor. The indoor quiet felt pronounced, like someone had pressed a mute button. Shadowy walls of lockers and darkened classroom windows lined the hallway. They crept toward Room 40. A long, low creak lingered behind them. Emily and James froze mid-step, then scrambled forward to a nearby stairwell where they could hide.

They huddled motionless for several excruciating minutes, waiting to see if the shadows would shift.

"You heard that, right?" James whispered. "That wasn't my imagination?"

Emily nodded, and then realized he might not be able to see her in the dim light of the stairwell. "Yes," she said. "Maybe it's the walls settling." That had been her parents' go-to explanation for any creepy nighttime sound in one of their rentals.

They couldn't hide in the stairwell all night, so they continued toward Mr. Quisling's classroom. Emily repetitively looked over her shoulder. When they reached the intersecting hallway, voices came from around the corner. One she didn't recognize said, "Seems unusual for a social studies teacher to keep a supply of sodium metal on hand. Are you aware this element is highly explosive when mixed with water?"

They heard their teacher's voice reply, "I have no idea how that jar got into my drawer. I swear, I've never seen it before in my life."

"They're in Mr. Quisling's room," Emily whispered.

A police radio crackled. "We're going to have to confiscate this, all the same. Traces of sodium were in that fog machine. I'm sure you understand."

"There's paper wrapped around the jar, too," a woman's voice said. After a light rustling, she added, "The handwriting here looks an awful lot like what you have written on that white board. Did you write what's up there?"

"Yes, but I don't know what that piece of paper is."

"Looks like a list of dates: October ninth—Ferry Building, November eleventh—Mission, December twenty-seventh—Washington Square Park . . ."

"Those are the dates of the fires," James whispered. "Mr. Quisling is being framed."

This time, Emily didn't balk at the idea of doing something. She charged down the hallway to Room 40, no longer worried about making noise. James was right behind her.

"Mr. Quisling, we have to tell you something!" Emily called out as they skidded to a stop just inside the classroom door.

Their teacher jumped up from where he sat on a student's desktop. A raised welt on his cheekbone and small white bandage marked where debris from the exploding fog machine must have hit him. Two officers were there as well. One held a brown bottle in his hand and had been leaning over Mr. Quisling's desk, writing something down, while the other was sealing a small piece of paper inside a clear bag.

The officer at the desk straightened. "What is this?!" A tag on his uniform identified him as E. Pike.

The other officer stepped toward them, shooing them with the plastic bag in her hand. "Back outside. Go, go."

Emily ignored the officers and talked to Mr. Quisling. "Coolbrith is impersonating you on Book Scavenger. Each of the dates on that list is a fire that was set after you found the copy of *Tom Sawyer*. You're being set up."

Mr. Quisling's brow wrinkled. "How do you know about Coolbrith? How . . ."

"All right." Officer Pike clicked his pen and tucked it in his front shirt pocket. "We can't have you kids in here."

Emily rushed on, knowing she had a small window of time before the officers made them leave. "James and I should have said something before, but we thought you and Coolbrith were trying to solve the unbreakable code—"

"The unbreakable code?" Mr. Quisling crossed his arms and frowned. "Emily, this really isn't the time."

Officer Pike nodded to his partner, who stepped forward and gently herded Emily and James backward to the hallway.

Emily tilted her head to shout around the officer's shoulder, "Coolbrith tricked you into thinking he was your old girlfriend leading you on a Book Scavenger quest!"

James leaned his head around the other side of the officer and added, "There was a man at Coit Tower yesterday who started a fire after you found the book. That was Coolbrith!"

Mr. Quisling's mouth dropped open.

Running footsteps echoed in the hallway. Emily braced herself to see more officers arriving to escort her and James away, but instead Mr. Sloan leaned against the door frame, trying to catch his breath.

"What in the world?" Officer Pike threw his hands in the air. His partner spoke into a handheld radio.

"I saw them sneaking around the school," Mr. Sloan said between gasps for breath. "I'm sorry they bothered you. I'll take them out front."

After so much anguish over whether she should say

something to Mr. Quisling, Emily couldn't believe her words carried no impact. Mr. Quisling might have been surprised by her outburst, but now the look on his face was the same as when he caught Emily and James passing a note in his class: disappointed, but not worried or concerned. The image of her teacher propelling back from the exploding fog machine replayed in her mind. The stifling smell of burning paper at Hollister's came back to her.

"It's Charlie, Mr. Quisling," Emily said. "He's trying to make you look like an arsonist. He was the DJ and brought the fog machine and must have put the sodium inside, knowing he could ask you to add the solution later. He probably planted that bottle in your classroom, too, and gave the police the anonymous tip."

"Charlie? My former student?" Mr. Quisling shook his head, refusing to believe Emily. "That's quite an accusation to make."

"I know, but someone really is trying to set you up. And you gave Charlie the only D he's ever gotten for a class. He's been holding a grudge ever since."

Officer Pike sighed and removed his pen. Clicking it open, he asked, "Do you have a last name for this Charlie? Is he still here?"

"I remember Charlie," Mr. Quisling said evenly. "He wasn't an angry or malicious kid. He also wasn't a motivated student—that's why he earned a D. He couldn't be bothered with homework. I cannot fathom Charlie taking the time and initiative to do what you are saying he did."

"Don't underestimate a disgruntled student," Mr. Sloan said. He rested his hands onto Emily's and James's shoulders. "We need to let the police do their job." He gently pulled them backward to the hallway. To the officers he said, "She was recently involved in a bookstore fire. Very traumatic, as I'm sure you can imagine. Tonight's events have probably retriggered stressful feelings."

Emily bristled at this. At first she thought it was because he was dismissing her concerns as some kind of hysteria, and she was tired of not being taken seriously. But then his comment fully registered with her and something clicked.

She pulled away to face Mr. Sloan. "How did you know I was at Hollister's bookstore the day of the fire?"

Mr. Sloan gave a clipped laugh. "Emily, come on now. You talked about it."

Emily shook her head. "At the first dance committee meeting after the fire, you said you were sorry to hear I'd been there when it happened. But I never told you I worked at the store. Only a few people knew I helped out at Hollister's on Saturday morning."

"That fire was on the news," Mr. Sloan said.

"But *Emily* wasn't on the news," James pointed out.

Emily dared to look at the other people in the room. Mr. Quisling studied the substitute teacher like he was a painting in a museum. The officers were as attentive as two cats watching a mouse.

Mr. Sloan smiled in a placating sort of way and spoke slowly. "The fire happened weeks ago, Emily. Word travels around a school. And didn't I see you two at Hollister's book party? Maybe that's when I learned you spent your Saturdays at the store."

"That party happened before she started helping Hollister," James pointed out.

Emily's vision blurred, and she was back in Hollister's Treehouse the morning of the fire, hearing the door chime over and over. If Mr. Quisling had found the *Tom Sawyer* and left, Charlie might have run out next "to feed his meter," as he claimed, leaving Emily alone in the store. If Mr. Sloan then entered, he could have assumed the store was empty when he set the fire, but realized he was wrong if he heard her call for Charlie, or if he had waited somewhere outside afterward and seen her race onto the sidewalk.

"*You* are Coolbrith." Emily threw the words boldly, trying to sound more confident than she was.

Mr. Sloan laughed. "I don't even know what you're talking about. What does that even mean—*I'm Coolbrith*?

Emily turned to Mr. Quisling. Her teacher was far from laughing, but she couldn't tell if the scowl on his face was directed at her, or if her theory was beginning to make sense. She forged ahead to make her case before the officers lost interest in what she had to say.

"Why did you fill the fog machine, Mr. Quisling?" Emily asked. This seemed like an important question. "Charlie brought it with his DJ equipment. Why didn't he?"

"Vivian told Charlie to hold off on the dance music and special effects until after the game, remember?" James interjected. "So maybe he couldn't do it himself while he was playing the music. Maybe he had to ask someone else to do it."

"Charlie did ask someone else," Mr. Quisling replied. He was calm—superficially calm—like a teakettle before the boiling water inside makes the whistle blow. "Didn't he, Harry? But you were too busy manning the snack table—or at least that's what you told me when you asked if I could grab the fog solution from the break room and start up the machine for the DJ."

Mr. Sloan rolled his eyes. "Don't let these kids manipulate you, Brian. It's been a long, stressful evening. I think you're getting confused."

Mr. Quisling took a step closer, and the officers tensed, like they were preparing to separate the two men if they had to.

"I remember who you are now," Mr. Quisling said. "It's been over thirty years, but it's coming back to me. You didn't go by Harry. When we worked together, you were Harvard Sloan, that odd friend of Miranda's."

Mr. Sloan snorted. "Now you remember me? Of course you do, *now*, when it's convenient for you. You

couldn't remember me last September at the literary labyrinth. You could barely spare a second to talk with me, you were so high and mighty about your win. But I remembered *you*. It's hard to forget someone who ruined your life."

"I didn't ruin your life," Mr. Quisling replied.

Mr. Sloan guffawed. "Oh, you didn't? I forgot, you're an expert about my life, too, even though you couldn't remember me until five seconds ago."

"If by *ruining your life* you're referring to when you were fired from Hamlet High School, that wasn't my fault."

Mr. Sloan shook his head, disgusted. "I've never met anyone so arrogant. So self-absorbed."

The two officers exchanged a look, and Officer Pike stepped forward. "Gentlemen—" he began, but Mr. Sloan ignored him.

"I had one chemistry demonstration go wrong, and off you raced to report me to the principal."

"You launched a fireball across a classroom," Mr. Quisling said evenly.

"*Accidentally.* It was my first year teaching. Nobody was hurt. But you couldn't wait to get rid of me. You knew it was only a matter of time before I would have taken your job, your girlfriend. You got me fired, and that started a chain reaction that ruined my life. But guess what?" Mr. Sloan leaned close to Mr. Quisling, spittle flying off his lip as he hissed, "I. Am. The. Phoenix. I always rise from the ashes."

"All right." Officer Pike stepped between the two men. He placed a firm hand on Mr. Sloan's shoulder. "I'm going to ask you to go with my partner while I finish up here."

The substitute teacher clamped his mouth shut and allowed himself to be led from the room.

CHAPTER 43

TWENTY MINUTES LATER, Officer Pike left, after finishing his report with Mr. Quisling and taking statements from Emily and James.

"So Mr. Sloan is the arsonist, then?" James asked. "He went to all that trouble to get back at you for something that happened over thirty years ago?"

"That appears to be the case." Mr. Quisling gave a heavy sigh and dropped into his chair, unbuttoning the collar of his shirt. "What a waste of a good mind."

"I would feel sorry for him if I wasn't so angry about him hurting you and Hollister," Emily said. "It's sad. That's a long time to carry a grudge. That's more years than I've been alive."

"More years than you and I both put together," James amended.

"Okay, okay." Mr. Quisling held up his hands. "I get it: I'm old." Their teacher gave a light smile and sighed.

"I should have known better, getting wrapped up in that quest. I accepted it at the start because, well, I have a hard time turning down a challenge."

Emily nodded. She could relate to that.

"Actually, at first I assumed Coolbrith was my son, Robbie. The quest title, 'For Old Times' Sake,' sounded like a nod to when he and I used to play the game together. But then after I found the first and second copies of *Tom Sawyer*, it seemed clear Coolbrith was someone who knew about my old fascination with the unbreakable code. That seemed a little odd coming from Robbie, but I've talked to him about it before. I even took him to see the code at the library when he was younger and enjoyed puzzles and Book Scavenger.

"Anyway, I didn't give it too much thought, because it seemed like a lighthearted game. When the book cipher in the second *Tom Sawyer* mentioned a map, I immediately thought of my old friend Miranda. Ina Coolbrith had been her favorite poet.

"Mr. Sloan himself never once crossed my mind. When I ran into him at Book Scavenger events this past year, he seemed vaguely familiar, but I assumed it was the Book Scavenger connection. I had long forgotten how I really knew him. He was a friend of Miranda's whom I barely remember. A blip on my life radar. Apparently I wasn't a blip on his."

"Don't beat yourself up over it," James said. "Mr. Sloan wanted you to think he was someone playing a friendly game with you. Someone who was interested in reviving your interest in the unbreakable code."

"I don't think Mr. Sloan actually even cared about the unbreakable code," Emily realized.

"No, I don't think he did," Mr. Quisling agreed. "He used it because he knew it would get my attention. Especially if I thought the messages came from Miranda." Mr. Quisling blushed. "Anyway. It's getting late. Have you called your parents yet?"

Parents! Emily and James turned to each other in startled panic. In their haste and worry about Mr. Quisling, they had completely forgotten about checking in. Automated texts would have been sent to the families of students attending the dance after the gym was evacuated. If anyone was trying to find them out front, they would be freaking out. They hurried through the darkened hallways with Mr. Quisling to the front door.

"My mom and grandma are catering a Valentine's dinner tonight," James said. "They probably haven't even seen the notice yet."

"Your dad may have," Mr. Quisling said, slightly out of breath.

"He's traveling. Again."

The bitter note in his voice made Emily think of Mr. Sloan and his decades-long resentment. Was that what had happened to him? A drop of bitterness at a time, revisited over and over again until he was carrying around a bucketful?

Emily wasn't sure if her parents would be out front yet, either. They didn't check their phones often or have them set with sound notifications, because they didn't like electronic disruptions. They might be at home assuming all was well and Emily was at school helping clean up after the dance.

They pushed through the front doors and saw the commotion had calmed down greatly from before. The fire truck idled, but the ambulance was gone. One police car remained—Emily guessed Officer Pike and his partner were still inside talking with Mr. Sloan. Many students had left or been picked up. Looking down from the steps on the front lawn to see the group of remaining kids and teachers adorned with Abraham Lincoln hats, George Washington wigs, and trailing balloons made it seem like a late-night picnic instead of the aftermath of a fire evacuation.

Emily saw Sal, the family minivan, before she noticed her dad standing in front of it with the principal. Both were scanning the crowd, the principal with a phone to his ear.

"Dad!" Emily waved.

Mr. Crane's head snapped to the school's front entrance, and a smile split his face. Principal Montoya rolled his shoulders in an exaggerated sigh.

"James!" a voice called. As Emily ran down the front walk, she saw James's dad stepping out of a sedan and waving.

"Dad?" James called. "What are you doing here?"

Both Emily and James reached their dads at the same time. Emily heard Mr. Lee say, "I decided to come back a day early." James threw his arms around his dad's waist and buried his head against his chest. Mr. Lee laughed lightly, then raised a hand and hesitantly stroked James's hair, patting down Steve.

Mr. Crane swung his arm around Emily and hugged her tight to his side. "What in the world happened?" he asked.

"A fog machine caught on fire." She didn't want to get into explaining Mr. Sloan the serial arsonist yet. She knew she'd only have to repeat herself to her mom, and then probably again to Matthew, since he'd want to hear the story, too. It suddenly hit her how tired she was, and right now all she wanted to do was curl up in bed with a book.

"Oh, before I forget," her dad said, "there was a phone call for you tonight. From a San Francisco public librarian?" His eyebrows were question marks.

"Ms. Linden!" Emily clasped her hands together. She'd forgotten about leaving her a message.

"Yes, Linden. That was the name. I asked her if you had overdue fines, but she said she was returning your call to answer your questions about boats." Her dad said the word *boats* with emphasis, like Ms. Linden had said *intergalactic space pigs*.

Emily realized something. "I need to talk to Mr. Quisling. Hold on, Dad."

The teacher was standing where she'd left him on the front steps of the school in his traditional stance: legs spread, arms tightly crossed over his chest, steely gaze (which now seemed more like "keenly observing" than "steely" to Emily) on the crowd.

"There was something else we wanted to tell you, Mr. Quisling. A good something."

Mr. Quisling raised an eyebrow. "Yes?"

Emily looked back to James, who was walking with his dad to their car. "Actually, I should let James tell you about it. He's the one who solved it."

"Solved . . . what? You don't mean the unbreakable code?"

Emily wished she could snap a picture of the incredulous look on Mr. Quisling's face. She may not have been the one to solve it, and she'd learned Mr. Quisling was much less cutthroat than she originally had him pegged, but it was still satisfying to think they'd bested their teacher.

"It would be better if we showed you in person. Could you meet me and James at the main library tomorrow afternoon? On the sixth floor at the History Center?"

CHAPTER 44

AFTER EMILY FILLED IN her family about the night's excitement, she collapsed on her bed planning to read for a few minutes, but she woke up in the middle of the night still fully dressed with her Scrabble boards on. She changed into her pajamas and went to brush her teeth, but had barely stepped down the hallway when she heard her parents talking in the front room. Her mom often stayed up late to work, and that night her dad must have joined her.

"You don't think it will upset Emily?" her dad said.

Emily froze at the mention of her name.

"It's the right thing for our family, David. It's a great opportunity."

"I know, but it's a big change. And we promised her—"

Her mom interrupted him, "I bet she'll surprise you."

Emily hurried back to her bed, not wanting to hear

any more. She knew what they were talking about, and it had nothing to do with the fire at the school or Mr. Quisling. Her parents had made only one promise recently: that they wouldn't move again. Her parents had promised they would call San Francisco their home until *Emily and Matthew* decided they were okay with moving again. That had been the deal. That's what they agreed on. And now her parents were about to go back on their word.

Emily tossed and turned in her bed, kicking her bunched-up sheet straight. The argument she'd overheard came back to her, about her dad losing a client and money. San Francisco was an expensive place to live. They had budgeted for only one year. But they had *promised* her they wouldn't move again.

The next morning, Emily didn't say anything to her parents. She kept waiting for her dad to drop the bombshell, but with every slurp of his cereal and cheery comment about how beautiful the weather was going to be that day, she imagined an internal needle inching toward her red zone, like some kind of gauge that measured anger.

Emily buried her nose in a book in her room for the rest of the day, biding her time until she and James could go to the library to meet Mr. Quisling. Finally, it was almost time to leave. As she double-checked her backpack for her notebook and extra pens, Matthew walked in and flopped on her bed. "I'm bored. Want to go do something? We can walk down to the beach at Fort

Mason. Or see if anything's going on in Washington Square."

"I can't," Emily said. "James and I are going back to the History Center."

"The place with the green-haired librarian?"

Emily nodded.

"You're still trying to figure out that old cipher?"

"Not *trying* to. We did figure it out."

Matthew sat up. "For real?"

"For real," Emily said, zipping her bag.

Their dad popped his head into Emily's room. "Oh good, you're both here. Do you guys have a minute for a family talk? There's something your mom and I need to discuss with you."

Emily took a deep breath in an attempt to calm that needle on the anger-meter so it wouldn't spin off it completely.

"Is it about last night?" Emily said evenly, already knowing the answer.

"No, no, no." Their dad rubbed a hand against his head and stared at the floor, looking a little sheepish. "Just some changes we might need to make."

Matthew groaned. "Are we moving again?"

Their dad looked up, surprised. "I thought you liked the moving?"

Matthew raised his hands and spoke to the ceiling, like he was having a conversation with James on the other side. "Why does everyone think that? Geez, you get misunderstood a lot when you try to be easygoing."

Emily couldn't believe her dad had chosen this moment, right when she was about to leave and do something she'd been looking forward to all day, to drop his big announcement. She knew her dad had done that on purpose, too. He probably thought it was a nice thing— pull the rug out from under her first, and let the fun activity distract her from the bruises. But it didn't work that way. She was going to the library as she planned: bruise free. His announcement could wait.

"Now isn't a good time. James and I have to do research at the library for a school project. It closes at five."

The doorbell rang, much to Emily's relief. She sent James a silent thank-you for his excellent timing. "Can we talk later?"

Mr. Crane sighed. "Yes, this can wait."

Matthew raised an eyebrow at Emily after their dad left the room.

"Since when is the unbreakable code a school project?" he asked.

Emily jerked her thumb to where their dad had just stood. "I'm not about to feel bad when *they* have been misleading us."

"You know something I don't know?" Matthew asked.

"Yes," Emily said, simply. "Anyway, James and I are meeting Mr. Quisling at the library. We're showing him what we discovered. So that's kind of like a school project."

"Well, if you don't want Mom and Dad to know the real reason you're going to the library, then you're going to need me to come with you."

"What! Why?"

Matthew shrugged. "Because I'm bored. And if you leave me here with nothing to do, I'll probably wander around the house in a stupor, babbling about the unbreakable code. I can't prevent what Mom and Dad might overhear."

Emily rolled her eyes. "If you really want to come, fine."

Matthew grinned and tugged her ponytail as he stood up. "Thought you'd never ask."

CHAPTER 45

EMILY, JAMES, Matthew, Mr. Quisling, and Ms. Linden all crowded around the original unbreakable code document as Emily and James took turns recounting how they deciphered the message. Emily pointed out the steps in her notebook, from using *hope* as a keyword cipher to writing the grid of letters in the order they fell if you read their columns from top to bottom and right to left.

Finally, she flipped a page to reveal the final message:

XTHIRDTREEEASTOFDUCKROCK

"Well, I'll be," Mr. Quisling said, shaking his head in awe. "Those are some excellent observational skills you two have. I never would have thought to question that brown mark or about the possibility of invisible ink.

Many people assume that's a modern invention and don't realize how long it's been utilized as a tool."

"Isn't it also fascinating," Ms. Linden chimed in, "how most people who have attempted to break this code over the years probably assumed the original gold miner was the stereotypical caricature of a white, Yosemite Sam type of guy?"

"Yes, exactly." Mr. Quisling nodded enthusiastically. "It makes you realize how much you limit yourself if you refuse to think outside your preconceived notions. Excellent work, you two."

"This is so exciting." Ms. Linden pressed her hands together and said to Emily and James, "I am begging you to let me be part of this adventure. I'd love to take you to Gull Island on my boat, whenever you'd like. Because of its small size, if Gull Island is actually what the map is marking and not Yerba Buena, then I think you'll have a much better chance of identifying this duck rock. There's probably only fifteen trees on the island all together, so even if the duck rock is elusive, you might even be able to happen across this final spot by investigating each tree."

Emily had been so excited about sharing how they solved the puzzle, she'd momentarily lost sight of the fact that there might be something waiting at the end of these directions. Something valuable that would change her parents' mind about the big change they were preparing to spring on her and Matthew.

"Can we go right now?" she asked.

"Oh!" Ms. Linden looked at Mr. Quisling, then her watch. "Well, I get off work in half an hour. If you wanted to meet at the marina an hour from now, I suppose we could do that. I'll need your parents' permission, of course."

Emily chewed her lip. "Can we have a minute to talk this over?" she asked, indicating herself, James, and Matthew as the "we."

"Of course," Ms. Linden said. "Just meet us at the front desk when you're ready."

"What do you think?" Emily asked once the adults had left the room.

"I'm game," Matthew shrugged.

"My mom likes Mr. Quisling, so she would probably say yes if he's going," James said.

Emily was less confident about what her parents would say. They hadn't talked to her teacher very often, as she'd lived in San Francisco for only four and a half months. After Hollister's fire and then the events from the night before, she wasn't sure they'd be so agreeable about her sailing off with two grown-ups they didn't really know, even if Emily promised they were trustworthy. There was one way she knew they'd agree to her and Matthew going, and it would probably make James's mom more comfortable, too.

"Can I use your phone?" Emily asked Matthew.

He handed it over, and she dialed their dad's cell phone number.

"Hey, it's Emily," she said when he picked up. "How

321

would you and Mom feel about going on a little adventure right now?"

Emily's parents were surprised about the spontaneous boat trip, but one of the perks of having parents who embraced new adventures was that they were often up for something out of the blue. Emily, James, and Matthew went home from the library, in order to change into warmer clothes and meet up with the Cranes, before the group assembled again at the marina.

In no time at all, the seven of them were wearing lifejackets in a small sailboat bobbing across the bay toward Gull Island. It was freezing on the water, and Emily was glad she had listened when her mother told her to bring her fleece jacket.

Much to Emily's amusement, Mr. Quisling and Ms. Linden were hitting it off. She would have pegged them as opposites. He was so rigid and rule-oriented, and Ms. Linden seemed anything but, with her color-streaked hair and tattoos. Mr. Quisling asked her about learning to sail, and the librarian pushed up her windbreaker sleeve to show him the tattoo that commemorated the first time she'd sailed to Farallon Islands. Mr. Quisling began asking about the stories behind other tattoos, and then to Emily's great surprise, he pulled up his pant leg to show Ms. Linden his own tattoo of a blue-inked compass rose.

While Mr. Quisling and Ms. Linden bonded, Emily

and James filled her parents in on the unbreakable code and where they were headed.

"Mark Twain once had this cipher in his possession?" her dad repeated, incredulous.

Emily's mom turned to Mr. Quisling. "How did you first learn about this legend?"

"It was back in 1978, believe it or not, when I volunteered with the recovery effort of a whaling ship that was discovered buried underneath the city. The unbreakable code has ties to that ship, the *Niantic*, so it brought the old puzzle back into the public's eye for a short time.

"I got so far as figuring out the paper might double as a map. An old girlfriend and I even hiked Angel Island once with a metal detector, hoping to find the gold." Mr. Quisling shook his head, humored by his younger self.

"You did?" Emily said.

Mr. Quisling nodded. "Yerba Buena belonged to the military at that time and wasn't easy to traverse, so we crossed our fingers and hoped we'd make a lucky find on Angel Island. When Coolbrith said there was new info about the map, I thought perhaps Miranda had figured out which island. Of course, that message was only a trick."

To Emily's parents Mr. Quisling said, "I realize this must seem absurd. A grown man getting caught up in book and treasure hunts."

Emily's dad waved him away. "You don't have to

explain yourself to us. We've been called the same for wanting to live in each state."

"And we know all about book hunting, thanks to Emily," Mrs. Crane added.

"And it's not absurd, at least not according to me," Ms. Linden said. "Are you kidding? I'm in my late forties, I belong to a competitive Yahtzee club, and spend my downtime coloring in coloring books. I'm not judging anyone for participating in a Book Scavenger quest, no matter what their age. I think more people should get off their keisters and do quests, as a matter of fact, that's what I think."

"Keisters?" James said, and Mr. Quisling gave a loud belly laugh in response.

Ms. Linden grinned. "Keisters. I said it, and I'm sticking by it."

The group fell into a contemplative silence for the next stretch, listening to the waves slap the side of the boat. Ms. Linden pointed ahead to a small mound of land that rounded out of the water, like a lumpy turtle shell.

"Gull Island, straight ahead," she said. "I can get us fairly close, but then you'll need to take the dinghy to the beach. I don't recommend more than three in the dinghy. I'll stay on the boat. It gets too busy around these parts for me to leave it unattended."

Emily's parents and Matthew volunteered to stay with Ms. Linden, as Mr. Quisling, Emily, and James had been the three working on the unbreakable code all along. Matthew stretched out along a bench with his hands behind his head and the sun beaming down on his face and declared, "*This* is what I'm talking about."

The dinghy was a small inflatable boat that barely fit Emily, James, Mr. Quisling, and the metal detector and two different-sized shovels he brought along.

Once the water was shallow enough, they dragged the dinghy onto the narrow sliver of pebble-filled beach. Birdcall chatter drowned out the sounds of the bay. Ms. Linden hadn't been kidding when she said the island had become a refuge for birds. White gulls waddled around the beach; another gray bird swooped overhead.

The island had a gentle rise that was easy to hike to the flattened top. The trickiest part for Emily was not placing her hand on a bird-poop-splattered rock as they climbed. At the top of the rise, they could see all the way across the island. It was sparsely covered with scrub brush, the occasional boulder, and a handful of trees. Because of the flat terrain and small size of the island, they could see all the way across it. It would probably take ten minutes to cross from one side to the other.

"Do any of these boulders look like a duck to you?" Mr. Quisling asked, and they began walking haphazardly around the island, scrutinizing rocks as if they were studying sculptures.

"This one?" James pointed to a rock that was not much bigger than a football. Emily tilted her head, realizing that one person's *duck* was another person's *bunny*. This might be as difficult as spotting the same picture in the clouds, but at least the rocks weren't changing shape.

They wandered and analyzed rocks for what felt like a long time. The sky was lightening into a beautiful shade of pink, which Emily knew meant they were running out of time for tonight's adventure.

"What about this one?" Mr. Quisling called.

As Emily walked closer, she could see it: The rock looked like a plain version of a duck resting on the water with its neck tucked into its body. There was even a lip of rock that extended kind of like a beak.

"I think this might be it!" Emily said, excited.

"This direction is east," Mr. Quisling said.

Emily and James ran in the direction of his pointing finger calling out with each tree they passed, "One . . . two . . . three!"

Tree number three was more of a stump than a tree. It hadn't been chopped down, but looked like it had been split by a storm or lightning a long time ago. There was a hollow area at its base that was almost solidly white, it was so completely covered with bird poop.

"Gross!" Emily said.

Mr. Quisling swung his handheld metal detector in front of the tree. When he arced it up the side of the tree, it beeped. The three of them froze and looked at each other. "Let's not get too excited yet," Mr. Quisling cautioned. "Could be a false alarm." But the beeping continued consistently whenever he combed over the trunk.

"It almost seems like there's something *inside*," James said. They studied the trunk hollow that had layers and layers of bird poop caked over the top. "It's like a fortress made out of bird poop." James grimaced. "I call 'not it.'"

If Mr. Quisling was grossed out, he didn't show it. He began to gently scrape at the white crustiness with the tip of a trowel. Gradually it chipped and peeled away until a dark opening was revealed. Emily bent close trying to see inside. She wished she'd brought Matthew's cell phone with them so they could shine the light in.

Mr. Quisling stuck the trowel in, this time swinging it around to get a feel for what was in the hollow. The trowel connected to something with a dull clank.

That didn't sound like bird poop.

That didn't sound like tree innards.

"That sounded like metal," James said.

Mr. Quisling reached a hand in the dark hole—an action alone that had Emily feeling antsy on his behalf. Even though the opening had been sealed with bird poop, what if this was still a nest for a snake or another animal? Maybe the occupant had a different entrance than the one they were barging through.

But Mr. Quisling didn't yelp, and nothing seemed to attack him. Slowly, he unearthed a large, rusty tin can.

"Oh, man," James said.

"I really hope that's what I think it is," Emily said.

Mr. Quisling pried open the top. He reached in and pulled out a black bowl. It was small enough to fit in the palm of his hand and simply designed.

Emily knew it was probably unrealistic to expect a treasure chest filled with gleaming gold coins, but the bowl was quite a disappointment.

"That's it?" James asked. "Is that the miner's treasure from the unbreakable code?"

Mr. Quisling removed a paper from the tin. He unfolded it to find a letter with Chinese characters on one side and primitively written English on the other. "It's difficult to make out the handwriting, but it looks like this says *Wong Ming-Chung*—this is probably a notice of ownership."

"You know what doesn't make sense?" James asked. "If this is ceramic, then why did the metal detector go off?"

"It's the tin," Mr. Quisling said. "It's known to be a false-positive for finding gold."

"Can I see the bowl?" Emily asked.

It was a dull black, like a chalkboard. Emily rubbed her thumb along the uneven side and was surprised to see some of the black came off. A dull brown peeked through. Emily rubbed more. More of the black coloring came off.

"This is like soot," Emily said. "Look, if you rub it off, the pot looks different underneath."

"Well, I'll be," Mr. Quisling said. He took the bowl and began rubbing it vigorously with the corner of his shirt. The shirt quickly became blackened. A patch of gold gleamed through the surrounding soot.

"We found the gold," Emily said, not quite believing what she was seeing.

James whooped. He threw his head back and hollered to the sky, "We found the gold!"

CHAPTER 46

BACK ON THE BOAT, Emily and James were like excited frogs hopping all over the place as they told how they had uncovered the golden bowl from the hollow tree. Ms. Linden laughed. "Settle down, settle down! You're rocking the boat! The last thing you want to do now is capsize us and lose the treasure to the bottom of the bay."

"The first thing we're going to have to do," Mr. Quisling announced, "is reach out to the owner of this island. By property rights, this bowl belongs to him."

Emily and James the hopping frogs landed splat.

"It belongs to him?" James repeated.

"Even though we did all the work to find it?" Emily added.

"It could, but that will depend on a lot of different things. It's entirely possible he might reward you for making the find. We'll have to wait and see."

Emily blinked back tears. She tried not to show how upset she was, but her mom noticed right away. "What is it, Em?"

She shook her head. "Nothing," she said. But then words came bursting out of her, directed to her dad. "I know what you wanted to talk about this morning. San Francisco is too expensive, and we need to move again. This was my plan to fix that." She jabbed a finger at the bowl. She blinked repeatedly, desperate not to cry in front of everyone.

"Oh, Em," her dad said. His face paled. "That's not what I wanted to tell you and Matthew."

"It's not?"

Ms. Linden had gotten the boat moving back toward San Francisco. Emily and her dad shouted at each other over the wind. Matthew leaned forward to hear what their dad was going to say.

"What I wanted to tell you is that I was offered a job at Bayside Press. But before I accept, I wanted to get your okay. I know Mr. Griswold means a lot to you, and with you two being on his teen advisory committee, well, I thought me working there might be similar to if I became a teacher at your school or something. I know you might not want your dad hanging around a place that's personal to you."

"Are you serious?" Emily leaped forward and hugged her dad. "That would be great if you worked at Bayside Press! Are you going to help Mr. Griswold with his games?"

Her dad laughed. "No, I'll be working on the publishing side of things. You know, the actual business part of the company? I'm going to be a production editor for their humanities and social sciences textbooks."

"That sounds really boring!" Matthew shouted.

Her dad laughed again. "I suppose it does. I'm excited, though. It's funny—for years I thought I never wanted to set foot in a nine-to-five office job again. Freelancing was the life for me. But now I'm really looking forward to the stability."

"And staying in San Francisco," Emily added.

"Yes," her dad agreed. "And staying in San Francisco."

"It's almost on!" Emily's dad called down the hall.

Emily sat next to her dad on their couch, a pillow hugged to her chest. A week had passed since their outing to Gull Island, and any minute now her face was going to be on the TV screen, talking with the reporter about the unbreakable code and found treasure.

"Coming!" Emily's mom hurried from the back of the apartment, bangles chiming as she ran. Matthew plopped next to Emily on the couch.

"It's starting," Emily said, ducking her face behind the pillow so only her eyes were visible.

Her dad smiled and patted her leg. "It's going to be fine, Emily. You did great!"

The news report began with a brief overview of the history of the unbreakable code. "There's Ms. Linden!"

Emily pointed. The footage showed Ms. Linden opening the manila folder to reveal the miner's original code and map.

The news report shifted to footage of the reporter standing on Gull Island next to the tree trunk where they had found the treasure. Wind whipped her hair as she said, "Thanks to the cleverness of two middle school students and their social studies teacher, this centuries-old mystery has been solved and treasure uncovered in this very spot."

Now the TV showed Emily, James, and Mr. Quisling sitting in his classroom, where they had been interviewed by the reporter.

"Did you imagine you would actually find treasure?" the reporter asked Emily and James.

James replied, "I imagined it the way I imagine flying in a rocket ship or fighting zombies. You know—I imagined it, but not in a really-thought-it-would-happen way."

"And when you uncovered the treasure, what was that like, Emily?" the reporter asked.

"It was exciting at first, because we found something—"

James interjected, "Actually, it was disgusting before anything else, because of all the bird poop."

Emily laughed. "That's true. And then when we found the bowl, I was disappointed. It didn't look like gold at all, so I thought maybe it was just old junk. And then it was exciting again when we realized it was gold after all."

"And, Mr. Quisling," the reporter asked, "how do you feel as their teacher?"

"Incredibly proud. We've solved a historical mystery, and it wouldn't have happened without the hard work and dedication of these two students."

Over footage of the found bowl, the reporter's voice stated, "What was the breakthrough discovery made by these clever kids? A Chinese symbol for hope, painted in a citric wash on the paper. The acidity turns brown when it is heated, making it an invisible ink commonly found in many households. Discovering that the map incorporated both Chinese and English eventually led to the children solving the mystery."

The TV screen now showed a woman from the Chinese Historical Society speaking with the reporter.

"It wasn't common for the Chinese in Gold Rush era San Francisco to know both English and Cantonese, but it also wasn't unheard of," the historian said. "We know of Chinese immigrants like Ah Quin, who maintained a diary in English in an effort to practice the language. The miner who created the unbreakable code was undoubtedly educated, likely a merchant who interacted with both English-speaking populations and Cantonese.

"The letter is dated 1853, and at that time there was a lot of antagonism toward the Chinese. They were the only group required to pay a special tax for mining. There was no legal protection if they refused, so they could be robbed or beaten or worse, without any legal recourse or protection from an entity like the police. Because of this hostile environment, Chinese miners sometimes melted their gold and molded it into an everyday object like a bowl, and then covered it with soot to conceal the value. For reasons we will probably never know, this miner took the extra step of hiding his gold to be retrieved later."

The news report ended, and Emily's dad hugged her sideways. "That was wonderful!"

"You're a regular Indiana Jones," Matthew said.

The doorbell rang. "That's James," Emily said. "It's time to go to Hollister's."

The replaced front window of Hollister's bookstore greeted Emily, James, and Matthew like a warm smile. The store hadn't reopened yet—Hollister said there was a long road ahead until that happened. But the structural damage had been repaired, and today he was having a painting party.

Empty bookcases huddled in the middle of the room, waiting to be painted. Every inch of floor was covered with canvas tarp. A long card table had been set up. Mr. Quisling had come to the painting party and was laying out paintbrushes, rollers, and drip pans at one end while Ms. Linden arranged an assortment of snacks and drinks at the other. Mr. Griswold ran blue tape around the new window and door trim. Jack draped the front counter in plastic.

Mr. Griswold's dogs were there, too. Angel had curled up on a mound of tarps, and Claus was sniffing every inch of the store.

"Dogs at a painting party. Leave it to Gary." Hollister shook his head. "You know they're going to get paint on their fur, don't you?" he said.

Mr. Griswold waved a hand. "They'll be fine! They're due for the groomers anyway."

James set down the plastic bag he'd been carrying and began unpacking the food his mother and grandmother had insisted he bring along: steamed banana leaves that held sticky rice and chicken, and fried spring rolls.

Emily and James had invited the dance committee, and they soon trickled in. Vivian was at a loss for what to do without her clipboard in tow, so she rearranged the painting supplies Mr. Quisling had set out. Kevin and Devin made a beeline for the dogs. Claus eagerly played a game of catch with them and a balled-up towel. Maddie and Nisha laughed when they realized they had both brought similar-looking dishes. Maddie's were empanadas with shredded beef and cheese, and Nisha's were samosas with curry chicken and peas.

Charlie wasn't at the painting party. Hollister had fired him. While Charlie hadn't started the fire as Emily had suspected, he did lie about feeding a parking meter, and it turned out that wasn't all he had lied about.

Hollister had hired him because Charlie claimed to be proficient in computer coding and web development, but in actuality, he had only recently begun to teach himself HTML. The reason he left the store on the day of the fire was because he didn't know how to fix something on Hollister's website, and he needed to check a how-to manual he'd left in his car.

"He was only learning HTML? That's so basic! And he said he was an expert?" James said, astonished that someone could lie so boldly. "Did he even know JavaScript?"

"It seems Charlie was a jack-of-all-trades, but a master of none." Hollister sighed. "Even without the lies, I would have let him go. Leaving my store unattended with only a minor inside by herself is not a responsible decision by any stretch of the imagination."

Even though Charlie hadn't been a good employee for Hollister, Emily felt a twinge of guilt for accusing him of being an arsonist to the police. If they hadn't figured out the real story with Mr. Sloan, her words could have caused an innocent person a lot of trouble.

Hollister looked around his empty store. "This little shop is ready for a new chapter. I want it to be a cheery one. Orange walls, white bookcases—I think it will look nice."

"It's going to look fantastic," Jack said.

"Like being inside a Creamsicle," Matthew said, and everyone laughed.

"Yes," Mr. Griswold said. "And who doesn't want to

browse for books inside a Creamsicle? Every biblio-phile's dream, I imagine."

Emily eyed a sunny orange test patch of paint on the wall. "I like the color you chose, Hollister. Maybe I'll paint my bedroom this color, too."

"That reminds me." James flipped open the top of the cooler they'd brought to reveal piles of It's-Its. "We pooled together a little of our treasure money to splurge on these for the painting party."

"It's-Its!" Hollister clapped his hands gleefully. "I haven't had one of these for years. Do you have mint?" He rummaged through the plastic-wrapped ice cream sandwiches. "Oh, yes you do!" He triumphantly raised his treat and did a little dance, which got Claus excited.

"Claus," Mr. Griswold said sternly. When the dog trotted to his side, he leaned close to his ear and stage-whispered, "Don't worry. I'll share some of mine with you and Angel."

After everyone selected their ice-cream flavor, Mr. Quisling asked Emily and James, "So you treated us to It's-Its. What other plans do you have for your reward money?"

When they had returned from Gull Island, Mr. Quisling had followed the protocol of turning over the found bowl to police. Since they had found the gold on private property, the owner of Gull Island had to be notified before anything else could happen. It turned out he was so taken with the story and moved by the historical significance, he donated the bowl to the Chinese Historical Society and gifted Emily and James each with a ten-thousand-dollar finder's fee. Since her parents weren't worried about money with her dad's new job, they had insisted she keep her share. James's dad had refused the money when James offered, and instead promised to cut back on his business trips. So she and James had come up with an alternative plan that they were excited to announce.

"Since you asked . . ." James looked to Emily, and she nodded for him to go ahead. "We'd like to give the money to you, Hollister. To help you get your store back up and running."

Hollister had been mid-bite of his ice cream sandwich. His mouth dropped open in surprise, but he closed it quickly, pressing a napkin to his lips. He mock grabbed his chest and stumbled backward, then laughed as the rest of the party clapped and cheered at James's announcement.

"You two." Hollister swung an arm around both their shoulders and hugged them to his sides. "You two are the sweetest. That is a very generous offer, but I'm going to turn you down."

"What?" Emily pushed away in surprise. "Why?"

"That's your reward. You two earned that money, and you should treat yourself to something special. Put the rest away for college. The fact that you would even consider giving that money to me is a gift in itself."

"But . . ." Emily looked around at the drop cloths and bookcases clustered together. "Your store?"

"My store and I will be just fine, don't you worry. In fact, I've been working up a plan of my own, with a lot of help from my old partner." Hollister nodded to Mr. Griswold and said, "Why don't you do the honors and fill everyone in, Gary?"

Mr. Griswold grinned. "I thought you'd never ask." He raised his It's-It. "I'd like to make a toast. To Hollister and the magnificent future your store will surely have. And to these young people for their generosity in donating their time today. As you know, I was so impressed by your ingenuity with the game you planned for your school dance last weekend. It was inspiring."

Mr. Griswold looked down for a moment and cleared his throat. "Truth be told, I have not felt like myself since I was attacked last fall.

"Watching your game reminded me that the energy we put into the world is infectious. There is a ripple effect, whether you are fostering fear or fun, cruelty or kindness. You heard the laughter from your classmates during your game—the positive energy you generated was palpable in that gym.

"You planted an idea in my imagination. I hurried home and called Hollister immediately, and now, without further ado, I'd like to announce my next big game."

The store had been silent, other than soft jazz playing behind Mr. Griswold's words, but at the mention of a new game, everyone started talking at once—even

Jack, who seemed just as surprised by this news as any of them.

"What is it?"

"What's the event going to be?"

"A new game?"

Claus sat up and barked sharply three times, and everyone laughed.

When the room quieted, Mr. Griswold asked, "Have you heard of an escape room challenge?" When nobody spoke up, he explained, "Participants are placed in a locked room and have to work together to solve a series of puzzles in order to break out before time is up."

"That sounds fun," Emily said.

"It's great fun, and I've decided to host one in the ultimate San Francisco escape challenge location."

"Where's that?" James asked.

"Alcatraz," Mr. Griswold said.

"*Alcatraz* Alcatraz?" James asked. "The old prison on the island?"

"The one and only."

Hollister whistled and shook his head. "I told him he was crazy when he pitched the idea to me, but Gary never thinks small."

"The event will be called"—Mr. Griswold swiped a hand in the air like he was unveiling a banner—"Unlock the Rock."

"Cool!" Kevin and Devin said. "Do we get to go?"

"Of course! I'll also invite some of the top Book Scavenger competitors from across the country, and the rest of the tickets will be auctioned off as a fund-raiser to help get Hollister's bookstore back up and running. What do you say? Are you onboard?"

The group erupted in cheers. Emily clinked her It's-It with James, then Nisha and Vivian.

Maddie leaned close. "Don't think you'll have an edge over me just because you found a gold bowl," she said, but with a smile on her face.

"How about we work on the same team for once?" Emily replied.

"And what kind of fun would that be?" They clinked It's-Its and joined in when Devin and Kevin started chanting, *"Unlock the Rock! Unlock the Rock!"* Everyone chimed in, except Mr. Quisling, who stood with his arms crossed on his chest, but he looked amused. Next to him Ms. Linden bounced her shoulders to the beat of the chant. She playfully bumped her hip against his, and Mr. Quisling grinned, shaking a finger to the beat like it was a waving pennant.

Emily couldn't remember a time she'd felt this light and happy. The first day she'd walked into Hollister's store many months ago, she wasn't even sure if she could call James a friend yet, that was how brand-new everything had been. Mr. Quisling and Maddie were so intimidating back then. Mr. Griswold existed only on the Internet and in her imagination. Emily didn't think she would ever know what it felt like to belong to a place or a group of people outside her family. And then, within a matter of months, she was surrounded by not just friends but a community. She never wanted to lose that feeling. She thought about what Mr. Griswold had said, how important it was to create positive moments and generate goodwill. She wondered if doing that would make this feeling last forever.

One could only hope.

AUTHOR'S NOTE

The Unbreakable Code is a work of fiction; however, I did draw on historical events and people for inspiration. Here are some of the facts behind the fiction.

Mark Twain, Tom Sawyer, and the Unbreakable Code

The legend of the unbreakable code is entirely made up, but Mark Twain really did live in San Francisco between the years of 1864 and 1866. He was known then by his birth name, Samuel Clemens, and worked as a reporter for the *Morning Call*. During this time, he wrote the short story that launched his literary career, "The Jumping Frog," and published it under his famous pen name. The Transamerica Redwood Park, where Emily and James followed Mr. Quisling, is a real place you can visit in San Francisco, also known as Mark Twain Plaza. The fountain Mr. Quisling circles has sculptures of jumping frogs as a tribute to Twain's story.

During his time in San Francisco, Twain met a San Francisco firefighter by the name of Tom Sawyer. According to *Black Fire: The True Story of the Original Tom Sawyer* by Robert Graysmith, Mark Twain and Tom Sawyer met at the very location where the Redwood Park is now. In 1864, there was a large building there known as Montgomery Block, which housed the Bank Exchange Saloon and Turkish baths, both places where Twain and Sawyer allegedly interacted.

It is Sawyer himself who claimed that Twain borrowed his name for his future iconic character. In an 1895 article in the *Morning Call*, Sawyer was quoted as saying:

> *[Twain] walks up to me and puts both hands on my shoulders. "Tom," he says, "I'm goin' to write a book about a boy, and the kind I have in mind was just about the toughest boy in the world. Tom, he was just such a boy as you must have been. I believe I'll call the book 'Tom Sawyer.' How many copies will you take, Tom, half cash?"*

Twain never refuted Sawyer's claim, but he also never confirmed it. It remains left to history to know whether Sawyer's account was true.

In an 1898 interview, Sawyer recounted a trip he took to Virginia City, Nevada, where he spent time with Mark Twain. In *Black Fire*, Graysmith writes of this visit that "Sawyer had an exciting few nights with his pal Sam and his friends. He drank and gambled with him and high rollers. . . ." From this I imagined the scenario of Twain accepting the unbreakable code for the payment of a gambling debt owed to him.

The fires that the unbreakable code was rumored to have survived were actual historical fires. The first was the great San Francisco Fire of 1851, the largest in a series of fires to overtake the young and rapidly developing city. The *Niantic*, which had been run aground and converted from a whaling ship to a place of business and commerce, burned to the waterline during this fire. The remains of the *Niantic* were left in the ground, along with the many other burnt store-ships, as the waterfront was filled in and developed over. The Niantic Hotel was built over the remains of the old ship, and when the hotel suffered a major fire in 1872, it was rebuilt as the Niantic Building, which was then destroyed in the 1906 earthquake and subsequent fires.

The second fire was one Mark Twain experienced in Virginia City while staying at the White House Hotel, shortly after Tom Sawyer had visited him. The third incident happened to Tom Sawyer's saloon, which he owned for the last twenty-five years of his life at 935 Mission Street. His saloon was destroyed in a fire in 1906, and Sawyer died later that same year.

The Gold Rush

In January 1848, gold was quietly discovered near present-day Sacramento, mere weeks before California was included in the large territory of land ceded to the United States as part of the Treaty of Guadalupe Hidalgo to end the U.S.– Mexican War. The Gold Rush became an international event, bringing fortune seekers from all around the world including China, Mexico, Chile, Australia, Germany, and France. In the span of two years, San Francisco exploded from a small settlement town with a population close to one thousand to over twenty thousand people. San Francisco was the main port of entry, and as there was no transcontinental railroad at this time, many people arrived by ship. Sometimes these ships were left abandoned and cluttering Yerba Buena Cove by crews headed north to the gold fields. Because building materials were scarce and expensive, these ships were sometimes broken down for their materials or brought aground and converted into commercial and business spaces, as was the case with the *Niantic*.

Yerba Buena Cove was gradually filled in and built up. The land closest to water was most desirable both because of the proximity to ships bringing in goods and also because the majority of San Francisco terrain was hilly and provided challenges for a newly developing city.

With the prospect of great wealth at stake, tensions between different ethnicities were prevalent during the Gold Rush. When California became a state in 1850, the legislature enacted the Foreign Miners Tax, which meant non-American miners had to pay a fee of twenty dollars a month. This was an often lawless time, with minorities especially receiving little to no legal protection. According to the Harvard University Library open collection, "the Chinese adopted the unique practice of melting down gold to make household goods, such as pots and other utensils" in order to protect their wealth from thieves. That detail, as well as reading *The Chinese in America* by Iris Chang, *Chinese San Francisco 1850–1943* by Yong Chen, and the fictional story from the Dear America series, *The Journal of Wong Ming-Chung* by Lawrence Yep, inspired my origin story for the unbreakable code.

Buried Ships of San Francisco

The dig that Mr. Quisling participated in to recover the *Niantic* in 1978 is an actual event that happened. The ship remains were discovered when a construction crew was excavating a lot in preparation for a new building. Construction was halted, and the Maritime Museum was brought in to see what could be salvaged from the old ship. At the Maritime Museum, Emily and James view part of the *Niantic* stern, a miniature model of the converted storeship during the Gold Rush, and artifacts from the 1978 excavation project. These are actual displays that exist (as of the printing of this book) and can be seen, although the exhibits are spread out between the Maritime Museum and the Maritime National Historical Park Visitor Center. For the sake of storytelling, I combined them into one location.

While the *Niantic* is the best known, there are at least forty-seven ships from the Gold Rush era buried underneath the city of San Francisco.

Gull Island

Gull Island is fictional, but I was inspired by Red Rock Island, the only privately owned island in San Francisco Bay. (And as of this writing, it is currently available for sale!)

Wave Organ

The *Wave Organ* is an acoustic sculpture commissioned by the Exploratorium in San Francisco. It's located on a jetty that was built from the remains of a demolished cemetery.

Sodium and Water

Certain alkali metals, like sodium and potassium, cause an explosive chemical reaction when mixed with water. Sodium, the element the arsonist uses in my story, is a silvery metal that is soft at room temperature and typically stored in mineral oil because of its ability to be spontaneously explosive. When a lump of sodium is dropped into water (which should only be done by trained professionals with appropriate protective gear), sodium hydroxide and hydrogen is produced, causing the metal to zoom around the water and ignite into flames. You can find many videos on YouTube to view this reaction.

ACKNOWLEDGMENTS

The Unbreakable Code would not exist if it weren't for my editor and publisher, Christy Ottaviano, who envisioned *Book Scavenger* as a series and nurtured it into the story it is today. Also vital to this book's existence is my literary agent, Ammi-Joan Paquette, who always makes me feel like I can do it, even when I doubt myself. It is an honor and a joy to work with you both.

This story is also indebted to everyone at Macmillan, who rejected my original title (and second and third—don't feel bad for me, they weren't very good titles). I received the "Could you come up with something else?" e-mail at the same time I'd written myself into a wall, plot-wise. My publisher didn't know this, of course, but I was panicked and floundering, worried that I'd never be able to pull off this sequel. I was asked if I could come up with a title that sounded more fun, something like *The Unbreakable Code*. There was no "unbreakable code" in the story at that point, but I read the e-mail and thought, "Heeeeeey . . ." And voilà! I punched right through my plotting wall and was off and running again.

The whole team at Macmillan has been phenomenal to work with. Thank you to: Jessica Anderson, Starr Baer, Nicole Banholzer, Molly Brouillette, Lucy Del Priore, Katy Halata, Kathryn Little, Kallam McKay, Amanda Mustafic, John Nora, Caitlin Sweeny, Mark von Bargen, April Ward, Melissa Zar, and the many other people who have worked hard on this book's behalf. Thank you to Sarah Watts for your wonderful illustrations.

Thank you to the following people who generously answered questions for me as I researched a wide variety of topics for this book: Yong Chen, Pat Cordor, June Cutter, Lisa Shah Evans, Jenni Frencham, Neal Griffen, Vanessa Harper, Ann Kodani, Adi Rule, Ryan Russo of Walk SF Tours, Elaine Vickers, Steve Wood, and Laura Young-Cennamo.

A hug and thank-you to Tharind Bopearachchigedon, Joaquin Diaz, and Morgan Rieb, three young *Book Scavenger* fans who read an early draft of this book. Your feedback was very helpful and gave me a boost of confidence when I needed it most.

To my dear Writing Roosters—Tracy Abell, Vanessa Appleby, Claudia Mills, Laura Perdew, Jennifer Simms, and Michelle Begley who will always be with us in spirit—you lift me up with your encouragement, laughter, wisdom, insightful critiques, and friendship. Thank you so very much. I am also appreciative for the children's writing community at large. This story in particular, and my mental well-being while creating it, benefited from the advice and feedback of: Ann Bedicheck, Tara Dairman, Kari Anne Holt, Ingrid Law, Jeannie Mobley, Katherine Rothschild, Jennifer Stewart, and Elaine Vickers.

Thank you to my family and friends, always, for your love and support, and for understanding this hectic place I have found myself in the last two years.

A special thank-you to my husband, Justin: the list of reasons why would fill a book all by themselves. To our son: You were three and four when I wrote this story, and I'm giving you twenty-ten-ninety-nine hugs and smooches for being the best little boy a mama could hope for.

To the booksellers, librarians, educators, and others who champion children's books every day: Thank you for what you do. So many of you have embraced *Book Scavenger* and connected with me in meaningful ways. At the risk of forgetting someone and kicking myself later, I have to thank the following people for being so dang inspiring and awesome: Sarah Azibo, Eric Barbus, Lauren Baumgartner, Leslie Berkler, Kim Campbell, Kirsten Cappy, Jesica DeHart, Brooke Dilling, Drew Durham, Scott Fillner, Kristen Gilligan, Cressida Hanson, Brett Keniston, Sharon Levin, Angela Mann, Cheryl McKeon, Kim Parfitt, Kari Riedel, Angie Tally, Susan Tunis, Brianne Walterhouse, and Susan Whited.

Finally, to the enthusiastic fans of the first book: *Thank you*. I've had the chance to meet and hear from many of you over the past two years, and those experiences always left me motivated and excited to return to this book. I tried to honor you by writing the best sequel I possibly could. I hope you enjoyed it.

GOFISH

JENNIFER CHAMBLISS BERTMAN

The Unbreakable Code **involves a cross-cultural historical mystery; what was the most interesting historical fact you learned in the research process?**
I learned *so* many interesting things writing *The Unbreakable Code*. I've now written three books in the Book Scavenger series, and all three have involved a lot of research, but *The Unbreakable Code* spanned the widest variety of topics, and almost all of them were new to me. Though the most interesting historical fact was actually about the topic I thought I knew best: the California Gold Rush. I grew up in California, where Gold Rush history is part of the elementary school curriculum, and I remember learning about people traveling west in covered wagons, and the influx of people eager to find gold, and the process of panning for gold. What didn't sink in for me when I was young was how international the Gold Rush actually was, with thousands of people sailing from South America, Asia, and other places to America. There were 25,000 immigrants from China alone who arrived in the first years of the Gold Rush—which was also the very beginning of California as a

state. That amount might not sound very large by today's standards, but when you consider that the entire population of California when it became a state was 92,597 people according to the US Census (not including Native Americans), I think it's pretty exceptional.

What was your favorite scene to write and why?
My favorite scene to write was when Emily, James, and Matthew visit the Wave Organ in San Francisco, and I have several reasons why. First, that was one of my personal favorite spots when I lived in San Francisco, and so it was a lot of fun to take my characters there. Second, I re-visited the Wave Organ on a research outing with my mom when I was writing *The Unbreakable Code*, so the scene also reminds me of that trip. And third, the same day my mom and I went to the Wave Organ I received a phone call from a bookseller, Drew Durham, letting me know that *Book Scavenger* had been selected for the Indie Next list, as well as a finalist for the ABA Indies Introduce New Voices list. So there is a lot of happiness wrapped up in that one little scene.

Can you tell us a little about what to expect in *The Alcatraz Escape*? (No spoilers, please!)
I hope readers will find more of what they loved in the first two books. There will be puzzles, games, bookish fun, friendship, humor, historical tidbits, and mystery. Many of the characters return, and since it's in the title I don't think it's a spoiler to reveal the story takes place in large part on Alcatraz Island. The mystery of this book was a pleasure to work on—it might be my favorite of the three!

Did you love puzzles as a kid? Are you a crossword player?

I loved puzzles as a kid, but I am a horrible crossword player. Embarrassingly horrible. The puzzles I enjoyed most when I was young are the same type James works on: logic puzzles. I often like math puzzles more than word puzzles, which is perhaps odd because math was never my favorite subject. As an adult I like sudoku puzzles. And I've always liked jigsaw puzzles as well as what I call "pack a car" puzzles—games like Tetris that have to do with how cleverly you can fit shapes into a space.

What was your first job?

When I was in the sixth grade, I started a babysitter's club with my friends, modeled after the popular series of books. We named our club Sitters Anonymous until my mom suggested we check a dictionary, and then we realized our name should be Sitters *Unanimous*. We made flyers and had weekly meetings and assigned ourselves officer roles. That was a tricky process because we couldn't agree on whether we should match people to the character they were most similar to, or if we should pick the job we were best suited for. I ended up being the vice-president because we had the meetings at my house, just like Claudia, the vice-president in the books. As you can see, it was a very seriously run business. It did turn into quite a profitable venture for me, though, as I built up a stable of regular babysitting clients. By the time I was sixteen, I'd saved up enough babysitting money to pay for half of my first car (a used Geo Metro), which was something I was very proud of. I also discovered that I really loved working with children, and was quite good at it, too.

What book is on your nightstand now?
"Book" singular? Oh, that's funny. There is a teetering pile of books on my nightstand right now that includes *A Spool of Blue Thread* by Anne Tyler, *The Sky is Everywhere* by Jandy Nelson, *Blue Lily, Lily Blue* by Maggie Stiefvater, *The Arctic Code* by Matthew J. Kirby, *The Long and Faraway Gone* by Lou Berney, the original version of *The Mystery at Lilac Inn* (Nancy Drew #4) by Carolyn Keene, and *Memoirs of a Muppets Writer* by Joseph A. Bailey.

If you could live in any fictional world, what would it be?
Sesame Street. Or a Jim Henson's Muppets–inhabited world.

What's the best advice you have ever received about writing?
The best writing advice I've received came from the author James Howe, who replied to a letter I mailed him when I was ten. He wrote, "Don't think so much about what you 'should' do, or how you will please someone else, as much as writing to please yourself and create a story *you* would enjoy reading."

Do you ever get writer's block? What do you do to get back on track?
I definitely get writer's block, and there are many different things I do that help. Doing something physical for a

change of pace: going for a walk, vacuuming, playing with my son. Lots of breakthroughs come to me while I'm showering, for some reason. Sometimes I open a fresh document and free write about why I'm struggling with a scene, or I give the section I'm struggling with to a reader to get their perspective. I often turn to favorite books for inspiration. My two go-to authors whose writing almost always unfreezes me are Elise Broach and Rebecca Stead.

What do you want readers to remember about your books?

The books I loved most when I was young filled my life in some way outside the story. Like forming the babysitting club, or playing a version of *The Egypt Game*, or trying to create my own elaborate filing system like Mrs. Basil E. Frankweiler. So I hope my books will inspire young readers similarly so that twenty years from now, when they look back on their childhood, they will have memories marked by their experience of reading my books. And for my adult readers, I hope that reading my books will take them back to that childhood feeling of letting your imagination live large.

What would you do if you ever stopped writing?

Professionally, if I stopped writing, I would like to work with children in some capacity. I fantasize about becoming an elementary school teacher. I also like interior design. Owning a children's bookshop is another fantasy. I could also see myself working on the editorial or marketing side of children's books. For hobbies, I would do more gardening, dancing, snowboarding, reading, listening to music, scrap-booking, and making collages. I'd learn to crochet and I'd take drawing classes.

If you were a superhero, what would your superpower be?
The power to freeze time.

What would your readers be most surprised to learn about you?
I was a dance major in college, and for several years a career in dance is where I saw myself headed. But when I was a dancer, it was generally accepted that you only had a career until you were about thirty, and so you were encouraged (cautioned, really) to have a backup plan. I double-majored in English and fell back in love with writing stories when I took a creative writing class. In my last year of college I had to choose between taking an-other creative writing class I *really, really* wanted to take (but didn't need to take) or the last required class in order to graduate with my dance degree. It felt like a fork in the road on this path I'd been walking, holding the hands of two things I love. I chose creative writing and graduated with a degree in English and one class short of a dance degree. That creative writing class is what led me to the MFA program I went into the follow-ing year, and I haven't looked back or had regrets once about choosing writing.

A HIGH-STAKES GAME ON ALCATRAZ ISLAND.

A false accusation. And the most challenging mystery yet.

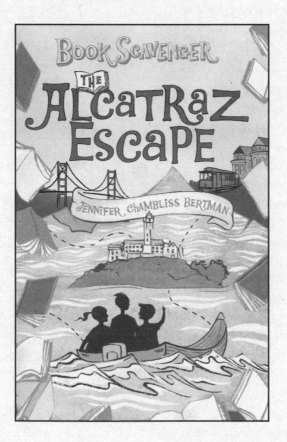

Keep reading for a sneak peek.

CHAPTER 1

I F ONE OF Errol Roy's fans had passed him on the street, they wouldn't have known who he was. With the wispy white hair that covered most of his head and nearly reached his shoulders, and his long cottony beard tinged with yellow, he was more likely to be mistaken for Santa Claus than for himself. Nobody knew what Errol Roy looked like, but his books were recognized around the world.

On this day in mid-March, the author stood at the bay window of his San Francisco apartment.

"It's been a long road, Dash," Errol said aloud to his cat, who was stretched across the windowsill. Dash swatted his tail in response.

Errol was thinking about his personal favorite of his own books. He doubted any of his readers could correctly guess which it was out of the twenty-some mysteries he'd written. It was arguably the most obscure: *A Body in the Alley*. A horrible title. Maybe that was why it hadn't sold well.

In *A Body in the Alley*, Mickey Jones is a crook who continuously finds himself in the wrong place at the wrong time but finally pulls off the bank heist of his dreams. At the book's close, he sails into the sunset while the detective on his trail watches him get away. The book ends with this line:

The boat disappeared over the horizon, rings spreading behind like a peacock fanning its tail.

Errol Roy had written millions of sentences in his lifetime, but that was one he had never forgotten. It wasn't so much the writing he was fond of, but the image it painted and the feeling of freedom it gave him. It was an ending Errol had always wanted to try, but it turned out critics and readers didn't like it when their detective hero lost.

Dash sat up and stretched out a paw to tap his owner, as though encouraging Errol to look up. The view below was of a hillside gouged from its quarry days, now covered in vines and shrubs. The scene straight ahead could be a San Francisco postcard.

On a crisp, clear day you could see all the way from the Golden Gate Bridge to the tiny stump of Gull Island, which had been on the news because two kids and their teacher had found buried treasure there. And if the bay was a stage, then front and center was Alcatraz.

Errol Roy rested his eyes on the famous former

prison, which had had a reputation for being inescap-
able. Now Alcatraz was a popular tourist destination,
attracting travelers from around the world, and soon it
would be the setting of the latest cockamamie game cre-
ation by Garrison Griswold, the city's beloved book
publisher and game enthusiast.

Errol sighed.

Last fall, his most recent mystery had been published
to great fanfare, not that he had participated in any of
it. He never did. That decision had started out as a spontaneous choice made decades ago, which grew into his

reputation. His "branding," as the publishing industry termed it today. The most popular mysteries in America, written by a man who was himself a mystery. Once, he had stood in line at the grocery store behind a woman who had piled produce, a plastic tray of muffins, and his latest paperback onto the conveyor belt. She and the cashier had had a lively discussion about his books, never realizing the author stood right beside them.

Errol had planned for his most recent book to be the final of his career, but when Garrison Griswold announced this new game, he knew it was time to tell the last story he had in him. There would be considerable risk, but it rankled him to leave loose ends dangling.

He was a novelist, after all.

"It's time, Dash," he said, and turned from the view.

The cat meowed, as though hoping his owner meant it was time for dinner, and dropped to the floor with a gentle thud. When the man crossed the room to his computer desk instead of the kitchen, Dash meowed again. His tail quirked into a question mark.

Errol lowered himself into his chair and opened his laptop. He bent over his keyboard and began to type.

CHAPTER 2

EMILY CRANE and her best friend, James, ran along a dirt alley closed in by a graffiti-covered fence on one side and a vine-covered fence on the other. The path cut horizontally across a hill. Emily couldn't see the two- and three-story buildings above and below them, but she knew they were there.

"They're going to catch up to us," James panted.

Emily looked back. The path behind them was empty, all the way to the arched trellis they'd entered under. Their feet pounded past weeds that grew to their ears. An enormous shrub spilled over the top of a fence like it was trying to jump into the alley and make a break for it. The path curved, and there was the exit back onto a street in Emily and James's San Francisco neighborhood.

"We're almost there—we can make it!" Emily shouted, but a hooded figure jumped in front of the exit and blocked their way. Emily hadn't anticipated that they'd be stopped from the front. She and James stumbled a bit, trying to change course and run back the way they'd come. Before they could fully turn around, there was a soft pop, and purple powder splattered across their shirts.

"Found you!" their friend Maddie crowed, her sweatshirt hood falling back off her head. She was nearly a head taller than both of them, so when she triumphantly held up the plastic bottle of colored cornstarch and squeezed, more violet dust rained down over Emily and James.

"You're out," Maddie said.

"Aw, man!" James stomped a foot in mock disgust. The purple-dusted black cowlick atop his head, which James affectionately called Steve, bobbed indignantly. "You could have let the birthday boy win, you know."

Maddie rolled her eyes. "Right. Like I'm going to do that."

James aimed his squeeze bottle at Maddie, and a puff of green powder blasted toward her. She jumped aside so only her shoulder got hit. Laughing, she said, "Too late! Purple team still won!"

Footsteps came up behind them, and Emily turned to see their other friends, Devin, Kevin, Nisha, and Vivian, coming down the path. Devin had been on their team, but he and his twin brother had blasted each other with powder within minutes of the game starting, leaving only Emily and James to fend for Team Green.

"I told you I could beat them to the end of the path, Vivian," Maddie called over.

Vivian frowned—she was more comfortable doing the correcting than being corrected—but she nodded and said, "Good job." Vivian looked even more crisp and polished than usual, being the only one of the group without green or purple splattered across her face and clothes.

"Do we win anything?" Nisha asked, removing her glasses. She attempted to clean them with her shirt, but only succeeded in smearing green dust across the lens.

"Here." James plucked Nisha's glasses from her hands. "The back of my shirt is clean." He tugged a corner of fabric forward and rubbed furiously, then handed them back. "Your team wins my undying admiration—even you, Maddie."

Maddie and James had a competitive history that dated back to their elementary school days, long before Emily had known either of them. Recently the rivalry had taken on a friendly tone. Which still felt totally weird, if you asked Emily.

"You can keep the T-shirts, too," James added.

Nisha lifted her shirt like an old-timey lady curtseying in a petticoat. She was the smallest in their group, and her shirt hung to her knees. "My mom's always telling me to wear more dresses."

Maddie peeled off her shirt from over her sweatshirt. "The winners also get first choice for pizza," she declared.

James shrugged. "Sure. Speaking of, let's eat!"

He led the group back the way he and Emily had come. The alley connected to a very narrow, vertical public garden that was broken into tiers, with stairs zig-zagging the slope. The group climbed the stairs, weaving around rosebushes and daylilies until they reached the halfway point, where James's mom sat on one of two benches that faced the San Francisco Bay.

His mom held two pizza boxes in one hand and slid her sunglasses onto her head with the other. "Wow . . . ," she said, taking in their green- and purple-stained faces, arms, legs, and clothes. "Your parents are going to kill me."

"It washes out, Mom. I told you," James said.

His hand darted forward and his mom yelped, trying to dodge, but James was too fast and wiped a purple streak on her cheek.

She laughed. "You're lucky it's your birthday," she said.

Maddie's team chose their slices; then the others took their turn. After distributing napkins and drinks, James's mom balanced the empty boxes on one hand and hiked the stairs that continued up the hill. She called back, "Parent pickup in forty-five minutes!"

Emily sat on a bench with James and Nisha; Maddie and Vivian sat on the other bench that was on the tier below them. The twins stretched out on the five stairs in between.

Everyone ate quietly until Maddie asked, "Is

everyone trying out?" She straddled the bench so she could face Vivian and the rest of the group sitting up the hill behind the two girls.

They all knew she was talking about Unlock the Rock, Mr. Griswold's upcoming game. From where they sat eating their lunch, they could see Alcatraz down below on the water, framed in the corridor between buildings on either side.

Vivian folded her napkin and pressed it to her lips. "My parents won't let me miss my flute lesson, plus it's a school night."

"Failed the entry puzzle," Devin announced. "Big time."

"You sound proud," Maddie said.

"It was a pretty spectacular failing."

His brother nodded in agreement. "If they gave grades for failing, he would have gotten an A-plus."

Maddie rolled her eyes and turned to Emily and James. "You two are probably automatically entered, being on Mr. Griswold's teen advisory board and everything," she said.

"Do you know what he's planning?" Nisha asked.

"We don't know anything." Emily spoke up while James finished chewing. "At least no more than what he told all of us when we were painting Hollister's bookstore: It will be like an escape room set on Alcatraz."